Finding
Majik

Finding Majik

amongst the chaos of trauma

Kelli Miller

Not just my story

In loving memory of Mardi

With deepest gratitude
Kimmi Diane Margarita

Deepest respect for Autumn

For all the many others who have also trodden this path, this book is dedicated to you: those whose story has been minimised, discounted, swept under the carpet. For those whose story involves family, friends, neighbours. Those whose abuse doesn't hold the same accountability in our society, court systems, legal language and most definitely not in compensation.

Your story is just as valuable, if not more, because you are the unseen, the one society wants to keep hidden. If we brought these stories into the open, then too many would have to look in their own backyards, under their own beds, in their own mirrors. We know our society will do anything to place ownership on strangers or institutions, rather than on family and friends. You have my deepest admiration that you are still here.

Let your voice be heard.

If you would like to view the artwork mentioned in this memoir, please follow this link:

And www.youtube.com/@findingmajik

Introduction

Trauma affects the way a person interacts with the world. It limits their ability or willingness to allow emotions to surface or to simply be present. These become daily, moment-by-moment challenges to be faced.

Detachment becomes first nature, especially after childhood trauma. The simple scent of burnt garden clippings, the tone of someone's words, a look, or an item such as sunglasses placed on top of a cap can remove from a traumatised soul all ability to be connected, to feel anything but the primal need to escape.

When interacting in any situation that involves connecting to feelings, many traumatised souls appear aloof. This is because they either don't give a shit (which a lot of the time is true) or they are not capable or don't know how to stay connected or present, or how to allow feelings in.

As the traumatised soul becomes aware of their triggers, then, bit by bit, when comfortable and safe, they may be able to communicate their feelings healthily.

This is not something that can be generalised nor even expected, but it is a possible outcome. However, things may change for any individual at any given moment. Based on my own lived experience, that's how traumatised souls exist – from moment to moment.

So, when you read or hear the story from a traumatised soul, it may appear different from your expectations of how someone should interact with their experience. Words will be missing, feelings unexpressed, messages all mixed and muddled, but there's one thing traumatised souls are very, very good at – rawness and a depth you may never have encountered before.

Allow yourself the opportunity to walk in their shoes and experience life through different eyes.

Trigger Warning

This book contains themes referencing abuse, especially childhood sexual abuse, domestic violence, self-harming behaviour, suicide ideation, alcohol consumption, drug use, nightmares about traumatic events, and panic attacks. This book shows depictions of the mental state of someone suffering abuse, CPTSD, or engaging in self-harming behaviour.
Some names have been changed to protect vulnerable people.

Joy Alert

This book also contains much
embracing of
adventures,
joy,
wonder,
excitement,
healing,
appreciation,
and
exploration.

With a deep sense of
gratitude
for Mother
Nature and the
Universe.

Glossary

Indecent Assault: (n) the crime of attacking someone in a way which involves touching or threatening them sexually but not forcing them to have sexual intercourse.

Sexual Abuse: (n) if a child or other person suffers sexual abuse, someone forces them to take part in sexual activity with them, often regularly over a period of time.

Child Abuse: (n) physical, sexual, or emotional ill-treatment or neglect of a child, especially by those responsible for their welfare.

Incest: (n) the crime of two members of the same family having sexual intercourse, for example a father and daughter, or a brother and sister, or grandmother and granddaughter.

Rape: (v) If someone is raped, they are forced to have sex, usually by violence or threats of violence.

*collinsdictionary.com 2021

Contents

Chapter 1

Bee – miracle bringer

Patrick O'Shanesy. She can smell him as the words blur, her body shaking with memories, her eyes leaking with pain. She can see his stinking breath creating waves in the falling dust particles highlighted by the sun's rays. Ana's whole being responds to simply seeing his name in writing, a name she wished would never scar her eyeballs, never, ever, ever again. She wants to run, to hide. She no longer feels safe, safe in this new place she calls home, Tasmania. Has she been disillusioning herself these past five years?

Something's buzzing around her head. Angrily she swipes at it, then hates herself for doing so. It's a bumble bee. She loves their furry huge bodies, their tiny wings. How they manage to fly when being so disproportionate is well beyond her comprehension. No wonder they are miracle bringers. Maybe this bumble bee is a sign from the Universe, reminding Ana to believe in miracles. Yet how can she, when she's now been found?

Originally, she'd run 2000 km to get away from him, then another 2500 km, finally finding this space she feels safe in. She even changed her name, removing any connections to family, her past, her old self. She loves Ana Suci. She spent considerable time and reflection choosing a name that resonates with what she wishes to embody. She wanted a name that sounded like it didn't come from here. She doesn't want to come from here. Ana meaning gracious, Suci meaning clean, pure, innocent. Qualities she feels so lacking and so desires within her being.

But now he's here, and this space, her space, is tainted by his presence. She hasn't invited him in, but he's here, and she wants him gone. Wants to wipe the image before her clean, like wiping the scratched chalk markings made by a child on a blackboard.

Patrick *fucking* O'Shanesy. She sees it written with a child's trembling hand, unable to hold the chalk as the sweat seeps from her palm.

#

Ana remembers leaving her hometown of Melbourne some thirty-odd years ago. She remembers what it was that set the despair within her to surface, that made her want to run as far away as possible.

With her then partner Troy, she arrives for Christmas lunch at a friend's home. When they walk into the typical Australian backyard, her heart drops through the dry cracked summer dirt. She's unable to comprehend who she's seeing. Patrick O'Shanesy's there. Like why? Why is he in her space, among her friends, among her family? She believed she'd got rid of him. Thought she'd wiped and scrubbed him from her being until she bled. So why was he at this party?

There's a lady standing next to him, it's his wife Maria, looking as though they're part of him but also looking like they too want to run from his putridness. The poor stupid woman.

Walking towards the hosts, Troy notices Ana's absence. Turning, he sees her looking like a ghost. He quickly goes to her side, pushing her from behind, trying to act as though everything's normal. Troy often wonders about normality as far as she's concerned. Sometimes he has no idea where she's coming from, no idea why she's reacting the way she is. Ana truly has some unusual behavioural ways that even she doesn't understand. Troy has no idea what's happening right now, why Ana's body's shaking, why it appears she's about to have a panic attack. All Troy knows is that people are beginning to stare, and he doesn't like that.

She knows exactly why she's reacting this way. Patrick O'Shanesy is here, and he's not allowed to be, it's all so wrong.

Throughout the day she tries her best to avoid being even remotely near POS, keeping Esi, her six-month-old, close to her sweating skin, not wanting Esi to be an opportunity for POS to engage in conversation.

Ana can see him out of the corner of her eye, he's trying to be included in the group Troy's part of. Troy doesn't know, not many do, who POS is. Over the years, the times she has shared her secret, her shame, she'd been shut down, punished, not believed, ignored, so she's learnt to try and lock it away, pretend it never happened. Many times, she's wanted to rip out her eyeballs, wanting the movie that randomly drops in her mind's eye to stop. A shiver runs up her spine as images invade her being. She wants to vomit, but she can't leave Esi, not even with Troy. Fighting the vomit back down, deep down to that part within her where all of POS lies, she stays.

A game of backyard cricket starts in the park across the road. Ana knows she's good at cricket. She's good at most sports, always has been, and needing something to take her mind away, to relieve her body of the tension it's holding, she joins the game. She's been drinking a bit, it's her go-to crutch when feeling like this. No longer breast-feeding, she just keeps drinking and drinking, knowing her behaviour's appearing socially unacceptable, feeling herself not being totally there with all the others, with him. It isn't just the effects of alcohol influencing her behaviour, it's the memories invading her vision, it's the body memories she's trying so hard to keep locked within her being, they're now breaking free, she can feel them, she can taste the rottenness dripping down the back of her throat.

Suddenly she sees POS walking towards her. She freezes, unable to move, not knowing how to, not believing she has the right to. He's there right in front of her, his mouth's moving, his breath's invading her clean air, causing her to stifle a gagging motion, oh how she wants to throw up all over him. Words are spilling from his lips, though she's finding it hard to formulate their presence in her space.

"Maria and I would be more than happy to babysit should you ever need one, Ana."

She wants to run as far and as fast as possible, her grip on Esi tightening with each breath. She senses her nails digging into their young skin, yet she can't stop herself. Esi must sense their mum's distress. They remain silent despite the loud screams they can clearly feel. She turns and flees, uttering, "I need to change the baby", grateful for the excuse Esi offers. She's unable to offer herself a way out. She never had a way out as a child. Instead, she remains silent, his words "I'll kill you if you ever tell" ringing in her head.

Later that night, the words pour from her mouth. She's not thinking, not knowing how they're forming the sentences. Simply letting them come, she blurts, "I'm leaving. You either come with us or not, but I'm going."

Within two months they've sold most of their belongings, changed their cars to a 4WD and caravan, and set off on a journey to the unknown. Any where's better than here. She knows she must run; she must hide. She needs to find a space that's safe for her, for Esi. Up to this point, she's spent most of her life running. Hiding from real and imagined threats, simply to minimise the risk of seeing him or any of them ever again.

When Ana left Melbourne, she had a bad lisp and stutter. She'd had that ever since she was a kid. She was sent to speech elocution lessons when she attended a private school, making her feel even more of an outcast, more different, more not normal, than all the other girls. She hated that school, she knew she was different. Not only did she dress differently, go on different holidays, and ride in a different car to all the other girls, but she also knew she was different on the inside; she knew she was tainted.

She hated herself back then, believing that all the other girls hated her too. Watching them play from the hill where she'd sit most play times, separate from everyone, she wondered if the same things had happened to them. Like all the shit things POS did to her. Did they have their own POS? She didn't think so then, but now, as an adult, she knows the statistics, and the reality is that more than likely there were others in her school if not in her class. It's such a sucky shit thing.

The farther away from Melbourne she got, the longer she remained absent from that space, the better her speech got. Her lisp's still there but now only commented on as an endearing feature. Her stutter shows itself whenever she feels overwhelmed or less than, a sign to remove herself from whatever situation she's currently in. So as far as Ana's concerned, her stutter has now become a gift to self.

#

Unfortunately, though it doesn't matter how far she runs, the memories are ever present, their focus becoming clearer and louder with the birth of each kid. She always believed she'd never have kids. She didn't want to bring them into a world where people could do horrible things. She felt unable to live with that responsibility.

When she was 19 years old, a gynecologist told her that it would be highly unlikely she'd be able to carry a baby to full term. It didn't faze her. She was always struggling to keep herself alive, safe. How was she ever meant to keep others safe too?

She feels such a failure, knowing she's a crap parent, trying so hard not to pass on her anxiety, her fears, to her kids. Instead, she tries to be brave, when inside she's ever so shit-scared. She doesn't want them to see her like that, but she's pretty sure their young open beings pick up on all she tries so hard to hide.

As a result, she appears aloof, unavailable to her kids. It's hard. She has always loved kids, having pretty much always had something to do with them, if not through work, then through volunteering. But after having her own kids whom she loves deeply, she quite simply doesn't know how to relate to them. She's afraid of fucking them up, of them being abused by her failing as a parent, as a human. Instead of nurturing them as they probably need, she does what she can in the only way she knows, detaching anytime things get overwhelming, and with kids that happens a lot.

At first, she wasn't too bad. Being a new mother to Esi brought challenges – no space, demands upon her being, responsibility for another. By the time Rey arrived she was doubting her ability to ever be a worthwhile human. Zeb's arrival didn't even register in her world, she was already so overwhelmed and detached that nothing seemed real, even the birth of a child.

When Esi reached the age Ana was when first abused, it became like one terrifying roller coaster after another – the constant fear that something could happen to Esi, that someone could hurt them, was too much for her mind to deal with. When Rey turned six, Ana really struggled. It was all too hard, the memories all too present.

She wanted to love them, to protect them, to teach them, to show them. Sometimes she feels she's done this, seeing their abilities, their compassion and empathy for others, their intelligence. And then right beside that seeing her own failings. She never wanted to parent like Mother Blobfish, but feels she has in a different way, still just as dysfunctionally.

#

Many years ago, before she'd moved yet again, she had received a phone call. Caller ID didn't exist back then unfortunately, if it had she'd never have answered that call. POS was on the other end. She smelt his scent before she heard his voice, it permeated through the telephone line, invading her space.

She'd left Troy by then, realising there was some stuff she needed to deal with, and had started hypnotherapy, hoping to gain some clarity, some validation within her memories. She'd talked to Mother Blobfish about this in confidence, wanting, hoping that maybe she'd feel the love, the connection she so desired from her mother.

She had no idea why POS, of all people, was calling her. More importantly, how had he got her number? Those were the points of focus as her body started to shake violently, her can of bourbon comforting her like a faithful companion. She took a huge gulp, hoping to calm her being. The lounge room spun faster and faster. She felt like throwing up, wished she could. Wished she could vomit out all the yuck that was him.

POS is talking, she can hear a sound, a horrible tone coming through the thing she is holding in her hand. She feels as though POS is in the same room as her, breathing the same air as her. In that moment, she wants to stop breathing, to simply die. The thought, the prospect of hanging up the phone doesn't enter her mind. She feels so powerless, just like she did as a child for all those years. Within minutes he was gone. POS had wanted to know why she was doing hypnotherapy, what she had uncovered. Was there anything she hadn't already known? She didn't know how to respond. She felt so removed from her being. She spoke words but was unable to hear their meaning. She didn't care about his words; all she now cared about was getting the fuck outta there. She no longer felt safe.

Ana didn't know if POS was where she'd left him in her past, or if, in fact, he was here in her new space. All she knew were the feelings within her being. The feelings that were telling her to run – fast and now. Within a week she'd packed up and moved to yet another home. She was so used to moving, having moved twenty-two times in the last twenty-three years. One good thing about moving so much is that you're never in one place long enough to accumulate too much crap. If she didn't have Esi she'd be able to fit all her personal belongings into her faithful wagon. She liked it that way – as little physical baggage as possible. She feels she's carrying more than enough psychologically.

#

Ana loves Tasmania, the spaces, the water, the trees, the mountains. She needs them. She can sit with their wondrousness and simply be, feeling safe here. She believes she's far enough away that her past can never find her, that she'll never have to see, hear or smell him again.

So, why now? Why is he in her space, again? Why is she holding a letter with the name Patrick O'Shanesy written on it? She didn't invite him in – she never would. She'd kill him before he came even a hundred feet near her. She knows POS is not a nice person. To her, he's a manipulative, dominating, fear-inducing arsehole. And now, apparently someone else feels that way too, and they want Ana's help. That's how his name came to be in her space. She never found out how the letter writer found her. She didn't care, simply wanting him, them, gone. She burnt the letter, taking great glee in watching his name go up in flames, the wind carrying the smoke away from her, away from her space.

A drink, that's what's needed, to feel the familiarity of the cold amber liquid running down the back of her extremely parched throat. But she's not drinking like that anymore. Well, not like she used to. Nowadays it's only one can at about 5pm, before getting dinner ready, before having to be ever so present. Some may say that even one can a day classifies her as an alcoholic. "Come spend a day in my brain," is always her response. The kids aren't due home from school for an hour or so, she hopes Daren, her latest partner, will be working late. Things between the two of them are pretty crappy, she doesn't want to have to deal with his shit on top of today's shit, instead she simply wants a hug, no words, no nothing, just to be held, to feel safe.

#

The smell of a burning incinerator invades her nostrils; her skin becomes moist with summer sweat. She's no longer here in the cool of Tasmania, she's back there where it all began, in that house, that shed, that space that's all too familiar to her. The space where her whole being changed, where something so precious was taken by others with no regard or right.

She sees herself as a child, being introduced to people, hiding behind her eyebrows, believing if she couldn't see them properly than they couldn't see her. She's always done that, still does. It's her way of not having to look anyone in the eye, afraid that if they see into her eyes, they'll see her ugly truth. Looking down, she sees young, tanned arms and legs, the colours of yellow and orange stripes glaring at her from the home-made overalls Ana was wearing that very first time her world went drastically wrong. That outfit scratched into her eyeballs, most likely the reason why she hates straight lines, instead preferring the gentle smoothness of curves.

Chapter 2

Going back – not an option

She sits for a while, listening to the gentle lap, lap of the river tides washing over the pebbles on her local beach, reflecting that even though she's burnt the letter it's like she can't let it go, let him go, let what happened to her go.

Deep within her being she knows that receiving that letter was a sign. It's the Universe's way of telling her she needs to deal with this, whatever this really is. The problem is, she doesn't want to talk to anyone at all connected with her past, it's just way too hard. But she has a feeling deep within her soul that not dealing with it is going to be so much harder, so much more damaging, to her.

Years ago, she was physically assaulted by a female neighbour, the neighbour literally king-hitting her five times, resulting in a perforated ear drum and immense pain. Her hand now places itself over her ear, trying to soothe the body memory. When this happened, she was really taken aback. She had told herself that her experience as a child was sort of kind of normal. That it was ok. That it was not as bad as some. She'd minimised her experience by saying, "But I was never hit". Weird logic, hey? So, when this physical assault happened, it sent her spinning out of control, all the abuse from her childhood, and all the shit crap things that had happened to her since, wouldn't leave her alone. Night terrors, even in the day hours.

Prior to the assault, she'd spoken to her then-partner Jason about wanting to deal with her childhood shit. After the assault, Jason pretty much said Ana had to deal with it or they were over. Jason said that her past was destroying their relationship. She wondered how much truth was in that. From where she was sitting, Jason's abusive controlling behaviour was what was doing the real damage.

But again, she remained silent. Again, she felt she had no voice, no choice.

She had a solicitor for that case. Going to court, the neighbour had done a runner, leaving their daughter behind. Ana struggled with that, feeling in part responsible for the daughter no longer having their mother present. One day in the solicitor's office, she disclosed some of her past, saying she felt that perhaps she should try and do something about it, as in, try and press legal charges. The solicitor recommended that at that point in her life she should not, saying that the defence team would rip her to shreds, that every single part of her life would be put under the microscope, that any behaviour that could in anyway be constructed as "slutty" (yes, his word) would be used against her, to discredit her story. Was she prepared for that? He didn't think so.

As a teenager she hadn't known how to say no. Any time a boy had wanted a part of her sexuality she'd simply let them, never feeling she had the right nor the ability to turn them down. This was the kind of behaviour the solicitor was talking about. He didn't think Ana was strong enough in that moment to be able to deal with what would happen to her.

She was so, so angry with the solicitor's response. Once again, she felt less than, not worthy of being heard, seen, validated, but also knowing he was right. It was hard enough living each day in an abusive relationship, trying to survive that, without dragging up her past as well.

Since then, she'd put the prospect of legal proceedings out of her mind, instead choosing to have faith in karma, so that they would all get what they deserved, all of them, the whole gang. They were all part of it in one way or another, Patrick, Otto, Donny, Donna.

#

Part of the assault case required a psychological diagnosis for the victim impact statement and compensation. She had never seen a professional before, let alone told her story to one, but now Ana couldn't stop the words pouring from her mouth. She spent the next year in the safe space the psychologist provided.

Not long before starting these sessions, she'd had a dream. In the dream, there was a lady with long curly red hair who was teaching her how to dance. The psychologist Ana saw had long curly red hair just like the lady in the dream, and in a way, she believed they did teach her to dance, and so much more.

The psychologist diagnosed PTSD from childhood trauma exacerbated by the recent assault. Having a label enabled Ana to better understand herself. It made her feel not so crazy. There were reasons why she was the way she was, reasons why she reacted as she did. Part of the therapy, apart from talking, was some EMDR treatment. It was a tad controversial back then, but she can still feel the effects of it some twenty years later.

All the time she was seeing the psych, talking about the past, about how the recent assault was affecting her, she kept quiet, so quiet about her home life. So scared of saying anything that would suggest to the psych that she, Ana was in what is termed a "domestic violence relationship", so scared Jason would find out she'd talked to someone about him. Jason always told her not to talk to anyone, not to talk to the neighbours, not to have friends. So, for that year and a few more after she kept silent about that part of her life.

#

A year to the day after starting therapy, at Christmas time, Ana found herself locked up. Yes, locked up in the local hospital. She'd been given the diagnosis of Graves' Disease. Apparently, she could go into thyroid storm or thyrotoxic crisis. Basically, her heart could beat so fast that it would explode. "Much like a Monty Python skit," she thought, smiling to herself.

She waited for a surgeon to appear. Thankfully she'd done the shopping for Esi who was then six years old. Now she just had to sort where Esi would spend the holidays, as spending them with her in hospital wasn't an option.

She'd found this really cool robot, about the size of a three-year-old, thinking that Esi would love it. You could make it talk, change the voice, make it move – such a super cool present. On Christmas day Esi rocked into the hospital with Scooter leading the way, the smile on their face letting her know how happy they were with Santa's choice.

In that moment she felt like she was an ok person.

After the operation, once she was back home, she did some research. Graves' Disease has "stress" as a contributing factor, and she has just experienced possibly the most stressful year of her life, talking about the most damaging six years of her life ... Is it hard to join the dots?

When Esi was young and feeling unwell, they would lounge on the couch playing join-the-dots on one another's faces, arms, and legs. Like her, Esi has freckles, and what better use of freckles than using them to create majikal drawings? So now, as she's resting and healing, Esi comes over, sits by their mum, smiling as they start joining the dots upon her body.

Weirdest thing, a couple of months after the operation Jason goes, "You've changed since you've had your op."

"What do you mean?"

"You talk now."

Is that a good thing? Going by his actions, she doesn't think so. She knows something's shifted within her. She discovered metaphysics about ten years earlier and it makes so much sense – the mind-body connection with everything. Being told that she speaks now, after having a huge lump removed from her throat, interesting.

#

"Sometimes you have to kick karma along."

The words were spoken by her friend Gianna, a beautiful Italian soul, embodying all that it is to hold space unconditionally for another, someone she's so grateful to have in her life. Gianna's words echoed in her head, seeking attention. Within a few days they got it. If she simply lets herself be, she can hear her body calling her, begging her to do now that which for so long she felt unable to. It's time. It's her time.

She's so much stronger now, much surer of who she is, she's left Jason and now is in a space where she feels safe and has great supportive friends around her. Now she can, no, she *will* do this. This letter from some random stranger has actually done her a favour. It's the fuel aiding her to put out the fire within her soul.

The next morning, she gets up, puts on her big-girl pants and goes into the local police station. It doesn't look like a police station – more like a hotel out of some B-grade 80's movie. Memories of a time long ago when she was a teenager come flooding back.

Back then, she'd walked into a police station, though not by choice, she was led there by two policemen. She'd been busted shoplifting. Shoplifting when she was young was just like any other activity. She wanted someone to simply see her, to ask her why she was acting this way. But no one ever did, so she kept stealing. Next to smoking, this was the only regret in her life. These are the only things she would change; she was so ashamed of her behaviour back then.

The police had been really good, especially when she'd begged them not to tell her parents. She was nearly an adult, she didn't speak to them anymore, anyway. Even though she wanted someone to ask her why she was behaving this way, that someone wasn't them. A chuckle escapes her mouth as she remembers the funniest part: On the day of her court appearance, a group of school kids and their teacher walk into the court; these school kids just happen to be the legal studies class below her from her old high school. The teacher looks at Ana in the guilty chair and shakes his head with a smile on his face, saying, "I knew, I just knew".

Now some thirty years later, Ana's once again walking into a police station, feeling slightly more empowered, feeling more like she's floating than walking along the walkway. That's probably because with each step towards her destiny she's separating more and more from her physicality.

Reaching reception, she looks down upon her being, seeing herself move uncomfortably as each word leaves her mouth, the sounds muffled by her soul's absence. The police officer listens with respect, allowing the space for breath as required. She thought that this would be it, she'd go to the police, she'd tell them that she'd like to press charges, she'd give a statement and then it would all be over at least for a while. But that's not what happened.

Apparently, when filing a complaint like this one, the one Ana struggles to say out loud (childhood sexual assault, is that even a thing?) there is more to the process. The officer tells her that she needs to go home. That a police officer from the sexual assault's unit in Hilcock, the station covering the area where the abuse happened, will contact her soonish.

What? Wait. No, no, no, no. This isn't making sense. Why can't it all be done now? Why must she wait? That the contact may be from someone who possibly knows POS or lives where she used to, only heightens her rising anxiety. None of it makes sense within her mind. She turns away, mumbling a thank you, placing the business card handed to her into her jacket pocket, feeling in that moment the Universe conspiring against her. Somehow, she makes it home, not remembering if she drove or caught the bus. She's in shock.

Now she has to decide how much she's willing to share with Daren, how much she's willing to let him in on her journey. She knows their relationship's over; the challenging part is working out when to actually end it. Especially considering the wheels she's just put into motion. She feels that possibly that ending may have to wait, just a little bit longer. She needs her strength at the moment to deal with this and an impending operation she knows is on the horizon.

#

Ana didn't know the process, how could she? There are no how-to books written on dealing with legal proceedings to do with childhood abuse. There's nothing she can follow that would explain that everything she's about to experience is normal, considering the circumstances. Thankfully she can talk to Kimberly, the psychologist she's seen for the last three years. She shares with Kimberly what she's just gone and done.

The days turn into weeks, and finally Ana gets a phone call from the Sexual Assault Unit in Hilcock. The police officer introduces themselves, "Hello I'm Senior Sargent Monica." The phone slips from her hand.

A year or so ago, she'd had a dream in which Patrick O'Shanesy was trying to appear changed. For a moment she believes him. Then he tells her about his baby and how he gently fondles the baby's genitals when changing the nappy. She's in the shower when POS tells her this, she wants to vomit, wants to run away, wants to kill the motherfucker. She tries to get out, tries to open the shower door, it's in a change room. POS comes through the door naked, locking it behind him. She can hear herself calling out the name Monique, wanting Monique to come and help her, having no idea who Monique is. Yet now here's a Monica who's going to hopefully help her hold POS accountable for his actions.

That's what she wants, that's her motive behind all of this, she wants him held accountable. Wants her story told, to be heard, to be believed. At this point in time, she's not sure if she wants the other three charged – Otto, Donny and Donna – of that she's not too sure. But she knows she wants POS charged. Even though she's now in her 40s, it's like she's a six-year-old again. She feels unable to speak, to say no, to breathe without fear. She doesn't know how long all of this is going to take, she doesn't know if she is going to be able to walk it each day.

#

There are so many triggers: names, smells, places, appearances, tones of voices, words used. Sometimes it's really hard being her, interacting with others and pretending to be normal. Sometimes she feels herself relax, then a word, a tone, a scent will invade her space, and she's gone, she's so good at not being present without anyone else being aware. That is, unless they actually see her. Some of her friends know the signs, they too leave their bodies, so many injured souls out there.

#

Ana visits the local printing place, carrying some recent artwork rolled up under her arm. She wants to get some prints made and possibly sell them. This in itself is a huge thing, her art being so much a part of who she is. Each piece tells a story; each piece has some of her in it. Allowing others to see that makes her feel vulnerable. As she's talking to the man behind the counter, discussing her wants, her eyes move up to his name tag.

"Patrick"

A deep gasp invades her being.

Realising what's happening, that she's leaving, disconnecting, disassociating, she starts to name five things she can see 1) the countertop 2) the printing machines 3) the promotion flags that flutter anytime the door opens 4) her shoes, she loves her shoes, they're so cool with coloured flowers all over them and 5) the carpet under her feet, after all she is already looking at the ground.

Four things she can feel 1) the cold laminated countertop that feels so good under her sweaty palms 2) the sharp angles of the keys she's clutching tighter and tighter in her hand 3) the pen she picks up trying to fill out the order form and 4) the paper underneath. She wishes the paper would cut her, offering some physical pain for the pain she's feeling inside, unseen by anyone, but so felt by her.

Three things she can hear 1) the sound of the printing machines 2) the traffic going past outside and 3) the sound of this Patrick's voice.

Two things she can smell 1) the scent of the melting lamination that has obviously just been done before her arrival 2) her own body odour, stinking as the sweat pours out of her.

One good thing about herself? Now this catches her up, this is always the hardest part. Struggling to answer, her gaze falls to the countertop to where her art lays exposed for anyone to see. She loves her art. She is ever so proud of herself. So there, that's one good thing about herself 1) she thinks she's a good artist.

Taking a deep breath she rights herself all the while talking in her mind, "This Patrick is not him; this Patrick seems kind and gentle, his tone is soft." She breathes in; her order is finished. She leaves, not knowing how she drives home, knowing she's once again left her body, once again run as best as she can to escape him, to escape the memories. She gives thanks to her guardian angels for getting her home safely.

#

As a younger person, she'd read Stephen King novels as though they were nursery rhymes, her dreams always being so much worse than anything she'd read on the pages. She loved horror movies, though not ones that involved mind games, those ones scared the crap out of her, they would leave her with even more horrific nightmares for weeks. She finds reading scary books and watching horror movies to be spaces that allow her to escape, to escape her own horror movies that at times play consistently across her mind's eye. So now, as the legal stuff proceeds, she finds herself watching them night after night, sitting in front of the television, screaming, jumping, pulling back, slapping herself, as the images unfold and the emotions from the movies make their way through her body.

Kimberly said that watching horror movies was good for people with PTSD. That in doing so, their bodies can experience all the flight, fight, or freeze processes without actually being in any real danger. So, she watches, she watches until her eyelids can no longer stay open, watching even when Daren's condemnation of her choices causes unease within her. She knows this is what she needs to do for herself.

No one, herself included, seemed to realise just how much of a detrimental impact having to retell her story would be. It left her wanting to simply escape, for it all to be over, for the pain to stop, for the images in her head to stop, for the noise in her head, the noise that never stops in her head, to simply no longer be. Thoughts of ending her life become more and more pressing in her reality with each passing day. The not knowing when the police will make contact, the pretending that everything's normal, her failing relationship, her hatred for self, it's all taking a toll. The body pains she's experiencing just add to the mix.

Ending her life will end all of it, then she'll be no more, her pain will stop, her family will be free, and POS will continue along whatever bullshit life he's living without ever being held accountable for the choices he made, the choices that removed any choice she had as a child. Can she die with all of that being ok within her dead soul? Probably not.

Chapter 3

Dreams – an untold reality

One night, she's watching a show on television. There's a lady in court trying to convict her abuser. It's too close to home, leaving Ana unsure if she can do that, be present in the same space as him. She hadn't thought that far ahead, and watching, feels sick in the stomach, her breathing becoming shallow, rapid.

"Holy fuck, this isn't even my story and it's affecting me like this, what's it going to be like when it really is mine?"

That night, she dreams. It's a good dream, a wonderful freeing dream. She's in this place that has so many different lands, it's awesome. She's in the bottom land, which is beautiful. You walk into this cave and there's an oasis, the water's a lovely deep blue and the sky the prettiest of pinks, there are three crescent moons of different phases in front of her and another one off to the side.

It's so beautiful, it leaves her wondering, "Why is this only a dream? I would love to go there. Why can't I be there now? It's so much nicer, more peaceful and surrounded by space to simply breathe. Please God, take me there."

In another dream she's given a baby girl who she names Grace. It makes her cry; she feels so unworthy of such a gift. This dream throws her, leaving her feeling even worse about herself. You would think such a beautiful dream would be good, but no, it brings in such strong feelings of worthlessness, leaving her feeling she has no right to be on this earthly plane.

The next day she rings the police.

"I can't do this. In this moment I can't continue. The desire to kill myself is pulling me more to its side and I can't let that happen."

She's burbling to Monica, her breath barely audible above the heaving sobs escaping her soul.

#

It's weird how many times in her life she's felt out of control, as though an invisible force, Spirit, God, the Universe is the one actually controlling her life.

She dreams again. Dreams are so much a part of who she is. She remembers dreaming as a child, the dreams never stopping. She is 34 years old before she has her first good dream. How sad is that? Thirty-four years of nightmares.

Like so many other dreams in her lifetime, she believes this dream's telling her something. In the dream she's taken prisoner, not knowing by who or why. She's in a room, and this lady's trying to get her to talk but failing. They grab her and push really hard into her left ovary causing extreme pain. They are in Ana's face shouting, "TELL ME! TELL ME WHO IT IS!"

Her mouth remains shut, not a word escaping, not even a sound. They grab her even tighter, harder, placing their hands on either side of her ovaries. Inflicting so much pain.

"TELL ME! WILL YOU JUST TELL ME!"

She feels this dream's telling her that someone's not happy about her not speaking out. Someone wants her to talk no matter what the pain, but she just can't.

The dreaming becomes regular, invading the dark time, disrupting her peace.

#

When she was young, she didn't want to sleep, she was afraid to sleep. She remembers waking up from nightmares, calling out to Mother Blobfish, to be yelled at by Father Bullshark, "Shut up! your mother's sleeping."

She taught herself how to escape the dreams when they'd become too much. It took practice. She couldn't do it all the time, just sometimes. The more she tried, the better she got. She would check under the bed every night before sleep, always believing she'd find something, snakes most likely. Not knowing why she'd see snakes, not realising as a child that in fact, she's a snake in Chinese Astrology. It's always empty under there, but in the absence of anything, so much more can be present.

Dreaming's like seeing Spirit. She remembers being three years old and seeing Spirits for the first time in the house where they lived, on a road near the railway line. She had a night light next to her bed and every night these "things" would appear, scaring her. No one explained what they could be, but they must have been something, as every night at 5pm, but only Mondays through to Fridays, Mother Blobfish would line all of Ana's siblings up in front of the open fireplace, which was on the other side of her bedroom wall. Mother Blobfish would tell them to rub their eyes, hoping it would remove the images. It never worked, and Ana never understood why they didn't do this on Saturdays and Sundays. Maybe it had something to do with Father Bullshark.

Years later during a re-birth session, these images, the ones that haunted her early years, appeared. And they weren't evil at all. They were, in fact, her guardian angels, there to help and protect her. If only she'd known that back then, but they were perceived as a threat, as something to fear, leading her for many years after to fear all the Spirits she saw, and she saw many. Still does.

#

The dreams keep coming, filling her head with images. Sometimes wondrous divine images, sometimes haunting scary images. She never knows which is going to appear. As dreaming is such a huge part of who she is, she's kept a dream journal for at least the last 25 years, reflecting on her dreams, seeing what the dreams were telling her, finding that helpful and supportive. So now she listens, she pays attention to her dreams, even the crap ones, believing that those ones are teaching her the most.

In a dream at the beach, it's a rather rocky outcrop, she sees something moving behind the rocks. As it moves closer, she realises it's a seal. There are heaps of them all lazing around or playing. She's loving them, watching, embracing their seal energy. There's such joy in this dream; it's such a welcome change. Seal energy: of trust and integrity. She likes that meaning. It gives her more validation of what she's feeling.

Unfortunately, just because there's a good dream one night, doesn't mean that the next night will be the same. A few nights later there's another dream. She's in a space like a warehouse. A guy's running around yelling at everyone, telling them to get rid of anything that can act as a conductor. He throws all these tools on the floor, then starts pulling shit from his body. He pulls out a tool from his ankle, it sort of looks like a stun gun, but it has all these wires sticking out of it. It's very strange. Then moving his hand to his cheek, he pulls the skin down under his eye. There's a Stanley knife hidden in the skin. It's so very creepy as the man pulls the knife out of his cheek. He keeps yelling at everyone to throw their stuff as far away as possible. Now the man's running through this really big factory space, from one building to the next, yelling at everyone, "The aliens are coming! You have to go!"

Ana runs over to the school building and goes into the hall space. She can see the principal, who appears all confused. They thought they had to address the students about the aliens coming, but there's no students there. She tells the principal to run as there's not much time left. The principal heads down the corridor. Ana follows, then stops, sure she's heard a noise. It's probably a child. She hesitates. If she runs back, she knows she won't make it out, but can she leave a child?

Suddenly the child appears.

"Run!"

The child reaches Ana. Leaning down, she pulls the child up piggyback style and together they race down the corridor.

She can hear the speaker shouting, "Twenty seconds until shutdown!"

All the doors are closing in front of them. She must get through before they're fully closed, otherwise that's it. They sneak through the first door as a gas is being released through the vents. They hear its hiss, smell its poison. She tells the child not to breathe, wishing she'd worn a scarf, knowing the gas will kill them. They run to get through the last door. It's closing, but they make it. Ana gulps in fresh air, putting the child down. She looks at her ankle, it's really hurting, there's an open wound and it looks as though its badly burnt. The principal walks over, looks at the ankle and says that the gas is between 500 and 900 degrees Fahrenheit. She's lucky to be alive, let alone still have her ankle.

They have further to go to escape, there's a big wooden tower in front of them that she has to climb. With the child still on her back, she starts climbing. When she makes it to the top, she can hear others at the bottom. She knows she hasn't got long, that she needs to get down the other side and keep going. She climbs down, and in no time they're both safe.

She feels this dream's telling her that the aliens (her childhood abusers) will try and stop her. ("Well, that part's right," she thinks. Though it wasn't them that had made her stop, it was the effects of their actions that made her stop. So, in a way, yes, it was because of them she'd stopped. Now she's so confused.) But that she can and will overcome their attack. And she'll do so carrying and caring for her inner child, knowing that no matter what, she'll be safe. Now she just needs to believe it.

The next night, there's yet another dream. Sleep is seemingly unimportant. There are all these things flying at her and everyone else, killing most people. They all run and try to hide as she watches the mass of killing flyers going past, searching for the next victim. Someone's standing still, covered in what at first looks like the killer flyers. They watch and wait for the kill, but instead, the insects are dying, all of them. She's unable to figure it out.

Some guy says that they are "such-and-such insects", that they survive by zoning in on human emotions. Ahhh, so that's how the flying killers are choosing their victims, by picking up on emotions. So now everyone must avoid being killed by not showing emotion of any kind.

Everyone's in the open, the killing mass is approaching, looking, seeking. They all sit quietly, keeping their minds blank and their hearts empty as the killers fly right past.

Wow, it worked!

Oh shit, she's shown an emotion. A flying killer turns back. She's frantically trying to blank herself out. The flying killer picks up on someone else and she's safe, for the moment.

She's running with her friend Malia; they're trying to find somewhere to hide. They go into a bathroom and see a secret door. It's hidden in the wall. Pulling it open, they see there's a toilet and enough room for two people to hide. Quickly they get inside, pulling the door tightly shut. They can hear voices. The insects are looking for victims. Something tries the door.

"Hold the door," she mouths to Malia. But Malia seems very much out of it, so she slaps them across the face. Malia comes to. Together they hold the door shut by grabbing hold of the latch as hard as they can. They keep that door closed, their lives depending on it.

The flying insects give up. Faces look through the window, so they keep their heads low, hoping not to be seen as they leave the room. It seems that lots of others have also worked out that as long as they don't show an emotion, a mood, they'll survive. So, there's all these people walking around, empty, blank, but they're alive.

She feels that in this dream, she's telling herself to remain emotionless, to remain detached from the memories, to simply blank everything out. To simply survive.

#

The simple joys of a toasted cheese and spinach sandwich. This she loves, this she savours.

Chapter 4

Anaemia – lack of joy, fear of life

Art becomes her saviour, her sanity, a way of expressing herself. The simple meditative process of dotting helps to take her away. The colours, the action, just that repetitiveness, the result, they all allow expression of self. She's even started making her own frames. It cuts down costs but also allows the image to continue past the limitations of the canvas. It's kind of reflective, like her. It gets her to think outside the norm of conventional thinking, of limited perceptions. She paints the beautiful dream she had a month or so ago where she was present in many lands with the four moons. This makes her happy. This image soothes her eyes. She has no plan, no idea of how it will be. She's simply letting her hand get in the zone, the dotting allowing her to enter a space of relaxation, of peace. It's so colourful and it does, in part, reflect what she saw in her dream. She's really happy with it, titling it *Ascension*.

#

The operation, the operation she's known is coming, the one she's been trying not to think about, is in a few weeks. The anxiety associated with that is beginning to build. She's grateful she's withdrawn her complaint, but she doesn't understand why she has to go into the police station to complete the withdrawal. That action only adds to the trauma. Why can't she just tell them over the phone? But no, it needs to be in writing.

She feels as though her words are lost. Her saying how damaging it is to retell her story, to have any association with her story, how much that affects her. Her voice is being lost amongst the taboo of sexual assault, as she once again needs to be physically present for something she's spent her lifetime leaving.

She knows she needs to be present, but she knows she needs her strength for the operation. She's already left her body, before even arriving at the police station. The challenge now is to bring herself back in before the anaesthetic removes her further. Knowing what's ahead, she's prepared for the discomfort, for the horrible floating effect of the anaesthetic, the floaty feeling that isn't hers by choice. The hysterectomy's necessary. She's chronically anaemic. First, they tried injections, then transfusions. Neither helped, the operation seemingly the only solution. Well, the only one that sits comfortably within her being.

The specialist tries to get her to have an IUD inserted. She sits in his office, tears rolling down her cheeks, as he tries to justify his wanting to shove a foreign body into her most sacred-ness.

He looks bewildered, wondering why this woman's crying over something so basic. Surely having an IUD is much better than having to go through the trauma of an operation. He doesn't get it, he doesn't know, even though Kimberly's written a report explaining some of Ana's her-ness to him, he still doesn't get it. How could he? He's male. He's probably never had unwanted, uninvited things put in places nothing should go in someone so young. He simply doesn't know, but his ignorance doesn't help.

She's made up her mind, she's having the operation and there's nothing he nor anyone else can say to stop her. She decides, in the process, to also have her ovaries and cervix out. There's so much pain in her ovaries, especially the left one, just like in her dream. Having had stage one cervical cancer when she was younger, it seems like the smart thing to do – eliminate more possible cancer sites.

#

In yet another dream, she's walking aimlessly around her childhood town. Lots of thick green yucky phlegm is in her throat and mouth.

It just keeps coming up, making her feel as though she's going to choke. At times there's even blood in the phlegm. It is so thick and gross, and she so wants it out of her. So, there's this gooey sticky crap inside her – the parts of her past she's tucked so deep inside have become a blob of shit, sometimes containing blood – joy, life-force, family … interesting.

#

The crappiest part of all of this is the pretending. Pretending to be normal, pretending that everything's ok. Still making lunches, dinners, cleaning the house, taking the kids places, talking to people she'd rather not.

She has a little cleaning job; it's only a few hours a fortnight. She doesn't even know why she does it – she hates cleaning, but it's right next door. One day, as she's cleaning, everything feels weird. All the spaces seem so much smaller, closer together than normal. She feels so detached and realises that she probably has been since she had to go back to the police station two weeks ago.

#

It's time, and like most people, she really hates hospitals. At one point in her life, she felt she should write a guide to Melbourne hospitals. You know, like a travel guide. She'd been in just about all of them.

She doesn't want to be away from her space, from Big Dog and Little Dog, needing their curliness, their silkiness, their feel, their knowing. When she's feeling anything, they'll come and make her pat them, looking at her with so much love in their eyes. Little Dog's such a godsend. When she's waking from nightmares, Little Dog will come and dig under her hand, making her pat them, bringing her back into her body.

Why aren't dogs allowed in hospitals? It sucks. She knows she won't stay, she'll come home straight away. She's scared, scared of not being able to protect herself whilst under anesthetic, of not being able to control her environment, of feeling so vulnerable. They're taking everything. She'll be an empty cavern of nothingness, a whole abyss of ... what? It leaves her wondering what will soon fill the void left by the operation.

She's had the experience of lots of operations previously, each one hurting more than the last, but now she wonders why this one's hurting, like big time. She doesn't want her family to come and see her. She doesn't want to have to put on a face, pretend everything's ok when it's not. It's the pain that's scaring her. When the family calls, she tells them to stay home, its late, she'll see them tomorrow.

There's a catheter invading her her-ness, she hates it, it's hurting, she wants it gone ... Now! She's screaming at the nurses. They say it can't come out yet. Fuck them, if they won't take it out, she'll rip it out herself. It feels so much more than what it is physically. She's hating herself for yelling.

She's unable to sleep. The pain is huge, intense, deep. It leaves her questioning why. All her kids' births were caesareans; Zeb's birth included a tubal ligation. That really hurt. But this, this, this is different, this pain is deeper.

She searches for the core of it, the meaning behind it, wondering if it's psychosomatic, if the recent journey back into her past, to the childhood invasion, was having an impact on her physicality. The catheter's making her feel like that, it feels like such an invasion of her being. The catheter a penis, an unwanted intrusion into her femaleness. She just wants to go home. To curl up in a ball comforted by Big Dog and Little Dog. To simply block out the world. But she can't, she has to stay to endure this pain, this discomfort, for God knows what fucking reason.

The family comes in.

"Just go away, leave me alone," Ana screams. Then sees the hurt on her kids faces. Dying would be such a welcome relief right now.

Finally, the catheter comes out. She pees the right amount. She's out of there.

Tears stream down her face. She's unable to stop them, they're like a river flowing after the dam walls broken. She just wants to be held, to be told, "I love you, everything will be ok." But no arms come to envelop her. Instead, she's alone, shivering uncontrollably, so wishing she wasn't here.

#

Alone in bed with too much time for the silence in her head, she gently places her hands over what is now an empty space, the centre of her femaleness. Quietly she asks Spirit, "What's this all about? What do I need to learn?"

A vision appears, this happens lots, so she's neither afraid nor in awe, it's simply a part of who she is. There's a pool. In the pool, swimming happily, are five Koi fish. The pool has black and white checked tiles above its waterline. Lying on her back in the centre, arms and legs outstretched star-like, she floats. The song *Free From the Past* seems to come out of some invisible speakers in her room.

That song, she knows it, she heard it many years ago from a random busker on the street one summer night. She bought the CD, having connected so deeply with the lyrics. Now it's in her head. What's it telling her?

She lies there some more, embracing all the teachings her vision and tones are imparting, breathing in and out and repeating "Ok, I believe I get the message" to no one in particular. No one's there.

She's left feeling that Spirit's telling her to restart legal proceedings against POS.

"I know what I must do, may I just rest for a bit first please?"

Two days later she rings the police station, informing them that she'd like to restart her complaint. They tell her that the Hilcock Sexual Assault Unit will contact her shortly. She already knows that shortly can be a very, very long time.

#

The dreams start again. There seems to be these big grains of sand around the rim of her camera lens. She tries to wipe them away, then realises they're not grains of sand, they're crystals. All these amazing crystals are falling from her lens. How awesome. Thank you.

Ana feels this dream's telling her that she'll see many wonders through her camera, that it will offer her great joy. "Like really, how cool that would be? Crystals falling out of my camera lens. I'd just walk around taking photos all the time, collecting the crystals, adding them to my ever-growing collection."

#

Her mouth hurts so much, her teeth feel all cracked. She's sure that's from grinding them nearly every night for the last forty-odd years. Teeth, metaphysically, are indecisiveness. Well, that's true. She's *ummmed* and *ahhhed* about the legal proceedings for many years really. Now she's sure she's going to follow through. Nothing and no-one is going to stop her.

The local public dentistry, which she's been going to ever since moving to Tasmania, is fantastic. They have students there, and she knew when she made the appointment that she'd be seeing one. No worries, she didn't care. She simply wanted the pain in her mouth, like the pain all over her body, to stop.

As the dentist chair reclines, anxiety starts rising. She feels herself becoming agitated, her hands doing the nervous repetitive actions that betray her increased anxiety. Her breathing becomes shallower and shallower. She starts talking to herself, "This too will pass, this too will pass," but it doesn't, it gets worse.

The bewildered look of having no idea what to do is written all over the student dentists' face. Ana fears she may bite their fingers off if they aren't removed from her mouth immediately.

You see, she's not seeing a student dentist in front of her, much less a grown woman with a lovely gentle face and open smile. No, all she can see and feel in that moment is being held down, trapped, with a penis being shoved in her mouth. That's why she wants to bite down on the fingers, she wants to bite down on the penis, severing it from the owner. Then with great glee, she'll spit it out and wait for some bird of prey to come and take it away. Her whole body's reacting to the embodied memory, not the reality of the moment.

Thankfully the student realises that whatever's going on is way past their understanding, so they stop, raising the chair back to its upright position.

Ana feels such a failure. Unable to be a normal person. She feels so trapped, claustrophobic and ever so vulnerable. She wants to run but doesn't know how, so instead she finds herself on the ceiling of the dentists' room, floating, watching herself squirm in the seat as she's told she has trench mouth.

Thankfully, she's given some written documentation on what exactly trench mouth is, otherwise she'd have no idea what had been said. Apparently, trench mouth is so named as it was quite common in the wars. The men stuck in the trenches suffered from it, their gums becoming inflamed, much worse than gingivitis. It was the stress of the war that the doctors believed was the cause of this condition.

Ana knows she isn't in a war. Or is she? Isn't she waging a war against those who have done unspeakable acts to her? Isn't that what war is? People doing unspeakable acts of cruelty to one another. Her teeth are still cracked; her pain is still real. At least now she understands why.

#

The first blood-test results since the operation came back and look really promising. Her iron levels are good. She has absolutely no idea how. She hasn't eaten much meat, nor any of the food substitutes she should, yet here is the evidence. She is no longer anaemic.

Metaphysically, anaemia is lack of joy, fear of life, not feeling good enough. All of those things are so relatable. Maybe, just maybe, placing the complaint against POS is actually going to heal her physically. Time will tell.

Chapter 5

Ancestry – the origin of being

Over the years she's figured out that who she speaks to, who she interacts with, the memories she's having, all of these things influence the dreams she has. So, it is no surprise that she has shit dreams when dealing with anything from her past.

One day, she speaks with Mother Blobfish – not exactly something Ana enjoys, as Mother Blobfish chooses to live a life of denial. They refuse to see, refuse to accept what happened to their daughter. After all, if Mother Blobfish did accept it, then they'd have to accept responsibility for the trauma that was done. Father Bullshark's slightly better. At least they believe her, trying in their messed-up way to support her. Mother Blobfish instead took sides, choosing the other side, and basically removed Ana from the family. So why is she even wasting a moment of her energy talking to Mother Blobfish? Because she's always held onto the belief that maybe, just maybe one day, she'll finally have the mother she so longs for. She knows that's never going to happen; however, that doesn't stop the wishing.

#

A new passion is walking aimlessly around the streets, the town, the bush, the beach, anywhere where focus isn't required, though this has led to getting lost a couple of times. She loves exploring the local op shops. There are so many treasures to be found, usually at bargain prices.

Coloured glass becomes a new obsession. Glass of any colour. She places the glass on window ledges throughout her house with the intent of bringing colour into her world. Soon everything she owns is full of colour too, just like the glass. She hates plain, lifeless shades, instead wanting bright, vibrant shapes and patterns to fill her eyesight with life. Her family think she's becoming a hippy. They just don't get it.

#

It's hard not knowing when the police will contact her or where she'll be when they do. She knows she will once again have to repeat her story and wonders how through all of that she will manage to stay sane. She tries writing. Trying to make sense of what she's feeling by putting words on paper. Trying to sort her feelings into something that may make possible sense to someone, anyone. She writes now amid the overwhelming anguish; thoughts of suicide ever present.

I lie here, wondering if I can do it right, so I know it's final.

The abyss of emptiness is all so enveloping.

A little hand reaches out

Please don't show you care

It doesn't seem fair

But here I am

Wondering how

Wondering why

Wondering when

While all the time you talk and laugh

It's not your doing, it's not your care

You show that true

So why am I here?

No longer to be

Another time, another place

Then maybe there'll be a space for me to care

It's amazing how alone I can feel in a house filled with people

I'm drowning … silently.

The hard part is not feeling safe enough to express any of this outwardly. Not being able to share it with those who are meant to love her. So, she doesn't, she keeps it all locked inside, her journal hidden, tucked away in the back corner of the bedside table.

#

Dreams, dreams, friggin dreams. She feels as though there's no rest, no place to be at peace in her mind, her being. It's always busy trying to combat some unseen force.

In this dream, an upper left tooth is pulled out. It's full of stones. She's trying to run away but unable to do so, for some reason. When she's inside, she can't run, but outside she can a little bit. She's trying to run fast but it just isn't happening. It's like slow mo.

This is not much different from real life. In real life she can't run, having restricted movement in her ankle from a bad break when she was a teenager. So, running in a dream, no matter how weird, is still great in her mind.

Another dream. She's trapped in the entrance of her house by a dark energy. The door from the kitchen to the backyard is closed. She's trying to drag herself along the floor towards the steps, getting up, lunging for the door but falling short. She tries calling out, her shout but a whisper. She can hear the family in the kitchen, but they can't hear or see her. Suddenly Little Dog comes running in and somehow manages to disconnect the energy.

This is so telling, she feels unseen, separate from her family. She's so grateful for Big Dog and Little Dog, they seem to be filling the role of her greatest comforters. She doesn't know where she'd be, or whether she'd even be alive without them.

Walking Big Dog and Little Dog is good, it brings her joy and peace. The best part is that people can talk to them, and not to her. It's also an excuse to escape from home. She walks when everyone else has gone home for the day, when her family's home. She pays attention to the number of people she encounters, then adjusts her walks to minimise contact.

The rawness of Tasmania is so appealing. Its rough edges, its wildness, its intangibility, its unwillingness to conform. It reflects those qualities Ana so wishes to embody.

A trip up the mountain to snow-covered Mt Field, her most favourite local space, brings a smile to her face and a sense of peace to her soul. She feels alive in the white wonder, so free, so unrestricted by anything. She so wishes she could stay. She'd build a hut, find some water, sit under the stars, be grateful. She knows it won't last, that she'll have to return to the normality of life, yet she'll come back here time and time again to simply be, to simply breathe.

#

Family comes to visit. She likes that, likes seeing her kids interact with their cousins. This is all her family, the only ones who have stood by her, apart from Father Bullshark and Mitria her step mum. It saddens her greatly. Her kids only have a little extended family, they know there's more out there, though they're not sure why they're not part of their family's lives. One day she may tell them, one day when they're old enough and understand enough to not carry her shit.

Most things were never shared in Ana's birth family, there's so many secrets even to this day. She shared her secret, but it didn't help, it just divided the family she knows so little about. Maybe that's a good thing, though she does know that part of her comes from here, Tasmania. There's a genealogy group at the local hall, so she decides to try and find something that may connect her to the history of this land. Some progress is made and a road trip is planned. They head north to Scottsdale on a search for where she believes an old family home may still be standing. A family adventure, yay!

#

Why are all family road trips like oh so shit? Daren's driving, but she wants to drive. At least then she'd have something to focus on. Instead, she's sitting on the passenger side, letting the landscape blur before her eyes. Father Bullshark and Mitra are visiting, they're in the back with Rey and Zeb, adding to her stress, her unease. She hates the tone of Father Bullshark's voice when he speaks to Mitra, when he speaks to her or the kids, his arrogance causes discomfort within her being.

They find what's believed to be the ancestral home. It's run down, unloved, weathered, much like her, she thinks. On the trip back, the mobile rings; there's no caller ID, they're the worst calls. She doesn't want to answer, feeling she'll be found if she does. That's how her brain works: no caller ID means that it's someone that doesn't want her to know they're calling, so in her head that must mean someone from her past; therefore, someone she doesn't want to talk to … but sometimes it's not.

Thankfully, there's no Bluetooth, so only Ana can hear who's on the other end. It's a vaguely familiar voice, a woman. It's the police officer from the Hilcock Sexual Assault Unit – Monica.

She needs to get out of the car, not wanting to speak about such filth with her kids only inches away. Her whole body's spinning, it's leaving this space, she can feel herself floating away over the lush green valley out to the sapphire blue waters, never to return. Now she must wait for another phone call to organise giving her statement. She didn't get this far last time. That's the hardest part – not knowing when that will be.

It's interesting how that phone call comes as she's returning from a journey to find out where she's from, how she's connected.

Sometimes she manages to remove all of the shit from childhood out of her mind, her space, and be sort of normal. It's called self-preservation. She moves things, crap, yuck things, to places within her where she can be sort of ok. As in, still appear normal. But this, this phone call, this invasion into her reality, moved them from there to here, now, right in front of her, with no more hiding.

In the end, the Sexual Assault Unit in Tasmania is pretty quick. It's not long before she finds herself giving her formal statement. It's all so surreal, she knows she's talking, she knows words are being written down, but it so doesn't feel like her. She imagines herself with fairy wings and a wand. She waves the wand and it all disappears. She flies away to a wondrous majikal land where there is no yuck, only joy and wonder.

Vomiting seems like such a good option right now. That's what she wants to do, throw up all over everything, over the yuck written on the paper before her. She wants the vomit to seep through the ink, the paper, onto the desk, leaving its stain, its stench for all those who come after to bear.

She so doesn't want to carry this anymore. She wants it all to be gone, to be cut out of her, scrubbed out of her. Cutting it out seems like a good idea, but oh where to start? It's in every cell of her being. Start in some random place, letting the knife dictate the direction and depth. But then there'd be blood. Then others may see. You can't have that, 'cause then they'd ask questions. Don't want people asking questions. So, she remains unseen.

She thinks a jump into the ocean may be the answer. She could keep swimming out until the water was high over her head. She could sink her feet into the muddiness of the sand, let it hold her, ground her, until a wave would come, its force lifting her up, pulling her along, then smashing her drained on the shore.

In the retelling, the writing of her statement, she feels it all. She can smell the smells, hear the laughter, see the dust particles dance among the sunbeams shining through the cracked louvers.

Do you ever get the chance to have a different story? One that would make you someone completely different. Wouldn't that be nice? But you can't. At least not at the moment. Maybe in, like, sci-fi time you'll be able to. Now, instead, she simply leaves. Floating away until she feels she's far enough away that she can't get hurt.

Afterwards, she takes a walk along the beach, her feet tingling as the cold water touches them, the wetness feeling so welcoming beneath her weight.

Quicksand, that's what's needed. It will allow her into its space, opening up offering itself to her. She will gladly accept, allowing it to envelope her, suffocate her, hold her.

Away from her body, away from everything, she stays that way for weeks. A return visit to the police station is required for her to reread her statement. As though she doesn't know her own story. She has to sign her name, claiming all of this as hers. That part is good, though it's somewhat strange to see her birth name scrawled across the paper. It's so foreign, she never uses it, hasn't seen it written for years. Yet here it is, a record of her existence, of her story.

#

So many great friends help to keep sanity in Ana's world. The terribly horrific and sad thing is that so many others have stories just like hers. The cruelty of human against human is something incomprehensible. Then again, humans are horrible to animals and nature too, why would they be any different to their own?

It's taken her many years to allow friendships into her space, to trust in another. Especially females, is that weird? She doesn't like being touched, that physicality, that intimacy. But Gianna, someone she trusts, senses so much built-up tension within Ana's body, she wants to give her a massage. Ana lies there, like an empty shell. Not flinching, not reacting at all, and this lets her know she's further out from her body than she'd thought.

She feels so removed that it's hard to feel things, to actually feel anything. One evening when cooking dinner, the smell of burning skin gets her attention. Not the actual physical pain associated with it, the flames don't seem to be hurting; however, the scent of charred flesh brings an awareness that this isn't good.

Yay, another scar to add to the ever-growing design upon her body.

It's dangerous to drive at the moment, she knows this, yet she still does. She needs that freedom, that ability to take herself away at the drop of a hat.

There are so many wonderful places in Tasmania, each corner revealing a "wow factor". When she actually feels something, after being numb for so long, she gets all excited. She had forgotten what it felt like to have emotions. They seem so foreign. When they reappear it's a strange sensation. Antidepressants don't help, she hates being on them, they numb her even further. Yet she needs them, she needs them so she can still be here.

Chapter 6

Crutches – not just under your armpits

Sometimes, no, lots of times, Ana feels it's weird being her. She feels so different from most people. Space is something she craves. Not just physical space but space within her head. She needs space to breathe among all the tainted boxes of memories she's filed away in her attic. The weekdays are pure joy, the school-time hours a blessing. The hard part is the ending of the day when the kids come home. Their noise creates deafening sounds within her mind. It's not bad noise or yuck noise, it simply is noise, and she has no room in her head for it. It's hard to explain.

Any outside noise is something she needs to have a space for. A place to file it away in her brain. It's like, say there's a book on the table, she's placed that book there. It's not straight or in alignment with anything else, it's simply there. However, if someone else comes along and moves the book, it becomes something that now needs to have a new space in her head. She needs to find a new space to file away the new information.

Not many people understand this, another reason she feels different from most people. Sometimes she's perceived as controlling, but it's not that. There simply isn't space within her mind to continually rearrange the filing system. When the silence is shattered by the presence of others, her frustration and annoyance come across as anger, which in turn makes her feel horrible about herself, ever so remorseful of her behaviour.

"Oh, how my family must hate me. I do wonder why they tolerate me. Why do they stay? Why don't they simply leave?"

She wishes she could disappear into the earth, becoming dirt again. That's what she feels like, dirt.

Her body's crumbling under all that is her life at present, it's in so much pain. The doctor, bless his ignorance, says there's nothing to account for the amount of pain she's experiencing.

"Then why does it hurt so much?" she asks.

Her knees (stubborn ego and pride/fear) feel like lumps of concrete, unyielding, heavy, impenetrable. Much like how she's feeling all over, physically, and mentally. She feels like she's trying to knock down a concrete wall, to achieve the impossible. Can she? Is she strong enough? Sometimes, many times, she doesn't think so.

Her skin's so itchy. She feels the need to constantly scratch deeply, to remove the upper layer and get rid of whatever's beneath, whatever's causing this constant annoyance. She feels like she's trying to escape her own skin. Like a snake.

Maybe that's what this is all about – a shedding of the old to allow the new to be seen. She wants to escape who she is, wants to step out of this flesh representation of herself, into a new and more updated model. Like a doll that wears different clothes to reflect their different personalities. This is what she's been doing with her change in dress code, her behaviour.

She's becoming more *her*. Dropping restrictions that she's felt have been placed upon her by society, schooling, family. Now she simply doesn't give a shit. She so wants to be herself; the person she believes she should have been if he hadn't intruded into her being. Silly walks across the road become normal.

Often, she wonders who she would have been if all that yuck hadn't happened all those years ago. Would her life have been different? And if so, would that have been a good different? No-one will ever know. The only thing she can do now is to live her best life, learning about who she is along the way, what her great points are, the things that make her unique. Embracing them, not discounting them, being proud of who she is. That's what she needs to be doing.

As she feels like a lump of concrete, she decides to do some art around that. After some research, Hebel blocks look like a good option.

Sitting outside in the warming sun (the seasons are changing, spring's coming) she starts sanding, chiselling this block of nothingness before her, wanting to create something, though not too sure what that something is, simply letting her hands take over. She loves the feel of the Hebel beneath her hands. It has a seemingly hard impenetrable presence, yet the reality is its light, filled with air. With patience, time and mindfulness, an image starts to form. She's loving being filthy, covered in dust. She doesn't care. She's having a great time. Her hands are busy. Her mind is stilled. Art takes her away from the shit, putting her in the now. It's a way to tell her story, her truth. No words, just images.

There's a mental health week exhibition coming up, *Minds Do Matter*. She reads the requirements, and realises that, hey, she has a mental illness. Holy fuck! She is crazy.

Though PTSD doesn't mean you're crazy. To some, your behaviours may seem crazy, but you're not. Ana's not crazy. She's simply different, unique. She sees things differently, interprets things differently. She's different, but that's ok.

She decides to enter some paintings. It's kind of scary, showing herself to others, being exposed. Her name out there in public.

#

Not working actually enables the opportunity to remain apart from society. She doesn't have to go to work each day, talk to people she really has no interest in, do a job she has no interest in. Instead, she stays home in the peace, simply collapsing into her own misery. She just wants to be left alone, so please, everyone else fuck off. She sucks, her art sucks, her parenting sucks. What was she expecting, opening herself up, showing her art in public?

Did she expect others to go, "Oh wow your art's amazing, you're so talented, incredible!"

Probably.

It's weird. As much as she doesn't want to be seen, to be found, she also so wants to be seen, but she's not.

#

Lucia, one of Ana's close friends whom she met through the kids' school, has moved to a super cool house near the beach. There's a blood moon eclipse happening and they're going to watch it from the balcony, just the two of them, no one else. Some time to breathe, some time to simply be.

They both love the night sky. The darkness, the silence. No-one can see you; you can't see anyone else.

Ana's senses are so acute, especially in the dark. She can hear like an elephant, has a memory like one too. She can see, sometimes better at night like an owl, and wishes for owl-like wisdom.

It's like she has spidery senses, like Spiderman. He's her favourite superhero, always has been. Though sometimes she imagines that instead of shooting webs from her wrists, she'd shoot them from between her legs to capture and imprison those who are yuck, those who go where no one should. She'd wrap them up in her sticky, unbreakable goo, leaving them to rot. That's more than they deserve. Better yet, maybe a bigger being will come along, see a free meal and proceed to rip them apart, limb from limb, enjoying the bitter taste of their yuck with each mouthful. That sounds so much better than simply leaving them to die. Let them suffer, just like she has. It's in those moments, the dark moments beneath the night sky, that the pain that's constantly present throughout her body lessens. It's still there, it's always there. But when she can sit in wonder of all that Mother Nature has to offer, it no longer rules her focus.

She realises she needs to do this kind of thing more often. She needs to get herself up the mountains, into the water, under the stars. But her body's so sore, it hurts so much.

But still, no excuses, one day.

#

Her back's sore. It feels as though it will dissolve at any moment. Pretty relevant metaphysically – your spine/your back is your support, and she's not really feeling she has any, not at home at least. She wishes she had the strength right now to end her relationship, but she doesn't. So, she stays, growing resentful of Daren's inability to be present for her, to try and understand her, to simply hold her. Or is that all her? Does she allow him to? She doesn't think so.

#

Weird, bizarre breast dreams are the latest phase of dark time hours. In the first one, she's standing in front of a female doctor half naked; the doctor's discussing Ana's breasts, commenting on how the left one's so much bigger than the right, saying how they can move her nipples up to sit more aesthetically correctly, especially with the implant. She's like, "Yay! Finally, I'll look normal." She looks down, expecting to see cleavage, but there is none. She doesn't understand why.

In another dream, she's walking around half naked, trying to keep her breasts covered, unseen by others. Yet another dream she doesn't understand.

Breasts are nurturing, something Ana knows she's not very good at, especially for herself. But why is she covering them up or seemingly having them disappear? At the moment she doesn't have the space to try and figure these dreams out, so she lets them go, adding them to her ever-expanding dream journal.

#

Her spidery senses are on full alert. Everything's heightened. It feels like there's no room to be her. The faintest whiff of an intruding smell, a book placed – not by her, a dirty dish left on the kitchen bench, they all become so much more than their reality. There's simply not the room in her brain to process their place in her space – a space where there is none. Added to this, its wintertime, work's scarce, and Daren's home. He shouldn't be, he can't be, there's no room for him. Ana needs him gone, and he senses this. It just makes things worse. She's such a bitch.

She wants to stop the antidepressants, hating what they do to her even while knowing they provide some kind of relief from her reality. They're stopping her feeling anything. She wants to feel. She needs to be able to experience the roller coaster of emotions that everyone should. She can't keep being numb.

She also wants to stop drinking. She's not drinking the way she used to. Gee, back in the day, drinking was her escape. Now it's only the one can at 5pm. Though lately she's found herself wanting more, wanting to get drunk, to wipe herself out, simply so the reality of the choices she's currently making will stop being so present in her space. Also, she doesn't want her kids to think drinking's a way of dealing with shit. Instead, she wants to show them that there's much healthier methods, though she's not too sure exactly what they are at this moment in time.

Anyway, without thinking, she stops both at once. This is no time for playing games. She has a feeling that she's pretty shocking to live with, remembering how when giving up smoking all those years ago she was psychotic for three weeks. That was nicotine. She remembers telling Esi at the time, "This is why you never start smoking – at some point you will have to give up and then you too will become a psychopath."

She can't imagine what the result of the antidepressant withdrawal is going to be. One thing she likes about herself is her stubbornness, so stopping the drugs and stopping the drink is easy in that sense. On the flip side, she's now able to somewhat empathise with drug users – cold turkey's a bitch. What a journey the first 72 hours are. You're literally living in hell. It's horrible, but she does it. She sits in the sauna, feeling, tasting the drugs as they sweat themselves out of her system. Then sleep and silence, lots of it.

The harsh reality of no longer being numb hits. It hits like a hurricane in full force, leaving her feeling so raw that everything prickles. It grates on her senses, she's unable to find peace. Everything seems to be on full volume. It's all so harsh, Ana finds herself crying most of the time, unable to watch or hear about anything that's yuck – it just rips her soul apart. So, she blocks herself off from the world.

It's a horrible experience. The drink, her saving grace since she was 14 years old, something that she'd normally be doing right now, is gone. There are no crutches, nothing to help support her through this shit storm. She is left raw, exposed, vulnerable.

"Why the fuck do I do this shit to myself?" she screams at the Universe.

Good fucking question.

Chapter 7

Metaphysics – mind-body connection

Reading an article on social anxiety, Ana thinks, "This is me." She feels so much smaller in public than in the safety of her home. She always arrives when things have already started, leaving as soon as something ends, minimising the participation in small-*fucking-bullshit*-talk.

"No one will want to talk to me anyway. *I* don't want to talk to me. I don't want to talk with anyone. I don't want to share parts of me. If I do, then it's possible they'll see the real me and be disgusted with the reality that's before them." All this runs through her head at the very thought of having to interact with others.

The times Ana does talk to others, the moments she allows herself to be vulnerable, are dictated by the tones, words, smells, and appearance of those around her. If something invades her space, causing anguish, then she'll leave. She'll run away, usually to the toilet, all the while wondering how others don't see her dissolving into nothingness. They expect Ana to be normal – to talk, laugh, smile like everyone else. But she's not. So, "Please, oh please, just let me go!" The screams echo in her already full head.

Big Dog and Little Dog don't expect that from her, they accept Ana just as she is, asking no more than what she can give in any particular moment. She has space within her space for them.

#

It's so visible what proceeding with this legal crap is doing to her kids, her relationships. But she can also see and feel what not doing it will do to her.

Climbing a tree seems a good option.

She used to climb trees as a kid, the tallest pine she could find. She'd sit in its tallness, swaying with the wind, waiting, wondering if anyone was missing her. Back then she'd walk through the bush behind her house, wanting to be unseen by any eyes.

One day, as Ana was ducking and twisting through the branches, she heard voices. In the clearing, waiting for her, were Patrick and Donny. Patrick was holding a white paper bag, saying it was full of lollies and that if Ana kissed Donny, then he'd give her the bag of sweets. She felt she had no option, she felt trapped. She kissed Donny and heard the laughter shattering the quiet of the bush.

"You'll grow up to be nothing but a prostitute." The words whispered between the trees as Patrick and Donny ran away.

That space, that bush she used to feel safe in was no longer her respite. Afterwards, she never walked through its nurturing goodness again, instead walking the hot unrelenting firmness of the newly laid asphalt.

Now, she doesn't care if anyone misses her, believing that they'd all be better off without her, believing she brings them nothing but pain. She can stop this legal crap, she's the one in control, or that's what the police and Kimberly tell her. But Ana doesn't feel like she is in control. She feels more like a puppet in a show with someone else pulling the strings.

#

Mother Blobfish is dead. Ana's sad. No, she's *angry*. Now Mother Blobfish is unable to answer so many questions.

Ana wants to dig Mother Blobfish up, to make their skeleton tell the truth, to provide some answers. Like, who actually is POS? How is he connected to Ana? Why did Mother Blobfish insist on him living with Ana in her flat? Did they not see changes in their daughter when Ana was young? Did Mother Blobfish know that stuff was being done to Ana? Why did they choose POS when Ana told them about what happened? Why did they always seemingly hate their own daughter?

Ana wants to shake the skeleton until the bones all fall apart. A mess in the dirt, much like how she feels. Instead, she dreams.

She's in a bathroom, its rather messy and dirty. She needs to go to the toilet. On the floor are all these little girl clothes. Looking at the clothes while sitting on the toilet, she realises they're covered in diarrhoea. She gets off, starts to try to wash the poo off the clothes, wondering what kind of mother would leave their daughter like this.

Next scene she's spitting up little balls of hard gristle. They're really dark and very solid. She pulls with both hands, pulling out string upon string of gristle. It's all joined together, side-by-side, coming out by the handful. She drops it into the sink, wanting to take it and show the doctor. However, in the sink it breaks up into individual strands. She washes it, amazed at how strong it is and how much it looks like the wool she recently used when she painted a triptych of the abuse. Go figure.

In the dream she then goes to the doctor and shows them her her-ness – all the strands of gristle she pulled from her depths. The doctor says that Ana's different from most people. They draw a diagram of the insides of the human body on a large sheet of paper saying that most people follow a path from the mouth to the anus. But not Ana. No, her insides go around and around, here and there. That's why she has all this shit coming out of her mouth; that's why her tummy hurts.

This dream, she believes, is telling her about a mother who wasn't a very good mother. A mother who knowingly left their daughter covered in shit all the time. All the hard balls of gristle are bits of dried-up anger and resentment she's trying ever so hard to get out. That the doctor tells her she's different from others doesn't surprise her at all. She knows that her mind works differently, that the pathways in her brain are more like squiggles then any form of road map. It's nice to know her body's just as weird as her brain. But
that's her: Ana Suci.

#

Ana paints many things, mostly things that others don't see, having always seen Spirits. Drawing them, well, it just seems natural for her. She loves seeing them become reality at the end of her fingertips, feeling their essence, their energy as they take form. A friend's making chocolates and asks if they can put her Spirit drawings on the chocolates. Such a trippy collaboration, but hey, chocolate and Spirits – perfect match.

#

"How would my mind and body work with a thyroid?" she wonders. Would having a thyroid enable her to better deal with all this stress shit?

One of the main contributing factors to Graves' disease is stress. So how much would a functioning thyroid gland help in balancing the stress that's currently impacting her health? It seems no doctor can enlighten her.

It's time for a check-up about her knees at the local public hospital. They have been so very painful for years. Now the pain has intensified as the psychological load has become heavier (knees – fear, inflexibility, won't give in).

Even before getting to the hospital, she's not in a good space. She's had a near miss in her car, her spiffy convertible, and a near miss with the other car's driver. In that moment of confrontation, she feels psycho, invincible, as though nothing can touch her. She believes she'll smash the other driver's head in if needed. The lady's so annoying!

Ana knows she isn't present, she knows she should just walk away, and she does. But she so wants to smash something, preferably something that bleeds and hurts, like her own head.

In the hospital, she's in tears. The intern says that the amount of pain she's experiencing doesn't relate to the MRI and X-rays, and asks if there's anything else going on that could be causing the pain.

"Of course there's more going on. What are you, fucking stupid?" she screams at him silently.

Instead, "No" leaves her mouth.

What part does he not understand? There's pain, her knees hurt so much. Simple, do something about it.

She wants, *needs* the pain within her to stop.

"Sorry Ma'am, but you'll have to wait another year or two for things to get worse."

Like, what the fuck? She's left with no choice but to go through private health. The cost, the actual reality of having an operation that isn't exactly required at this moment, none of that matters. She simply wants the pain to stop. That's what matters in this moment.

At least having scars will allow Ana to feel the pain and for it to be validated. She doesn't think about how both knees having done at the same time will mean having to sit on her bum for a few days.

"Sometimes I'd like to slap myself."

#

The human body's amazing, how it manifests unease into a physical reality. The unseen mental and emotional anguish hidden within Ana's body is retelling her story. Even her vagina's behaving weirdly, so a visit to the doctor is needed.

As she's describing what's happening in her vaginal area, she remembers a dream from the night before. In the dream, her vagina's bleeding. The dream doctor says that what Ana's experiencing is common after a hysterectomy.

"Your vagina can seize up, like its giving birth, and get stuck contracting. Here, just take this pill. It will fix it," says the dream doc.

Having no limits when it comes to sharing her dreams, believing that everyone sees dreams the same way she does, Ana shares her dream with her real-life doctor.

The real-life doc goes, "Sure, that can actually happen."

"Go figure. Could that be my problem too then?"

"Possibly."

"Great. Do I get to pop a pill?"

"Nope."
Oh well.

#

Dreaming allows her to better deal with her harsh reality.

Ana's in the back of their boat, which is on the back of their car, which is out of control driving down a road somewhere. Ana yells out to Daren for help, fearing that she's about to die, Daren says not to worry as it will all be over in two weeks.

"What will be over? Life? The Universe? Like how?"

In the dream, Ana's in not just one out-of-control mode of transport, but two, reflecting how she's feeling at the moment.

Going back to sleep doesn't stop the dreaming. This time, there's so much water. There are floods happening everywhere. She moves to higher ground. The water's rising so damn fast. She goes into a house, and collects supplies, not knowing how long this is going to last.

That rings true. Water stands for emotions. They are seemingly coming from everywhere and there's no way to control them. The worst part is having no idea how long this thing's going to go on for. Another dream, another car. There are road works happening. Before she realises it, her car has driven over some concrete dividers. They stop Ana from either moving backwards or forwards. She is totally stuck. When on the way to an appointment in the afternoon, Ana turns down a road she doesn't normally take. There in front of her are these road dividers, just like in her dream. She feels the anxiety rising within.

This dream's so telling, saying that she's stuck, unable to go either forward or backwards. That she's stuck in the place where she is. And as Ana's the one driving the car, this is a result of her actions. She needs to accept where she is and try to deal with it as well as possible. She's stepping out, speaking up, believing she will be supported, understood by her family. Yet she's not feeling that way. In fact, she feels more aggression aimed at her for doing this, for the discomfort it's creating within others.

So naturally, Ana's back is so, so, so super sore, especially on the left side. It hurts to move, to walk, to bend. It's physically stopping her from moving, leaving her feeling physically stuck just like she feels emotionally stuck.

"Thank you, body, for reflecting my current reality."

#

Yet another dream. There's a family, they're all big woman of dark skin. Ana watches them talking. The oldest one's out the back of a hall that's connected to the sea, which is exceptionally clear. Ana joins in the conversation; she's mesmerised by the clear water.

The elder asks, "How did you know we needed help?"

She replies, "I just trust in what I feel."

There's a toilet behind a brick wall, which a man shows her, saying that all the other toilets are being used at the moment. The man makes the wall open, revealing a space behind, where there's another toilet.

What is it with these dreams of toilets behind doors or walls?

Toilets are where we get rid of all our shit, so she's guessing it's good that she keeps ending up in them. She gathers that the toilets being behind closed or secret doors is saying that she's getting rid of all the shit that's been kept away from view, away from others. And that's exactly what she's doing.

Go dreams!

#

There's pain in the left rib now. It's worth getting it explored. She's pretty sure it's just part of her body working its way through the old hurts. She needs to accept that her body, in so many ways, holds on to pain, to trauma. That now, as she's speaking out, her body is reacting with body memories, as the mind memories become more present. None of that logic stops the hurting though.

#

She vomits during dark time. She doesn't know why it only happens then, especially as vomiting isn't one of her chosen expulsion techniques. In fact, far from it.

As a kid, Ana dreamt about vomiting. Vomiting all over the backyard. Not being able to stop. It was everywhere – on the concrete, the grass, up the trees. Since then, she's been afraid of vomiting, believing once she starts, she'll never stop. Maybe that's why the vomiting's only happening in dark time, when she's less mentally present, when the vomit has a longer time to explode before she can stop it, before she can control what's happening. If the vomit's stopped though, it then comes out the other end. It's like her body has all this crap, this shit inside, and one way or another it's getting out, no matter what.

Ana believes Daren thinks she's a hypochondriac. Shit, she'd think the same too if the roles were reversed.

"Maybe I am. All I know is my whole-body hurts. It hurts in ways that can't be explained."

Over the years, she's had lots of operations, resulting in lots of missing parts. You could play the game *Operation* on her, but you'd have to put the organs back in, not take them away. You can certainly play snakes and ladders with all the scars covering her skin. Holy crap, she has a lot.

As a kid, she so wanted scars, believing if she had scars then she'd be tough and no one could hurt her. That all the bad yuck shit that was happening to her would stop. Ana got what she wished for, never thinking of how or why she'd get those scars. Did they make her tougher? Maybe. At least she's scary. Her thyroid scar is, or was, especially scary after that op. She had a line of staples across her throat.

Esi said, "Hey mum, you should put bolts in your head, then you'll look just like Frankenstein."

#

Some of the pain within her body makes her feel like a bad person – shameful, not good enough, damaged, weird. So, she asks if her left side's trying to tell her anything. An image of this prickly reddish thingy, sort of like a caterpillar, stuck near her ribs, appears in her mind's eye. Ok let's let that sit for a moment.

The annual Gem and Mineral Show is on. Loving it, Ana heads there with her friend Danika, one of the first friends Ana made in Tasmania. Danika's kids and her's come to the show too. It's good walking around, visually stimulated by the wonders of crystals, feeling their energy, trying to remind herself not to pick any up. She'd done that last year, picked up some crystals, and in doing so she'd taken on the energy of the people who'd picked up the crystals before her. Sometimes this is too much, carrying other people's shit. Now, Ana doesn't touch, instead, she simply looks.

Then she sees it. There's a crystal in a clear cube. It looks just like the prickly reddish thingy that's sitting in her ribs. It's a Crocoite.

Excellent stone for self-healing. It helps heal stress and dispel negativity. It can also bring emotional healing as it has a strong loving energy that flows out from it. It's an excellent stone to keep in your environment to stimulate creativity.

"So why is it stuck in my body, causing me so much pain?" she screams silently to no one in particular as she hands over the money.

Returning home, Ana places it in her collection, hoping that one day she'll receive enlightenment as to its presence in her body.

#

A lightbulb moment. Is there really such a thing? She guesses so, as she's just had one: The physical pain that she's experiencing, that she's always experienced, is what makes all that childhood shit real. The other thing that lets Ana know it's real is that it's just not the story of herself and POS. There were others, like Otto Bowman and his brother Donny, not forgetting their crazy friend Donna – now there's a trippy person.

Ana wonders what's happened to them all.

"Why am I even thinking about them? I don't give a shit. They can all be dead as far as I'm concerned. Pieces of shit, watching, doing, never stopping."

It hurt Ana more in some ways, having a female about six years older stand there, watching and laughing, as shit was done to Ana. Donna never did anything to stop it. No wonder she doesn't trust other woman. Getting back to the pain. If her story isn't real, then the pain can't be real either. She knows the pain's real, her body hurts so deep inside. So her story *must* be real.

#

The police are calling what happened rape. Like, holy crap! Rape, that's a really ugly word. She finds it hard to have it sit within her and wonders why that is. It sounds so harsh, so wrong, so bad. Too close, but not close enough to the reality. The police officer goes on to explain that if Ana had been abused by a relative, then what happened to her, what's now being called rape, in her case would in fact be termed incest.

"What? Hang on, I don't understand."

She's too far gone to fully comprehend what's being said, to take in the severity of that word, as she floats away to some kind of sanctuary.

It does make sense though, for none of this to be real. She looks in the mirror, not seeing herself, but someone she feels no connection to. She has no knowledge of that person. So, if they aren't real, obviously she's really not real, and her story then is certainly not real.

"Oh my, I get myself so tangled up sometimes," she laughs.

Chapter 8

Ants – patience, strength, cooperation

She's weird in a good way – carefree, different, creative, inventive. She guesses she should be grateful that others see these qualities in her. She sometimes struggles to see anything in herself but yuck, often deflecting compliments by saying, "Ahhh, but I merely reflect you." That way she doesn't have to accept the fact that someone else can see good in her.

Maybe they do see the bits of her Ana hates, is ashamed of, rejects. Maybe others hold that within themselves too.

#

Walking on the beach brings so much deep, deep gratitude. As a kid she wished to live by the water, surrounded by bush, belonging to the milkman's family. She had hoped she was adopted – that the milkman really was her father. He had red hair and freckles just like her.

Now Ana does live by the water, surround by bush. Now she wishes she was married to the local farmer, who owns the most amazing cows ever. Black cows with white stripes, Belted Galloways, her most favourite. She loves cows, their big innocent eyes, their sweet smell of cow-ness. Maybe one day.

There's a lady down the road who does kinesiology. Feeling the need to get some body work done, she pays Rosemary a visit.

Rosemary's really good at what they do. She doesn't know exactly what it is they do though. A bit of this, some of that, with a touch of Spirit thrown in for good measure. Ana likes their energy, their weirdness. They're not quite standing on the earth.

Rosemary works with whatever they feel is most appropriate in Ana's pain. Sometimes Ana's so super sensitive that even Rosemary's fairy-like touch creates intense anguish, and then, thankfully, a release.

#

Sometimes Ana really amazes herself with insight and wisdom. Driving into town one day she shied away from the normal carpark – the energy just way too much for her head at the moment, the skills required in actually finding a park involving too much thought. Instead, she decided to park in an abstract place, making herself walk and breathe a bit before getting to wherever it was, she was going. She parked in this space; it's sacred space in her mind. She probably shouldn't have, but she did anyway.

Arriving back, she found her car surrounded and blocked in by lots of cars – there was a funeral at the centre. There was nothing that could be done in the moment but to simply sit in silence. To read for a bit, then maybe a nanny nap. Maybe this was the Universe's way of telling her to simply stop, take a break, have a rest, and breathe. Thank you, Universe.

#

Sometimes, lots of times, she thinks about ending her life. About simply walking in front of that truck, walking into that bush, never stopping. Wading out into that water until it consumes her whole being. No-one will know. She'll simply disappear. She believes her family won't miss her, nor even care. She believes they think of her as annoying, certainly not someone they want in their lives. She doesn't blame them, sometimes she doesn't want her in her life either. You really shouldn't go deep into thought when death is such a pressing reality.

Stupid Buddhism. Why oh why did she ever think embracing that philosophy would be a good thing? Now she believes she can't kill herself. That if she does, she'll have to come back and live this shitty crap life ten times worse. Like, no fucking way! As much as Ana doesn't like herself, she certainly doesn't want to spend a lifetime ten times worse doing this shit. So, for the moment, she stays.

Rosemary gave Ana some flower essences after the last treatment, and at first, they made her feel like crap, shitter than normal. She reminds herself that sometimes with alternative health medicines you can feel worse before you feel better, "So bring on the better I say." Now she feels like a newer her. Wow, that's pretty trippy.

And then, a dream – death, blood, being trapped, no choices. POSs face, large and in her face saying, "Not guilty." A very disturbed and restless night leaving her unsure about this dream. Death in a dream can symbolise rebirth, blood can be life force, family.

#

Even when she finds herself sitting among the wonders of Mother Nature in this most incredible space, she calls home, she still feels ever so ugly, like she's this big stain of shit wiped over the natural beauty.

"I taint it just like my past taints me."

So instead, she stays home, trying to be at peace, embracing the passing rain showers, feeling the soft droplets cleansing her soul, feeling a lot more alive than is comfortable or necessary.

Ana simply wants to die, to end her life. She's away together with her family and Lucia's family at the moment. They are in such a beautiful space and yet she so wishes to end her presence in it.

As she walks by herself along the country road, a truck approaches. She could so easily step in front of it. It would possibly end her life or possibly leave her fucked up. Either way, she would be inflicting her pain onto the truck driver. She can't do that, it's her pain, not his, to carry.

#

Ana believes there's a reason why she can't remember all of her past, sensing there's memories tucked deep, deep, deep within her mind. Sometimes dreams tell her she'll remember. Part of her doesn't want to, maybe there's a really good reason she can't remember everything. She reminds herself of this as the thought of wanting to see the police statements from the other witnesses enters her head. One incident she does remember happened one autumn afternoon.

After six summers, she'd finally had a whole summer with no abuse. She was in her school uniform, kind of embracing its cloak of anonymity among all the other girls from her school. She walked past the monkey bars, a piece of equipment she used to love. Her breath was taken away as she spotted Otto and Patrick sitting on top. They were trying to look cool, but they just looked stupid. They were nearly 18, the pair of them, far too old to be hanging around playgrounds.

They saw Ana and start snickering, looking at one another with big lecherous smirks.

Otto called out, "Hey Ana! Soon you'll start bleeding, and no one will want you."

She dropped her head, hoping no one heard those words of disgust and shame.

She had no idea why she'd start bleeding. She wondered if she was going to die, having completely no knowledge of female development into maturity. She wondered why Otto seemed to know this. After all, he had no sisters – there was just Donny, his brother. Patrick was looking on, enjoying the embarrassing flush spreading over her freckled face.

At the time, she'd found it a really weird, out-of-place statement. Now, as an adult, she's really struggling to recall this memory and not vomit. It doesn't sit comfortably within, though she's not too sure why.

#

Ana's done the unforgivable to her own kid. She's checked their iPad and found evidence of peer self-harm. She wishes she could un-see what she saw, although she's very grateful, she did, at least

75

she's now able to offer help and support. It truly must be hard being a teenager when the world is so accessible, the horror of humanity, the destruction of nature. It's a lot for adults to comprehend. How can young, as yet undeveloped minds even remotely grasp and make sense of the fuckedness of this earth? No wonder so many are choosing to end their lives. It's so sad, and yet another crap thing that those so young have to deal with.

Now though, she needs to find space amid everything else to be present for her kid too.

Shit, fuck, poo.

#

Her friend, Alice, is dying. They have breast cancer.

Ana only met Alice about a year ago. But you know when you meet someone and you have an instant connection? She has that with Alice.

And now Alice is dying.

Ana admires Alice's strength, Alice's attempt at trying to stay present here on earth until the last breath, with no physical reprieve in sight. And then there's her, knowing logically that there's an end in sight to that which is causing her so much pain. So how can she possibly think of taking her own life?

This state, this all-consuming lump of crap that is seemingly drowning her, it will pass. Alices won't.

A few weeks later Lucia and Ana attend Alice's funeral. This is a hard one. Alice died of cancer. Alice was her age. How come Alice died, and so far, Ana's survived? It doesn't seem fair. None of it is fair.

The funeral's beautiful, everyone's singing with joy and love in their tones as Alice's body is laid to rest.

#

No wonder she dreams.

There's a little girl, she's standing on an ant's nest, and the ants start to bite her. Ana believes Spirit is telling her to be patient, to be strong, to co-operate with all that's around. To lean into the support of friendships, instead of denying it. That's the message of ants – patience, strength, and cooperation. They all need each other to achieve their desired outcome. Ana needs others for hers. Thanks for the lesson, Spirit.

#

Her relationship is seriously like *so* over, so why is Daren still there? She has no idea what's to come, she just knows she can't keep living like this.

In a dream she's with some soul who's portraying this absolutely beautiful feeling. She has no idea who this person is. She just knows how amazing she feels in their presence. She's so looking forward to that reality as she tries to navigate her current reality. Trying to work out how to procced with a separation. Adding that feeling of yet again failing to the list of inadequacies, concerned how the kids will take it, shamed at her lack of ability to sustain or form functioning relationships. Sometimes it can all be way too overwhelming, so Ana does what she does best – disconnects. Removing herself and her emotions from the moment. It's the only way she knows how to stay alive.

She feels so sick. This shit's seemingly part of her life now. She's vomiting again. Naturally, it's dark time. It doesn't seem to want to stop this time though. Fuck, she hates vomiting! The stench, the feeling of burning acid in the back of the throat, the watering eyes. The "after" feeling's so worth it though. But this time the vomit's red. Not carrot red but blood red. Like, what the fuck's going on? She knows that vomiting blood isn't a good sign.

It's the middle of the night and she's ever so tired, so she jumps back into bed, sure that whatever's happening will be gone in the morning, or she'll be dead. Either option's good as long as sleep arrives. She feels it's all connected with what's going on with the legal crap. Some interviews are meant to be happening in Victoria.

Still, she really should go to the doctor … in the morning.

The doctor immediately sends Ana to a gastrologist that afternoon. Like, how come a person who deals with that part of your body is so easily accessible? That doctor thinks Ana has some major intestinal issue going on and admits her to hospital so he can stick a camera down her throat and look for anything that shouldn't be there. They believe that possibly there's a tear in her intestines that then resulted in the vomited blood. There's a little sign of the tear still remaining, "Our intestines heal really quickly," says the doc, who then goes on to tell Ana that she has diverticulitis. Yay, more anal shit.

The weird thing is she doesn't feel this pain belongs to her. So, she asks, "Where's this coming from?" An image appears in her mind's eye: her stomach's getting pumped after an overdose. She has no idea what's going on, she hates pills, always has, so this is obviously not something from this life. A past life, perhaps.

Well, there you go. The police ring, letting Ana know that the same day she was vomiting blood, POS was being interviewed.

"Like how did my body pick that up? Did my soul know and just manifest into the physical?"

She's wondering, guessing. There's no way to know. It's like POS is connected to her energetically, genetically. What if he is related? That would make all of this so much worse. How could she possibly live with herself, knowing one of those people, more like her than any other in the world, could do that kind of shit to her … It just adds another layer of fucked-up-ness.

#

She feels really blessed to have the friends she does, truly not knowing where she'd be without them. Ana can cry with them, laugh with them, simply sit with them. And she does.

Giana asks, "Why? Why are you doing this? As though there isn't enough shit going on in your life. But to add to it, like, really?"

"It's too hard not to."

She knows that if she doesn't stick with this, no matter how hard it is, no matter how much it hurts, no matter how much it's destroying those things she loves, if she just gives up, pulls the pin, stops it all, then she'll be dead. She knows she can't keep living with all of this inside of her. It needs to come out. She needs to tell her story.

Most importantly, it needs to be heard.

She sees herself as a jigsaw puzzle with many missing pieces. She needs to find those pieces, to put them back where they belong. But where to start? More importantly, she has no idea where they would go, once found. She feels as though she's been swirled around, like a spiral galaxy floating in the universe ten billion light years from Earth. All those missing parts, they all need to be brought back in, to try to be made whole.

"I need to find me," she says to no-one. "The only way I can do that is by doing this, this shit, fuck, stink legal crap, by giving myself a voice, a voice I never had as a child. I want, no, I *need* another to take accountability for the actions taken against me when I had no choice. Now I have a choice and a voice."

The saddest part of all of this, the part Ana so wishes she could remove, is how badly this is affecting her kids. She yells at them, gets angry with them, resents them for simply being in a space where there is no space. She hates herself so badly each time. She's such a bitch to them. She wants to tell them why, but she's so afraid that they'll look at her differently, that they'll no longer love her.

"I wouldn't love me. I don't love me. So how can I expect them to? But it's not fair on them, they think they've done something wrong, but they haven't."

One night while they're eating dinner it all just spews out. She obviously didn't put any foresight into it. She doesn't want food and family to be associated with such yuck, but it's done now. She's told them. The kids are actually really good, though Zeb seems more worried about POS trying to find and hurt them than anything else. She gets that. She's spent most of her life looking over her shoulder, afraid. This is not a conversation she ever wanted to have with her kids, but she has. It's done.

She tries to make it clear in their heads that this is her choice, that she's choosing at this point in her life to try and hold accountable the person who did that yuck to her. Though really, does she have a choice? She knows she has to do this for her sanity, needing to honour that child within.

Thankfully its sleepover night for both kids. Yay, some time alone with Daren. She watches horror movies; Daren plays on his computer. Totally functional.

#

Ana's yelling, ever so loudly. Zeb's done something to really piss her off. The thing is, she doesn't remember what it was. Her mind's so fried. It has nothing to do with Zeb, she's pretty sure. Unfortunately, they bear the brunt of whatever's happening for her and it's so wrong. She climbs into bed hating herself, unable to say sorry, which makes her hate herself even more. So, she dreams.

In the dream she's at Otto and Donny's house. It's been renovated. She's sitting at an outdoor area that is connected to the back of the house. Someone asks how she's feeling being back there.

"I'm ok at the moment but I don't want to go inside."

She does go inside though, and in there's POS doing shit to her. The others, Otto, Donny and Donna, are standing there at the kitchen window, laughing. No-one's doing fucking anything to help her, to stop him.

Chapter 9

How to kill yourself without committing suicide

Monicas in touch. The brief of evidence is being prepared and submitted to their supervisor. The police boss then decides whether there's enough evidence to prosecute. Enough evidence. Seriously?

She wants to yell. She yells. She wants to run. She can't. She wants to hurt. She hurts.

Not surprisingly, there are more dreams. Someone keeps pushing on the sore spot on her back. It's horrible and hurts so much. They just kept doing it, over and over again, seemingly on purpose, enjoying watching her pain. Why are these random people hurting her in her dreams? Isn't it enough that she hurts in awake hours? Does she really need to hurt in dream time too?

#

Wooohooo! Super coolness! There's bright blue glowing stuff, bioluminescence, happening in the waters of the River Derwent. She has no idea what it is, what it means, apart from a reason to go out at night. She heads over there in the dark, taking Rey.

It's incredible. So bright, like someone's in the water with a super strong blue LED light. It takes her away. It brings her joy. It's great to be laughing with Rey. It's great to be focusing on wonder, rather than shit, to be filled with joy instead of despair.

#

So much time is spent in doctor's rooms. Probably because she's in so much pain – pain that doesn't seem to have a reason, apart from it all being in her head. But Ana knows it's not, though in one way it may be, she knows her body holds memories, her body holds all the pain of trauma for so many years. However, surely there must be a physical reason for the pain in her back. There must be.

The back specialist sends her for a scan where they inject you with radioactive fluid. You have to stay away from pregnant women until it's out of your system, so she takes the opportunity to walk around the streets adjoining the hospital. The architecture of this space is kind to her eyes, the diversity's wonderful, it's a great way to pass three hours.

Having had cancer twice before, it's where her mind goes, and her doctor's mind too, whenever there's something wrong. The fear of it being cancer again is always present and probably will be forever. She thinks that unless you've actually had cancer, you probably won't understand. Anyway, she doesn't have cancer, thank fuck for that. Apparently though, she has Ankylosing Spondylitis, or AS, and it friggin hurts!

The scan shows that all the spots in her body that have been sore for well over the past decade are inflicted with this arthritis. In a way that's good.

It shows that:

1) she's not a hypochondriac
2) she's not a whinge guts.
3) it's not all in her head
4) there's a friggin good reason why her body hurts.

There's AS in her spine, majorly where the scoliosis is, in her wrists, her ankles, her hips, and ohhh the joy, her hamstrings. Who knew you could get arthritis in your hamstrings? No wonder her butt and the backs of her thighs hurt like hell at times.

Arthritis: feeling unloved, criticism, resentment. Her body's got that right. So once again, she has no-one she can blame. She just needs to take responsibility for her mindset and try to change it.

Metaphysically, your feet are how you connect with the earth. So, there is no surprise when she finds out she can now add plantar fasciitis to her ever-expanding list of medical complaints. It makes sense though. She's struggling to put her foot down comfortably at all and wondering how her body's so good at physically manifesting her mental anguish.

Painting is elusive, writing nonsensical. Her brain's flighty, and surprisingly her body is sore. This too will pass; this too will pass. Maybe saying it enough times will make it a reality.

She thinks about things, about life, about where she is right now, about where she's come from, realising that this is the first time since she was 14 years old that she is not using a crutch in any shape or form. She's doing this raw, no wonder her body hurts, her soul weeps.

#

Years ago, she was in a lift. The door opened and there, with those waiting to get in, was Otto Bowman. Otto saw Ana and smiled, his creepy scarred face looking directly at her. She wanted to run but was trapped behind others. She wanted to vomit but knew that others would then look at her. She wanted to kill the motherfucker; she could possibly get away with that. She wanted to scrub herself clean. Instead, she got drunk for about the next month.

#

The most bizarre dream: there are two books, both belonging to POS. One's a written journal, the other a scrapbook containing cut-out pictures of gay boys. Ana's disgusted, but also happy. She knows this will help her case. But she doesn't know how she got them or where from. POS finds out she has them. He tries to take them from her, but he can't.

Maybe the dream's saying that there's other information out there to help her. Let's see if anything appears.

#

She struggles to stay present in this world more times than not, wishing she could simply leave, leave it all behind, start again, afresh in another life. She knows this really isn't an option. So instead, she writes, because that's what she does, trying to make sense of everything.

#

Many years ago, when first dealing with what happened, Ana would hear voices in her head, laughing, calling her dumb. She remembers that they always laughed, the others, watching her be abused. They thought it was funny.

Just like this friggin' voice now thinking, "How funny it is that she thinks she can do this, thinks she can stay alive, stay sane and still have him held accountable."

Maybe if she leaves, if she simply falls asleep never to awaken, then at least the laughing voices will stop.

It's a dark and very disturbing time. She takes herself off to bed, hiding, not entirely sure what she's hiding from. She is told that this journey may at times be like a roller coaster ride; however, this is worse than any man-made ride. It's completely out of control. It costs a lot mentally, physically, emotionally, spiritually, and there's no end in sight. The hardest part is that her escape into art still has a huge block. She just can't seem to get it together, and with no crutches holding her up, she feels like she's drowning, needing to come up for air. Her body hurts ever so much, it's in pain, she knows that.

For years, what happened as a child was ever present in her mind, in her being, in her behaviours. Sometimes she remembered it clearly, other times, something would simply feel wrong, as though part of her was not right.

She hates all the excuses she hears over the years. People defending those who had violated another. There's no excuse for what was done to her, done to so many others.

"I was bullied." "My father was an alcoholic." "My uncle abused me." "The Scout leader did things to me." "I hate myself." "It happened to me." "She was asking for it."

None of these, nor any of the many other excuses that are heard across this world, make sexual abuse ok. Never ever, ever. It makes her so mad, hearing this shit. Having others defend, justify, horrendous behaviours. Like, holy fuck, how is their behaviour excusable?

She knows there really isn't a choice in doing this. That even when she yells at the kids for no good reason, appearing distant and not present for them, even when she sees the sadness and hurt in their eyes, reading it on their faces, she knows she doesn't have a choice. She has to do this. She hopes in the years to come that they may forgive her.

Mother Nature's now her crutch, her go-to for a bit of relief from life. She simply sits in the spaces in the silence. Thank God it's snowing. She immerses herself into its white purity, its majikality. The brash coldness of the snow brings her back into her body, washing her exposed skin with snow innocence. She hopes some will sink deep to her soul.

#

Different avenues of healing have always been an interest, and cupping (when little jars are lit and then turned upside down and the suction from the warm air grasps onto the coldness of the human skin sucking the toxins out) is the latest.

She gets some done on her back. Unfortunately, afterwards she feels really out of whack, unable to focus or sit still, confused, not present, and her head hurts. She spends the rest of the day in bed. Letting her body do whatever it needs seems like a good option.

There's an inner child workshop being held by a friend on the weekend. Having done lots of work on her inner child many, many years ago, she thinks, "Is this really something I need to be doing right now?"

She figures, why not? There'll still be crap that needs working through.

She's sort of happy she did go. An interesting part was writing wishes you had as a child. It can be very impactful, seeing thoughts and wishes written down in words.

Wishes from childhood:

I wish I was adopted

I wish the milkman was my dad

I wish I could fly

I wish I could die

I wish I wasn't me

I wish I had somewhere I could hide forever

I wish I had scars, because then I'd be tough, and no one could hurt me.

After the workshop, she spends some time reflecting on those wishes which were more like beliefs, mainly completely dysfunctional ones that she still carries to this day. It's time to do some reorganising of her thoughts.

Mother Nature must have known about this inner child stuff, as the next morning Ana awakes to snow in her very own backyard. How cool is that? Very childlike in the wonder and joy it brings.

She goes walking. The roads are all closed. It's wonderful seeing the neighbourhood covered in snow and hearing the squeals of joy from the kids playing. She's so grateful.

\#

Sometimes Ana doesn't think before acting, like really think. She just goes, "Oh yeah, that would be a good idea," or "That would help someone," or "That should take her mind off her own story," and sticks her hand up. Then, once she has a chance to breathe, she realises that maybe her hand should never have risen.

Some person's doing their PhD on domestic violence and wants people's stories, so she tells hers. It takes her mind off the other shit running around in it. Unfortunately, though, it brings up different shit, shit she still hasn't created a space to deal with.

"Oh my. How I wish I still drank."

Chapter 10

The unseen, seen

There's a photographic exhibition happening, and after seeing some promos Ana feels this is something she'd really like to attend. Before moving to Tasmania, she did portrait photography, usually children, until it became too much. Sometimes when she'd photograph children, she could see in their eyes that they'd been abused. When she was able, she'd share her insights with an adult.

One time she did share; three weeks later the girl whose eyes held so much sadness had to deal with their father killing himself. He'd been abusing all his children. Motherfucker arse, gutless piece of shit. It broke Ana's heart when she thought of this little girl; having seen into their soul, she'd seen the pain that probably only other abused people can see. She hoped that over time, this beautiful young child may be able to heal and live a life full of joy.

She stopped photographing children after that.

She was never really into landscapes. Now though, her focus is beginning to shift, there's so much natural wonder here in Tasmania that she wants to try and capture, in her way, with her eye. And as this exhibition is on night photography, she's curious to see what others capture. The photos are amazing. Even though she's been living here for the past six years she didn't know you could see an aurora. She didn't even know what an aurora was – the colours, the shapes exploding across the photos. Complete majikality.

Ana wants to be part of it.

She searches for information on night photography. She remembers many, many years ago, taking moon shots with an old 35-mm film camera, not knowing if any of the shots would work, having to wait until she developed the film. But that was another lifetime. Since then, her mind's become fried and then flipped, much like the eggs she dishes up to the kids on the weekend.

It's really weird sometimes, knowing how things were, adjusting to how things are, feeling such a pull to night photography, to the space beneath the stars, the quiet. She finds some social media sites that tell you when an aurora may happen. Woohoo! There's one forecast for tonight.

She believes she has it clear enough in her head what camera settings she needs in dark time: f2.8 or the lowest her lens will go – the smaller the number the more light allowed into the camera. ISO 1600–3200. Shutter speed 5–30 sec, that's when the number has, like, rabbit ears above it.

In the cold, but not caring, she heads to her local beach. While she's setting up the camera and tripod, a must for long exposures, a lady comes over. They are a science doctor and explain what Ana needs to look for.

"See that dark low-lying cloud to the south, that's what you need to look for, that's an aurora cloud."

"Oh, I see."

When Ana looks at the sky, to the space the scientist showed, in that moment of looking she's thankful she sees Spirits. Seeing the aurora's like seeing Spirits, you don't look directly at it like you do when you're looking at people or things. You look without looking. It's hard to explain, but easy for Ana. She believes she can see variance in the sky colour, and also what looks like beams of faint torchlight heading into the sky from the water's horizon.

It's hard to focus the camera at dark time. She tries to get a star as a pin prick on the LED screen, hoping she's got something right. It's really nice out there anyway, in the silence.

Arriving home, she puts the SD card into the computer. At first, all the pics look too dark, then with a bit of adjustment things start to appear. It's nearly midnight but she's jumping for joy, screaming with excitement. There's colour on the computer screen. Ana's captured her first aurora!

"Oh my, I'm so proud of myself. I'm in love."

The whole experience ignites such passion and joy within her being that Ana knows this is the start of something hugely impactful in her life.

#

She dreams of an aurora. It's like fireworks. She's in a city. The camera stuffs up, then the tripod, leaving her unable to take any photos. Obviously, the sight, the joy, the wonder is just for her. She's so grateful.

The night space is perfect, she doesn't have to see anyone else, or if someone else is there, it's so dark they can't actually see her nor her them. She doesn't have to hide herself; there's no need for talking, only whoops of joy breaking the silence. Ana can and does sit for many, many hours in the space it provides, becoming so hooked on the wonder of the night sky. It takes her away. She believes she's actually an alien, wishing she could go back to her home planet Zaphron, three stars on the right past Sirius, fifth galaxy straight ahead after that. She can't, not yet. But she can sit here under the sparkle, breathing in the solitude. It gets her out of the house, away from the noise of family. So, it's also avoidance therapy in dealing with her relationship.

#

There's a new police person, Police Officer David, who's now looking after her case. Fuck. She doesn't want someone else, she loves Monica, she feels their empathy, likes their tone. Now she has to deal with some stranger. A male, for fuck's sake. It means going over her story ... again. When are people going to get that doing that is just so bad? It retraumatises you every time you have to. Yes, it helps to heal, in a way, possibly. But not when you have to tell it for legal reasons. Then it's just fucked. Police Officer David is probably a good bloke, this new policeman. But she doesn't want a bloke, she wants her Monica back.

#

Sometimes when she puts her hand up it's a good thing. Well, actually, most times.

Once again, she's put her hand up. There's a post on social media asking new aurora chasers if they'd be interested in sharing their story on a current affairs program. "Woohoo! How cool would be to share my joy in this new obsession?"

She thinks, she believes, that the program will only be seen in Tasmania. She's so wrong.

The camera crew rock up to her home to do some preparation filming. Then they all head out to a local spot for a possible aurora show. There are some other dudes there, also new to chasing. Not much is happening, or so they all think. As they're all relatively new, they don't really have much of an idea. Ana does think that the horizon changes colour. One good thing is that she's learning very quickly where south is. A clear view south is what's needed to see the aurora.

She was always good with directions until she moved here. Now, there's water everywhere, so it throws her natural compass.

The TV thingy isn't shown for a couple of weeks. It's not local, its actually national.

"Oh fuck, I'll be found. I'm not safe."

She watches the report over and over, trying to see if anyone can work out where she lives by anything that's visible, hoping they can't.

#

The dark time is saving Ana. Every night she heads out, not caring if its cloudy, simply wanting to sit in that space, that silence. Things are taking so long on the legal side it's upsetting and confusing. The dark time allows a space physically and mentally removed from all the crap.

She dreams – somehow there's a million dollars in her PayPal account. She's unable to work out how it got there.

"I must get it out before someone realises the mistake."

She wonders what this dream's trying to tell her. Possibly that there's unknown riches being gifted to her? Maybe that she needs to accept good and not feel as though the good things happening to her are a mistake?

#

Esi comes to help celebrate her birthday, which Ana's ever so grateful for. But it also makes it so hard for her to be present, to pretend that everything's ok, that's she's ok, that her relationship's ok. It's not, none of it is, but she smiles, she interacts, all the while wanting to curl up in a ball and roll away. Wanting to be out in nature, feeling the wind in her hair, the wonders of it bringing joy to her soul.

A boat ride around the tallest sea cliffs is organised. It's such a wonderful experience, even in the five-metre swell when rounding the point past Tasman Island. The blowholes are all going off. She stands on the starboard side, watching the force of nature take control, feeling the rawness against her raw soul, becoming one with it, taking the salty air deep within. It's the only time the face that Ana puts on is able to come off. She's able to be herself, experiencing all of this, the simple joy of being present without pretending that everything's ok, that she's ok, when she's not. Inside she's crumbling, becoming a different version of herself, much like the water after each wave crashes it against the rocks. That's her – smashed, transformed, hoping to be rebuilt.

Thankfully there's an aurora forecast that night. What a gift from the Universe. She doesn't feel she can sit around pretending any longer. Esi's keen, so together they go chasing. They stand and watch as the sky dances before them, moving, changing colour, changing shape. There's some bioluminescence reported on the other side of River Derwent the day before Esi's due to leave, so naturally, they head over. It's a wondrous sight. And standing under the incredible Milky Way, they get the extra bonus of yet another aurora – the sky changing colours between yellow, red and orange while the ocean lights up with fluorescent blue waves, a memory Ana will cherish forever, feeling in that moment to be the luckiest person alive. She and Esi stand arm in arm, Esi the protector, she the vulnerable child.

#

She never knows what it will be – a tone, a word, a movement, a smell. Something triggers a physical response. It's right in her middle, her solar plexus, her gut. It feels like it's being torn, ripped, and twisted apart. It leaves her feeling tainted, bad, simply wanting to curl up in a ball and pretend her inside world isn't real.

It's the middle of Spring and work for Daren simply hasn't been there for the last six months, so Ana's had to go back on government assistance. At least this time they've allocated her a disability provider, which you would think would have a greater understanding of all disabilities. At an appointment with Ganlarice Work Services, Ana explains her issues with work, but they don't seem to have ears that hear her words, so instead she leaves her body, leaves the building. When asked what her triggers are she lists them: confined spaces, being indoors, white noise, different smells, the smell of cigarettes and alcohol, men wearing sunglasses on their caps, loud voices, kids' eyes that are haunted, stripes, straight lines, bright lights, adults yelling at kids, certain words, tones and many more, sometimes the list seems endless.

After they talk for about five minutes, they look at her and say, "Ok we have a job in a shopping centre taking Christmas photos, how does that sound to you?"

She stares back blankly. Like seriously, did they not listen to a word she just said? Ana leaves the office feeling like such a failure. Listing all her triggers made her feel as though she's really a basket case. But more than that, she feels that once again she wasn't heard or validated.

Getting into her car, she drives a few blocks further into town, parking the car without registering where she's actually left it. Walking back to where she thinks the car is, the anxiety and panic start rising. The closer she gets, the harder it is to remember where she's parked. She talks to herself as she walks around the blocks, trying to find her car, looking at her watch, seeing how much time's left before the meter runs out.

Finally, she finds her car by going back through her mind, step by step, from the interview at the disability services space where she knows she left her body, to standing, feeling lost amid the noise of city life until some distinguishing feature becomes visible.

"Wow that was an experience I'd rather not repeat." She shudders, feeling very lost, very alone and very unsafe.

Another aurora's forecast, and she feels grateful for the opportunity and excuse to escape her family after such a trying day, heading out to the space she's familiar with, where she feels safe.

Such incredible beauty, so humbling in its gift.

#

The *Minds Do Matter* exhibition's on again. She enters a few pieces she's managed to produce over the last year. This is one of her favourite exhibitions. The artworks are amazing and so raw. People's emotions, fears and hopes are displayed so openly. It's refreshing in a world full of fakeness.

Somehow, she manages two honourable mentions. One is for her painting from the dream awhile back of the planet with many moons.

Ascensions.

Ascensions is a riot of colours and symbols. It is very beautiful and demonstrates a terrific level of skill.

The other is for her painting depicting a being born from a tree. She feels this may be a self-portrait.

tREe birth.

This is an intriguing piece with beautiful colours and an unusual but very interesting interpretation of tREe Birth.

She's super impressed and super grateful. She manages to get through the night without talking to anyone about herself, instead finding other artists whose work she admires, focusing on their skills. It's a big test, putting herself out there, being seen, being acknowledged.

#

Daily walking of Big Dog and Little Dog is something that provides a break from reality, it helps ground her and brings in a space of sanity. Along the most common path there's a beautiful big blue gum. A large piece of bark has fallen to the ground. For some reason, this bark captures Ana's eye, leaving her wondering how difficult it would be to carry it home with her hands full of dog leashes.

"If it's still there in three days then I'll pick it up," she says, as for some reason that would then mean that the bark's meant for her. Go figure that logic.

Of course, the bark's still there in three days' time, so she walks home looking weird (nothing new there) carrying this long skinny piece of bark, trying not to break any of it. There's a canvas at home she's hoping will be big enough. It's long and skinny just like the bark. It fits perfectly. Turning the bark over, she reveals its underside, the side not normally seen. It's stunning, leaving Ana feeling as though she wants, no, *needs* to honour it.

"How can I? What kind of painting can I do behind it?"

She sits and reflects on what brings her joy: aurora chasing, sitting under the stars, being in the dark time, silence, being unseen, all these gifts are what brings joy. The meditative process of dotting is what's needed now.

The painting starts to take shape without any effort. Ana's never one to do a rough copy before doing the original painting, believing that's just a waste of time and materials. Instead, she simply starts creating. When it's not working, she goes over it and starts again. Some paintings have up to seven layers because of this process. It's not really logical in terms of saving paint and time, but it works and adds unseen depths to each painting.

This painting doesn't need that though; it just seems to be happening and coming together perfectly. Ana loves it, she's really happy with it.

There is a slight issue with the fragility of the bark, it would be so easy to damage, not to mention the amount of dust it would attract. She has an idea. What if a Perspex frame is put around it?

"Yes, that should work."

After searching through the local phone book, she finds a company that may be able to help. The guy understands what Ana's after, telling her to come back in three days. Three days later, she's taking the Perspex frame home and gently laying it over the canvas and bark. It looks amazing, bringing the whole creation to life, leaving it with a touch of professionalism. She calls the painting *Inspire*.

Chapter 11

Avoidance therapy

Ana feels like she's in no man's land. Words that used to fill the air don't come easily to her lips. Instead, she runs, afraid of her truth, afraid of being seen by others. If she's seen, there will not be enough words to cover the ugly silence created by her story.

She stays home, staying hidden, staying safe. She sits with Big Dog and Little Dog; they save her, they love her, they just accept her. They want nothing more than what she can give in any moment.

Then the family comes home. She can't deal with that, can't deal with the noise, the smells, the simple actuality of another being in her space. She hates what's going on. Hates how she's so absent from the kids. Hates how it's affecting them.

Ana could stop, she could pull the pin, she could walk away from the court case. But the thing is, she can't. It's part of her. It's what's made her. It's what's driving her. Even if she stopped the legal crap, the thing itself would still be there, even bigger and stronger, because it would be totally in control. She would have no control over it. At least this way she has some control. She can say yea or nay at any given moment. His life is in her hands, and she so wants to crush him.

#

Sometimes there's so much noise in general daily tasks it's overwhelmingly loud. Thankfully, the rain brings a blanket of shhh-y-ness, allowing for muffled tones, allowing for peace within her soul. At a dinner date with Lucia and their partner, Lucia asks everyone what's the one thing they wish for.

"You Ana?"
"Peace."

#

Confrontation. It's everywhere she looks. She hates herself, wanting to die, believing she must have been such a disgusting person in a past life to be having this kind of karma now. The kids agree, saying she's so fucked.

Some random lady at the local beach approaches Ana, believing her to be someone that they know.

"No that isn't me," she says, but they don't believe her response. The woman is furious that Ana would lie to them. They get angry, really angry. They start abusing her.

"Who do you think you are now that you live down here? Too good for the rest of us, hey?"

She has absolutely no idea who they are talking about, she hasn't even been to the town they are claiming she used to live in. It does get her wondering though. Who does she think she is? She feels at such a loss, not knowing who she really is. Maybe, just maybe, this random woman is right. Maybe she is this other person. Maybe she does have another life she knows nothing about. Maybe she really has lost her mind, her grasp on reality.

It feels like her brain's going to explode.

"I just can't do this anymore; I don't want to do this anymore. Its fucked, I'm fucked. It's all my fault, my ego thinking I've healed and that I've broken all my family cycles. What a load of crock."

She's unable to focus, unable to concentrate, crying, sobbing, crying, sobbing, not knowing what to do. She feels completely powerless.

There's no one to blame but herself. She feels like she's falling, falling through infinity, unable to see the bottom. She's not feeling an ending, just continual falling.

"This too will pass," she tells herself. "This too will pass," she tries to convince herself. "This too will pass," she disillusions herself.

It doesn't pass. It friggin doesn't.

"Please God, make it pass. I need to know that it will stop. God, please, make it stop, make it go away. Make it STOP. I hate ME, I blame ME, I know it's ME."

She screams into the dark time completely grateful for its abyss of nothingness encompassing so much.

Ok. She needs some sanity. She takes a photo, exposes herself. This is fucked, this is ME.

#

"Remove enmeshment. Enmeshment in trauma totally consumes – eating all in its path. I must change my path and live – not just survive. The world is my oyster; I am but a tadpole at the beginning of my existence. It's up to me whether I grow legs and hop away or become part of the stagnant water."

These random thoughts run around her head, occupying the already overflowing space. She clears her mind, shaking out all the cobwebs, because holding onto them lets "them" win. Must not let that happen. Must show the kids how to be a successful individual after experiencing trauma.

Ana knows she can do it; it just hurts so much and it's so fucking hard. She feels like a part of her wants to keep herself in the trauma mode. It's trying to make her head spin now, not letting her focus.

"Take back the power. It's mine not theirs. Move ahead, don't stay in the past. It's challenging reliving it, but I can do it. I have insurmountable strength." Ana knows this but sometimes she'd like someone else to help carry the load.

She feels better, simply breathing and repeating.

#

Thankfully Mardi, one of Ana's best friends, is at home. It's not good for Mardi, but it's great for Ana. Normally Mardi's travelling the world, sharing their learnings to many, but now they've had a back operation and need to rest, to stay still.

Like Ana, Mardi has a story, unfortunately too close in similarity. And like Ana, staying still and quiet, sitting with the memories, can be too much. Mardi's amazing at crochet. They crochet while they talk. Sometimes it's great to sit with another who's walked your path. They get you, they understand, they don't judge your weirdness. It's so fucked that this has happened to so many, females and males.

Mardi believes Ana should write a book.

Laughing, she replies, "Me? Write a book? Nah."

#

An update from the police … things take time. For fuck's sake, this is dragging on and on and on. Sometimes she's able to forget it or at least remove it from the front of her brain, managing this for possibly a day. Then something reminds her and the joy she's experiencing is once again taken away.

Dolphins are one of these joys, they seem to know when to appear and offer their healing energy, harmony and balance that's so needed. The simple joy of floating on the water, surrounded by the fun-filled antics of the dolphins playing, it takes her away, allowing breath in.

She's out in Storm Bay with Daren. Big Dog and Little Dog are there too. They're meant to be fishing. She doesn't care if she catches a flathead. The simple act of being on the water, engine switched off, the sound of nature invading her senses, that's why she's there. The peace is wondrous, the sounds of nature creating a symphony within her soul. The sounds are heightened by the presence of over a hundred or so bottle- and common-nosed dolphins circling the boat. They're everywhere, around, under, over the boat, adults, babies the size of a football. As she stands watching, her eyes leak, she's so grateful for all the support and gifts she's receiving from Mother Nature.

#

"I've made it!" This is what Ana feels when she finds out one of her aurora photos is being used as the banner shoot for the following month on social media. It's the equivalent of having your photo on the front page of a monthly publication.

In the photo she's standing on the beach in full awe of the wonder before her. An angel-shaped cloud gently touches the earth in front of purple and green curtains, as the beams of the aurora dance under a moonlit sky. This means so much. Being under the night sky truly brings inner peace, providing a space of sanctuary. Whenever she thinks her world is crumbling, she just sits under the stars. A tiny, teeny dot of existence amid the grandeur that is the Universe.

It's the music festival time of year in Tasmania. As she wants to spend time with Rey, they head to the Cygnet Folk Festival. There are too many people there, there's too much noise, too much movement. Ana stays, being physically present for Rey, but the whole time running away in her mind.

There's a concert by a deaf percussionist as part of the festival. They are totally amazing. She watches the crowd's discomfort as at first the musician sits in silence, waiting, at rest, reflecting their own inner world of quiet. Why as humans, do we so feel the need to fill silence? She doesn't get it. Sitting in silence is joy, a gift to oneself.

The percussionist springs into action. She loves the tones being created by this amazing musician. They're so tiny but able to create such big powerful sounds. Vibrational images are forming in her mind as the tones change.

"I must turn these images into creations."

One day.

Chapter 12

Mother Earth – a space to be

It's been a weird week. Ana was feeling so much lighter, then something happened. Now her ears are ringing, sometimes quite badly. This morning, she once again felt like vomiting. Like something's going to happen that will make her sick.

Her back and the spot on the left side have started playing up again. It's depressing. She felt so good and now she feels like crap again. She has no idea what's going on. Suddenly her eyes feel extremely heavy and tired, which is not good, especially when driving. It's a real effort to keep them open. She also notes that her left breast is significantly larger than the right and that both are hurting. A visit to her awesome integrative doctor is called for.

The doctor says that Ana's hyperglycaemic. They advise her to give up sugar, at least until the legal crap is finished. Stress can be a contributing factor.

Like, what the fuck? Really? There don't seem to be many joys left in her world at the moment, and now she has to give up sugar, which means CHOCOLATE.

Why???????

She knows she's being a Sooky LaLa but she doesn't care. This is chocolate, her one true love.

#

For some crazy reason she decides to hold a solo exhibition. It seems like great avoidance therapy. It's one way to take her mind off what's happening, or more to the point, what's not happening. Things in the legal system move ever so slowly.

Focusing on an exhibition is just what's needed. It may bring joy. It may also heighten her social anxiety. In fact, it will definitely do that.

She finds a space. It's far enough away as to not be in her backyard. It's by the water so peace can be found. The owners are lovely. This all leaves her feeling like the exhibition is a "coming out" for her. Coming out of what? She isn't too sure.

She spent the whole day hanging her works, something she's never done before. She kind of enjoyed the experience, and kind of hated it too. She basically had no idea what to do. It was the only way to learn though. It was like a jigsaw puzzle. She was trying to place all the pieces into a whole, so that it somehow appeared as a complete unit.

#

It's opening night.

"Like what the fuck do I think I'm doing?"

It's cold and raining, so she's super grateful that people still take the hour-long drive to be there, to support her, to enjoy her creations. Ana struggles though, struggles to be present for others. She hates small talk, so instead she pretends to be busy, avoiding everyone, not staying in one spot for longer than the blink of an eye. She's afraid if she talks, they'll see all that horrible shitty crap that's within her, the horrible stain she feels so visible over her being.

But others don't see. Some even lead conversations in directions that cause anxiety within. Sometimes she feels ok with a person, possibly opening up, just a touch. It's hard to not give too much away. Her art's so personal, so much a part of her, part of her story. Do others see the words or only hear the images?

#

The phone rings, it's the gallery. A customer who's bought some of her Spirit drawings would really like to talk to Ana. Is that ok?

What's she meant to say, "No way. Fuck off"?

As much as she'd like to, she doesn't. Instead saying, "Sure".

Thirty minutes later, after getting off the phone, she's ever so grateful, giving thanks to Spirit. That phone call, that lady's energy, their love for Ana's work, all of that, was just what was needed. Then to top off that feel-good feeling it snows.

She's so thankful.

The best thing to come out of the exhibition is the selling of one of her pieces. Her most favourite. Her treasured bee painting, *No Bees No Me's*. Mardi wants to hang it in their office. She feels so honoured that her art will create an image of peace for Mardi.

A slight problem arises on the day she's taking the exhibition down. There's a very strong wind whipping up from the south. Cold and powerful, it's the kind of wind she normally loves to stand in, feeling its rawness, it's cleansing power. It grabs hold of Mardi's painting while Ana's trying to get the car door open. There's nothing Ana can do. A huge force rips it from her hands and smashes it on the footpath. It's like the bees are being set free.

Thankfully, it's just the frame that needs redoing. And as it's home-made that's an easy fix. A few days later she's able to present it to Mardi.

#

She feels the need to escape her past. It completely envelopes her soul. She's unable to find any space without it being there. It's in the air she breathes, the sounds she hears. Contact from the police is just way too much, throwing her every time. It impinges upon her space without her having any control over it,

Ana leaves her body yet remains seemingly present for her family. They have no idea, or do they? No wonder she feels like there's more than one of her. Once again, Mother Nature provides an escape, more dolphins, more joy, more leaking eyes. It's truly such a gift to have her eyes blessed with beauty rather than horror.

#

There's a new diagnosis going around. It's attention deficit disorder – OSD. It's the *ohhhh shiny thing* disorder. Lots of her friends think they have it. The joy of finding new things, new *ohhhh shiny thing* distractions.

Bug chasing's the latest. Chasing these super cool insects called feathered horned beetles. They fly really fast, staying still for but a blink of the eye, looking like fairies in the sky.

A day can be lost simply being still, watching, waiting, trying to capture these majikal creatures in the camera. Oh, such joy, such a gift to self, being present in the moment. Such a rarity.

Adding to the gift, and even though it's summer, there's snow on kunanyi/Mt Wellington – the mountain that's almost in her backyard. She's so grateful to Mother Nature for bringing her this gift, the shhh-y-ness is just too alluring, allowing focus on wondrous distractions rather than past horrors.

On top of daytime wonders, the planets are aligning, seven of them. So she goes out at darktime with a new friend who found Ana through social media, asking if she'd take some pics of them under the night sky.

They get up around 3:30am. The early light brings in silence with its wonder. Ana's new friend Eve is sitting on the rocks by the water's edge, meditating, in awe of what's lining up above them. The sun's rising in the east over the water, a crescent moon's reflecting on the River Derwent. Venus, Saturn, Mars and Jupiter hang seemingly weightless amid the many thousands of stars visible to the naked eye. Planet Earth holds them.

What an incredible sight. So much gratitude.

#

Even though at times it was more than just POS doing shit to her, she can't remember exactly who did what. It's a bit hard to remember exact details, times, dates. After all, she was just a child. How could one so young remember the precise details, when so many were doing shit that should never be done to anyone?

The police ask, "Do you want to press charges against them?"

"I don't know, can I?"

"Probably not," comes the reply.

So why ask, then?

When things aren't clear, charges can't be laid. Ana can't be 100% sure who did what and when. This is bullshit. She knows someone stuck something in her mouth, and it wasn't food. She's pretty sure who it was, but she's being honest in saying she can't be 100% sure.

"How about a bystander charge?"

They stood there, the other three, many times. Watching, laughing, doing nothing to stop it. They were all older, they should have done something, anything to stop what was being done to her. Pieces of shit all of them.

"Nope."

Fuck, it sucks. She just wants it all to end.

#

Dealing with the police becomes too much. Her brain is unable to understand what's being said. She doesn't understand police speak, nor legal speak. She's noticing a huge decline in her ability to understand things lately. Her brain's truly fried. She knows she's not dumb, she's rather smart actually. She just doesn't have the ability, the knowing, the strength, the space, to take on all this legal jargon shit as well.

Layla is one of her most treasured friends. They're another soul who's unfortunately also walked this path, even trying through the legal channels to prosecute her perpetrator on three separate occasions, to only have it time and time again thrown out at different stages, for stupid reasons. Ana has no idea how Layla's still standing, still functioning and able to provide such amazing support. What an incredible being Layla is, and they're her friend! Super special.

Layla suggests Ana gets some support from another service especially set up for sexual assault victims. She hates that word *victim*.

She's not a victim. She's a fucking legend. She survived.

She goes to see the people at the new service. She's really nervous, sitting in a strange new space, new smells, new visuals, new people, needing to find space in her mind for all of this newness.

Part of her feels as though she doesn't belong, as though her story isn't that major, that there are obviously others who need this service more than she does. She's often felt like that over the years. Some of the story's others have shared with her are unrepeatable in their horror. All the stories have different levels of shit. But no matter what happened, or how many times it happened, it's equally as fucked.

A lovely younger lady enters the space and introduces themself. Ana's immediately put at ease by Melisa's manner, though she feels herself leaving the room as soon as they start to talk about the legal crap and ask what happened to her. Ana explains how she feels that the whole legal process is clinical and cold, how she's finding it all very confusing and struggles to make much sense of anything. This, in part, is due to her dyslexia and how her brain deals with stuff, especially when she feels emotionally overwhelmed, as though she's drowning and there's no life raft.

She tells Melisa how, at first, there was z female police officer whom she found to be very empathetic towards her, but that unfortunately Monica left. (She can completely understand why, it would be such a shit job.) Then she was passed on to the male police officer, David, who she's sure is a really nice guy, but he doesn't seem to get it, to get her. He doesn't understand why she doesn't want to speak on the phone, why she's upset at the lack of communication and the time taken for this whole process.

So, Ana asks Melisa if they would, if they could, please advocate for her. Could they support her in understanding the legal process and interpret what's happening with the investigation? Would Melisa act on her behalf with the police? Oh please.

Thankfully Melisa says yes, and Ana feels her body slightly let go of something, allowing a breath in.

\#

A copy of the statement arrives in the post. As she reads it, she feels weird. It doesn't feel like she's reading about herself, but she doesn't know if it's just because she's detached while reading it, or if putting it down on paper has enabled her to stand back from it, apart from it.

It's just totally weird reading your own words. It feels so clinical, so unemotional. Apparently, that's how it needs to be from the legal aspect, but for Ana it lacks truth. It's emotionless. It states the facts, but not the results. That's wrong, but it's the way it's needed for a conviction.

Apparently, she will get her chance to say her truth, the emotional aspect of it, should it make it to court. Should he be proven guilty, then she will have her chance to say her feeling truth.

Ana sits quietly with leaking eyes. It's all getting too much, the legal crap, dealing with the kids, watching her relationships crumble. She's sinking, and fast. Yet she's not able to, not allowed to.

"You're strong. You're my rock. You must be strong for the kids," is all she hears from Daren. All she wants is to curl up in a ball, close her eyes and disappear, forever.

To help ease the load, she asks Melisa if they can support her through the actual court process, should that eventuate. They discuss the options, Melisa explaining what services they can provide. Clarification will be needed on what exactly they can do, as the report is an interstate one. All these different state laws are really a piss off. Why should she have to go back to where it all happened? Why does she need to go to Victoria to have this dealt with in a court of law there? She'll have to leave her support network, her safe spaces, Big Dog and Little Dog, and go, and be present in a space that has so many triggers. This is what's so fucking wrong with our judicial system.

Some respite comes in the form of a Missy Higgins concert. Only Ana, Rey, Lucia and their family are going. It's a road trip filled with laughter and joy, all of them knowing that fun times await, sleeping under the stars beside the beautiful Mount Roland after a night of amazing tones from Missy. Pure perfection.

Chapter 13

Embracing the unknown

Another adventure. This time Danika encourages Ana's participation. She's feeling a tad nervous – new people, new spaces. She's thankful Danika's there.

The Bob Brown Foundation hold an art collective each year, hoping that creating many bodies of work will help promote and protect the unique temperate rainforests of Tasmania. The government want to log it. To log trees that are over a thousand years old. For what? Sawdust? It doesn't make sense. But then, lots of things humans do to the environment don't make sense.

They head north to the Tarkine, a space by Arthur River on the wild west coast. Artists from many genres have already arrived, many staying in tents. Ana and Danika are staying in a house – special treatment.

"Being a mental case like me has it rewards," Ana says, smiling at Danika.

There are two men in the house, which makes for some discomfort. They're both called Patrick. Go figure. She wonders if the Universe is playing some kind of cruel trick on her.

One of them is arrogant and condescending. She doesn't like him one bit. She doesn't like how he has the name Patrick, but he looks more like an Otto. She doesn't like his energy.

The other one is lovely and *so* not a Patrick. She asks him if he has a middle name.

"Yes, it's Dave."

"Is it ok if I call you Dave?"

"Yes," smiles Dave.

#

What an experience!

It's the first time away from family since moving to Tasmania. She can breathe; she can simply be. No-one apart from Danika knows her, she's anonymous, so is her story.

They visit some indigenous land, feeling the sacredness of sitting in its space as the roaring 40's winds lash against her exposed soul. Freshly caught abalone is gifted to all. Such an amazing sensation on her virgin taste buds. She's grateful for the experience of newness, understanding its high price tag as it lies like silken heaven inside her mouth. She doesn't want to swallow. She wants to retain this moment of pure joy forever.

There's a private dance performance in the burnt forest happening that night. Somehow, they manage to get invited. Neither of them is sure what to expect, but they are certainly not disappointed. Ana has never been so emotionally moved by a dance performance, or any performance for that matter. This one makes her eyes leak. The dancer is such a unique and divine soul, and she's so grateful for the opportunity to witness true art being performed with true connection to the environment.

Many thanks.

"It sorta makes sense now."

"What does?" asks Danika.

Ana thought she was talking in her head. Obviously not.

"In meditation about a week ago I was thinking about coming here. Asking what I was going to see? What's it all about? I saw a phoenix rising from a dark space. And this, this performance, is just that. There's the phoenix, our performer. The burnt forest – the dark space. This is what I saw."

"Ahhh," goes Danika, knowing not to question.

Now Ana needs to create what she saw. It's obviously significant, somehow. The whole amazing experience is complex and diverse, from the wild untamed Arthur River reflections, the quiet of Mother Nature, to the amazingly vibrant colours of the rainforest, were she wishes to be left to live amongst the fungi and what she's sure would be lots of majikal woodland creatures.

Due to the recent rain, the forest floor's covered in moss, making it all soft, adding to the shhh-y-ness of the space. She's never seen a space of such majikality. They walk, not very far, but it takes hours. Stopping, wowing, breathing in all its wonder, she can see herself composting into the forest floor, becoming entangled in the giant roots of the myrtle trees as they hold her, offering their goodness to her spent soul.

On the last day, they head to a place that had caught her attention on day one. The geology along this coast is amazing. It's filled with quartzite and granite, each little cove having different colour tones. In this particular cove, Bluff Hill Point, the colours start from the softest pink, nearly unrecognisable as anything but white, and go through to the deepest ruby red. Such a pretty sight.

Getting out of the car, Ana stands looking to the sea.

"There! Over there. That's where I need to go," she shouts with a hint of glee.

She has no idea why; she just feels that space is for her.

Along the way, she and Danika enjoy the wonders of the place – the incredible rock formations and flora, the flowering pig faces (her favourite) with the vibrant magenta flowers, the wild sea, waves smashing on the intense orange-lichen-covered jagged rocks. It's wild, raw, and extreme. Exactly what she needs. They make it to the spot; there's a rock ledge looking out to the water. Seating herself on the jaggedness, she feels the points sticking into her bottom.

"Sort of like acupuncture," she laughs to herself. "This is it. This is my space within this vast area. I feel like this is my home, that I know this space, and more weirdly, that this space knows me."

Her words are caught by the wind, lifted and taken out to sea, to be smashed and released by the force of Mother Nature.

Getting back in the car she feels a deep breath rising.

"I don't know what's happened. Something's shifted within me, I'm not sure what. I just know it's huge. Thank you, Spirit." The words expel from her mouth along with stale air.

Something's happened within her core, within her soul, that's fundamentally changed her forever. This journey, these experiences, this space, it's all changed her.

Returning home, Ana holds on tightly to the recent memories of joy as the familiar overwhelming pressures start to crush her soul.

#

The wonders of nature thankfully continue, along with questions from the police and communications with her GP to allow preparation of an impact statement about the physical side of things.

The night sky provides a place of sanctuary. Lady Aurora's dancing skirts and stunning beams. She sits below the dark skies, being present with Layla on the jetty near her home. The water is so calm, offering stunning star reflections.

They talk, they share, they cry, they sigh, they give thanks for Mother Nature, for Spirit, for friendship, for kindred souls, for shared journeys.

Ana asks when Layla voluntarily lost her virginity. As in, when did Layla first have sex that she chose to be part of?

Ana remembers years ago when she was asked at what age she lost her own virginity. She replied, "Do you mean voluntarily? Or forced?" The other person looked at her as though she was crazy and bad. She could feel the puke coming out of the other person's being as they heard those words.

It's so fucked, all these amazing, resilient, strong souls, all who share a common thread in their life journeys. It's so very, very wrong and so overwhelmingly sad.

#

Joy just keeps being thrown around.

More dolphins and a hint of a shy albatross. Ana loves the albatrosses. They just don't make sense with their wing spans of around three metres. Like, how does anything like that manage to glide so gracefully across the water. The tip of the wing the only thing briefly touching the surface. Such grace, such strength, such beauty. As a result of the journey to the Tarkine there's an exhibition, including some concerts that are the results of the musician's experiences. With each concert Ana sees images, visions of all varieties, depending on the tones. She decides to make some cards from those images, much like what she did after the percussion concert. This is a really great way to take her mind away from all the legal crap that's continually trying to grasp her attention. She wants to control it, and herself. It's absorbing her into its shit, so this is a blessing, this OSD.

She's happy with the result and hopes that they'll sell and generate some revenue to help protect the wild spaces.

#

There's a very special plant that grows in Tasmania. It's the fagus, the *Nothofagus gunnii*. It grows nowhere else in the entire world, it's that special. The best part is it grows at Mt Field when the ground is covered in white shhh-y-ness. It's a sight to behold – colours of red, yellow, gold and deep emerald green, popping out against the background of white.

So precious. She's so grateful.

#

Mother's Day has always been a day that's she's questioned. She never feels like it's a label that fits her. It leaves her squirming under its weight, its expectations. This year, especially, she feels like such a failure. She wants to be alone, so she doesn't have to pretend, or hate herself for getting angry at the kids. There's an amazing opportunity being offered through a social media promotion. Once again, she puts her hand up, resulting in a Mother's Day spent with complete strangers as they pass sea cliffs formed by 180-million-year-old dolerite, eating some of the finest local food and listening to the screams of the endemic animals. All while chatting with Ariel, a lady from Brazil.

Not being a mother.

Simply Ana.

A couple of nights later, she and Ariel head out. She's hoping for a clear evening, hoping to show Ariel the wonders of the night sky. They sit in silence as the Milky Way rises from the east over the River Derwent. The head of the emu, the coal sack, is visible, as the core making up the body of the emu rises like a giant image about to engulf all. Such divine beauty that she takes for granted.

Ariel's all ohhhs and ahhhs, saying how they have only ever seen the stars forming the Milky Way about four times before in their life. "That's so sad," she thinks, reflecting on the joy it provides her. She doesn't know where she'd be, or even if she'd still be here without it.

#

Her file has finally been submitted to the head honcho in the Hilcock Sexual Assault Unit for checking. It's six months after she was told this was going to happen. Why, oh why, does it take so fucking long?

Sometimes she forgets. Well, in a way. She doesn't let all the legal crap rule her mind's thoughts every minute of every day. So, when she receives notice of the submission, she's taken aback. It brings her back into that space. She needs to remind herself to breathe and repeat, giving thanks for progress.

Finally, the painting, the image that started this part of her journey, is finished. Giana's husband helps with the framing, resulting in what actually looks like a pool, complete with black and white checked tiles around the water's edge. It's such a cathartic piece in so many ways. It's huge, the biggest one she's ever done. Now the challenge is to find somewhere to hang it. It claims the space at the bottom of the exposed stairwell, a space she passes every day many times. Now she looks upon herself, swimming in a pool, surrounded by the Koi, lotus growing from her solar plexus, and she's reminded why she's doing this. Finishing the painting is emotional. She was hoping that it would herald the completion of the legal crap too. That's how she'd seen it in her mind anyway. Now she must accept that it's not so.

She's overwhelmed by the response to her painting, the feedback from friends. All of it crushes her with the weight of love.

Thankfully, Mother Nature knows exactly what's needed – a blanket of whiteness to cover kunanyi/Mt Wellington. Such a majikal space. She's so grateful.

She goes out in the boat with Daren again. Being on the water, being present among all the marine life, listening to the waves lap against the boat, being lulled into a space of sleepiness by the swell, watching the shy albatrosses with admiration, this is all gifting her with great faith that Spirit's always with her, offering strength, support, hope.

At darktime, the full moon energy keeps Ana awake. She's unable to find darkness behind closed eyelids, so instead why not embrace it? The night's calm, the sky relatively clear, Layla's jetty's calling. There's not a breath of air, the water is like a mirror, Layla joins her. She sits, accepting the gift from above, the gift of friendship. She wishes she could sit there forever.

Chapter 14

Value and worth

"It's going to court! It's going to court!" Ana yells, twirling in her space with no one home.

She likes that, not wanting to share this moment with anyone, preferring instead to simply sit and absorb all it entails.

"Oh my!"

This piece of information brings in so many emotions, so many memories, so much empty space. A deep breath is needed, a moment to gather herself back in as much as safely possible.

It makes up for the worst moment of being a parent – having to tell your kids you've been sexually abused as a child – when you can tell them that the person who did this to their mum is going to court. He's going to be held accountable for his actions. She truly hopes this teaches the kids that it's never too late to deal with anything. And also, that, hopefully, there is some kind of justice in their world.

This knowing, this information, helps her to open up to creating again. A painting from the trip to the Tarkine is complete. She titles it *Journey Within*. That's how she feels. She's unable to put it into words. She just knows that something happened within her being, subtle yet impactful, leaving her feeling stronger and more clear in her direction in life, in what brings her joy, in her connection with nature and appreciation of its value and worth.

#

Ana knows nothing about court proceedings, and court placements, so she seeks some help from Melisa.

There's still a lengthy process ahead. First, there's the committal, where all the evidence is put forward, where she needs to speak, answering questions directed at trying to undermine her truth. This doesn't concern her, her story has always, always remained the same, they can try all they like. But having to be present in the same air as POS, now that, that may be what breaks her.

This is where she gets to tell her truth, to tell her story. But the process of writing it, of trying to contain the victim impact statement onto paper, is difficult. How's anyone meant to write a lifetime of fucked up behaviours into a few pages?

As an adult, she's pretty much always kept a journal, as well as her dream journal. So, at least she has many writings to help her, to remind her. There's also doctor and psych reports, her friends' input, her own awareness.

Over the years, she's become more and more aware of her triggers. More able to limit her exposure to known people or places. But she's still unable, naturally, to control everything. Obviously, POS and Melbourne are major triggers. How is she ever going to go back there and be, ok?

There's a possibility that, at least for the committal, she may be able to be present via a video link up. Thankfully there's some time before she has to make a definite decision. She's floating between wanting to be there, to stand tall, proud of who she is, hoping it will make him squirm, and freaking out, thinking, "There is no fucking way I'm going to be present in the same space as that fucking arsehole."

The legal crap has escalated, and Ana has no idea what's going on or why all this paperwork needs to be completed. It's playing havoc with her mental state, leaving her questioning her comfortability on this earth, so much so, that together with Melisa she works out a safety plan.

Safety Plan

If I feel upset, angry, or overwhelmed I can:
- Walk Big Dog and Little Dog
- Sit under the night sky
- Have chocolate and chai
- Remind myself of the reasons I enjoy being on this earth:
  - Big Dog and Little Dog
  - Night sky
  - My home spaces
  - Being outdoors, finding new places, finding, and seeing things

If I feel I need to talk to someone I can call
- Layla
- Lille
- Asia

If I feel like I need someone physically to come and see me I can call
- Giana
- Layla
- Mardi

If I feel I need to have professional support I can call
- S.A.S.S after hours. 1800 697 877
- Lifeline 131114
- Mental Health Helpline 1800 332 388
- Suicide Call Back Service 1300 659 467

If I need to arrange to see a professional I can
- Contact Kimberly
- Contact S.A.S.S

If it's an emergency and I cannot guarantee my safety I can
- Dial 000 to speak to police or ambulance to take me to the emergency department.

She's not too sure how much better this makes her feel, but she can see by the easing of breath within Melisa that they feel better.

#

There's a person on social media, and there's something about their tone, their words, that creates a sense of familiarity and comfort in Ana. She feels she knows this person but can't understand how. When she reads their words, they create joy-filled feelings, tingles. She must push them aside for the moment. There's too much other life stuff going on without fantasizing over someone she hasn't even met. Someone she knows nothing about.

#

Olivia, Ana's high school bestie, comes for a visit. The visit makes Ana wonder how she has any friends now, let alone then. She believes she was a shit of a younger person. She had bad behaviours, she was unable to communicate healthily. Then there was the drinking, the unwanted sexual encounters, the one and only drug use, the stealing. Oh, the shame. She hated herself so much back then and assumed that everyone else did too. Yet here is a friend, someone she's known for over thirty years, and they still want to spend time with her. Why? Together with Ariel they head out on the town, so to speak, enjoying and embracing all the wonders of the *Dark Mofo* festival that happens in the darkest depths of winter. The best part for Ana was the house of mirrors. It makes sense; she can physically see there all the many selves that she knows live inside her being.

Over the days, she and Olivia talk. She has questions she's hoping Olivia can provide answers for. Olivia is one of the few friends she has who was never sexually abused as a child, so in that sense, Olivia doesn't truly understand what Ana's experiencing. How can they? That doesn't stop them being a good friend, offering support and input, even if it isn't what she wants.

She asks Olivia what they thought of her when they were teenagers, wondering if her own perception of self was the same as what others saw. "No way! You were fun. You said you didn't like POS but never explained why, so I never asked. I'm so sorry I didn't.

"I do remember when we were at the bottom of your street one day after school, we were like in Year 9. Patrick was there. He called you over. I remember you coming back about ten minutes later, shaking and looking like shit. I'm sorry I didn't ask you what happened, you didn't look like you wanted to or could actually talk."

Olivia cries, tears rolling down her cheeks.

"It's ok," Ana reassures. "I should have told you. That day, POS wanted to tell me about his new girlfriend, Judy and how he would never do to her what he'd done to me. That they were planning on waiting until they were married before having sex. He said he respected Judy."

In that moment, Ana's self-esteem had seemed to mix with the mud beneath her school shoes. She had been unable to move, to react. She had been only able to feel like absolute crap about herself, wondering, hoping that somehow Judy would see the true POS before it was too late.

Thankfully Mother Nature likes Olivia and knows that Ana needs some wonder and joy in her world. So, it snows, just for them, that's what she thinks anyway. Up kunanyi/Mt Wellington they head, playing and laughing in the snow just like two schoolgirls.

#

It seems that she's not the only one in her family who keeps journals or has memories of times long past. Rey shares a story as they climb into their mums warmed bed, hoping for comfort as the words fall out of their young mouth. Ana's struggling to hold back the tears, tears of joy because she's so proud that Rey can express themself so starkly, so openly, and then there's the tears of sadness, of regret, of pain, of guilt. She questions and wonders why she didn't leave earlier. Because of her inability to act, her kids now carry shit that doesn't belong to them.

Rey lies there wondering why their mum's sad, why she has that absent look on her face. They think to themselves that maybe this wasn't the right time. But then again is there ever a right time?

Rey leans over, laying their head on her chest, mumbling at first, the nervousness apparent.

"What?" Ana doesn't really want a conversation in this moment. The overwhelming feelings arising from Rey's writing still sit, so present in her being. She wants to run, to hide, but she can't. She's a mum, and she can hear in her kid's tone that she's needed.

"Mum I'm gay."

Ana shrugs her shoulders.

"OK."

They lay holding one another, mother and child, both immersed in feelings of shame, guilt, and for Ana, blame.

Chapter 15

Signs from the Universe

When a breast screen reminder comes in the mail Ana takes note. A couple of years ago she had been experiencing discomfort in her breasts. She had made an appointment for a check-up, cancelling at the last moment as the thought of an invasive procedure (as that's how she sees mammograms) was just too much for her to deal with in that moment. She had just started all the legal proceedings.

Now though, she knows this is a sign. The Universe is telling her, grabbing her attention.

An appointment's made. Naturally, her mind wanders to the possibility of it being cancer again. But nope, she's got this. She's feeling confident about this. Her breasts aren't hurting as much anymore.

After the mammogram, which thankfully is much more comfortable now than it used to be, she's advised she may possibly get a call back as it's been quite a few years since her last, like eight, and not to worry if this happens. She won't worry. It doesn't faze her. It's all good. She's got this.

The following week, the phone rings – it's Breast Screen.

"We need to make a follow up appointment for more invasive testing, please."

Ana's thinking to herself, "But wait, what? Nooooo. This is all good. I've got this."

But that wasn't what the receptionist was saying, so another appointment is made.

She hasn't told anyone in her family about her first test, so she certainly isn't going to tell them about this. Instead, she shares it with Giana, who offers to take her to the clinic.

"Be prepared for a long wait," she's told.

Wait they do. One small biopsy is performed in the morning. Then they are told that a more invasive biopsy is required, would Ana mind waiting?

The invasive testing machine is broken. A technician is required to fix it.

More waiting.

After lunch, she sends Giana home. She's got this. She's good at dealing with shit by herself.

She's called into an office. It isn't a good news office. She can taste the fear in the air, the stagnation of words left hanging. There's a lady whose title she can't remember. She feels herself leave her body as her bum hits the chair. The lady's name is the same as Mother Blobfish's, which is enough of a trigger, let alone everything else that's going on. There's also a man present; he's apparently a professor. She doesn't like him. Not at all. He seems pompous and arrogant.

They're explaining that it appears she has a high-grade multi-forma breast cancer. They need to do the invasive biopsy to confirm that it has spread. In normal terms, this means they want to remove Ana's right breast and do a lumpectomy on her left one.

She can see their lips moving, she can hear sounds coming out of their beings, but none of it makes sense. She had this. She was going to be ok. Why are they saying she needs an operation?

She asks, "Can I think about it? When are you wanting to do the operation?"

"Yes, you can think. We'd like to do the operation within the next six weeks if possible."

She comes back to herself with a bump. She and Rey are heading to Sydney in a couple of weeks. Rey's story, the one that caused such mixed emotions, has won a writing competition that requires Rey to read it at the University of Sydney. Now, more than ever, she wants to make sure that the two of them have time together.

"Can I have the op after that?"

"Sure."

She spends the afternoon waiting, sitting in silence, wondering why the fuck this is happening, again. She's present in her thoughts, surrounded by her memories of being here before. On dark, she rings Daren, lying, saying she's helping with a promotion for the Bob Brown Foundation, that she'll be home later. She's sure Daren knows she's lying. They probably think she's having an affair. These thoughts lead her mind to Jack, the man on social media who for some strange reason seems to have ignited a fire in her heart.

#

It's really hard not saying, pretending, not allowing anyone else to see your pain, to feel your fear. But that's what she does, and she does it well. There is normal life shit to deal with. Her relationship is at dissolving point. She's watching it disappear before her eyes.

"Can it just wait, please?"

The trip to Sydney is her only focus. She needs to do it, for herself and more importantly for Rey. Sydney, she hasn't been there for many years. She remembers journeys from Melbourne on the bus when she was young, how the excitement of such a huge space with so many people seemed an attraction, perhaps because she could lose herself amongst the many. Now, she prefers the quiet of small towns.

Rey's never experienced the excitement of being in such a large city. Their feelings of excitement are soon replaced with the anxiety associated with so many people and the sadness Rey feels on seeing many homeless, something that isn't very common in Hobart. Rather than being overwhelmed by it all, Ana decides that walking aimlessly will take some of the stress away, and hey, you never know where you're going to end up. The aimless wandering momentarily enables her to forget about all the legal crap, and instead, to be present for Rey in the moment.

Until a phone call comes. It's the police.

She asks Rey to go and find the shop they love so much, saying that she'll join them in a moment. She doesn't want Rey's experience to be tainted by the ugliness of their mother's past. She calls the police back, hearing sounds, but not really taking in the words. Police Officer David's telling her important information. It's about the charges, about how many charges POS is facing. She's not present, she left her body when she heard the tone on the other end, but she needs to be present. This is important, this is huge. Yet she remains absent. She asks for all these words to be emailed, wanting to see them in writing, to hold the information in her hands, to spit on it, to do whatever she feels.

Together they continue their aimless wanderings around Sydney. As they walk along a random road, they notice a queue outside a shop.

"Go line up," Ana instructs.

"Why?"

"Because obviously there's something good in that shop. Just stay in the line while I look inside."

Peering through the window, Ana can see bakers. Lots of them, all very busy, and lots of bakery workers, all busy too. She asks a person near the front what's it all about.

"It's a Japanese cheesecake, the best thing you can ever possibly eat." Cool. Rey likes cheesecake, she likes cheesecake.

"Stay in line."

After eating the cheesecake, she's so grateful for aimless wanderings resulting in delicious taste sensations. And for meeting new people, as Rey reads their heart-wrenching award-winning story to strangers.

#

An email arrives. Apparently, POS is facing eleven charges.

"Now don't get too excited," Police Officer David says. "The defendant's solicitor will try to reduce the charges, but it's a good start."

Not only has Ana's story been believed, but he is being charged. He is being held accountable for what he did to her. Holy fuck!

The charges are:

- Rape – common law (times three)
- Carnal knowledge of a girl under 10 years (times two)
- Sexual intercourse of a girl under 16 years (times three)
- Making threats to kill
- Indecent and unlawful assault of a girl
- Carnal knowledge of a girl aged 10 years or more but under 16 years

What's really sad, what causes more unrest in her mind and her soul than anything, is this stupid nonsensical bullshit: If you are a victim of sexual abuse as a child, and if the perpetrator is a stranger or friend (not a relative), then what happened to you is termed rape. However, if exactly the same actions are done to you by a relative, then it's classified as incest. And in a court of law incest holds a lesser charge.

Like, how? Who came up with that fucking logic?

If you are raped by a stranger, how is that so much worse than being raped by your own blood? Worse than being raped by someone that you will, more than likely, either have to live in the same house with, until you're old enough to run away. Or, at the very least, have to spend holidays and/or birthdays with.

Sure, that's so much less impactful than being abused by a non-relative, *not*. The act of betrayal, the sense of "no safe space", the divisions it can and does cause in families, the isolation the child can be subjected to, the blame, the guilt, the shame, these are the impacts. What the fuck?

This world is so wrong. She wants to bang her head against something that's really, really hard. She wants to jump off a building, play on the highway, get shit-faced drunk. How is this even real?

She snickers, when she reads how Police Officer David signs off: "Breathe and be patient."

He's learning.

She's feeling excitement over this news. Is it wrong to feel that way?

#

The flight home is in dark time. She's missing the stars, the quiet. Her fingers are crossed. She's hoping for an aurora, hoping that she'll have an excuse to simply disappear as soon as she gets home.

"Spirit does so love me." There's an aurora forecast. "Imagine if I could see it from the plane ... woohoo! How cool would that be?" She takes her camera as carry-on luggage. As dark appears, she takes practise shots out the window, trying to work out how to take a photo through a window with lights on inside and the plane moving at about eight hundred kilometres an hour, with bright navigation lights outside adding to the mix. This is a lesson in patience.

As they're crossing Bass Strait, she's sure she can see movement in the sky. She takes a picture and looks at the LCD screen, then proceeds to jump in her seat. People turn to look, once again Rey's trying to disappear, but she doesn't care. She keeps taking photos, happy to see that which brings her so much joy.

#

Back home, and the operation is looming.

While they were away, Ana and Rey talked, Rey asking if their parents are going to separate.

She couldn't lie, "If things don't change, and I don't believe they will, then yes, I feel that will happen."

Naturally this makes Rey sad, she gets that. Ana's so sorry it will make her kids sad, upset them, tear them apart, but she also knows she can't continue in the relationship. Not if she wants to be happy.

Her reflection in a shop window causes a momentary stop. She tries to visualise what she'll look like without her breasts. She used to hate them; they were part of her childhood stain. Whenever she'd see them or feel them, she'd see him, POS, with his smirking face and grubby hands touching her, invading her space, hurting her. It's only been in the last few years that she's grown to love them, their woman-ness, their vulnerability. And now she's going to lose them. She decides that possibly, visually, she wouldn't be able to live with an imbalance in her physicality, nor a reminder. So, she decides to have both removed. It will leave yet another scar. Maybe a tattoo will be needed to cover this one. She'll wait and see.

She isn't too sure at first that she'll have the operation. She wonders if she can possibly deal with it in her way, her belief in alternative medicines. But after spending time alone with Rey, she realises that this isn't only about her. She has kids to think about; two of them still young enough that they need her. Well, don't all kids need their mums, always? Is she prepared to risk her health, her lifespan, for purely selfish reasons? She doesn't think so. This is at least something she can do right for her family, for her kids.

Life really seemed so much simpler when she only had herself to think about. The term of her natural life never really mattered. But now there is more than just herself. She has three kids who, she hopes, love her and want her around, for a little longer anyway. It's weird how when the shortening of your life is dictated by something out of your control, the desire to end it is no longer a priority.

A session with Melisa is very much needed, to talk over and try and get her head around the latest developments. She's trying to absorb the meaning in the charges.

Melisa asks if she's suicidal.

"No. I'm not afraid of dying. Though sometimes I hope I won't wake up from the operation."

Does that make her suicidal? Having Big Dog and Little Dog stops her from doing anything stupid. Being under the stars helps to ground her, to keep her here, the silence offering peace amid the explosion of noise in her head.

#

Dreams have been a bit scarce of late. So, when they do happen, they can really knock her around.

She's in two different houses, both of them are old and in need of repair, both are huge with many rooms spread around inside. The first house doesn't feel that good. She walks around and even through it. There appear to be many rooms. Some have no windows and seem more like cells. There's only one toilet, in sort of like a lean-to right at the back of the house. It would get really cold out there.

The second house she likes better. It's an old library or school. There's this room that has awesome bookshelves covering all the walls. They aren't full of books though; they are full of old videos. There's this incredible old building attached to the property that's currently full of a tenant's furniture. She thinks it would be a great space for workshops, meditation and drumming. A market's happening alongside the property. The people living in the house smoke marijuana, as do the neighbours. Ana asks the lady what the neighbours are like, hearing the reply, "They're great!" She wonders how great they'd be with a neighbour who doesn't smoke.

The next night there's another dream. Sinkholes. Sinkholes everywhere. There's a sudden influx of them. She stands back, watching one form in her backyard. She's loving watching them, admiring their strength and ability to reclaim what's theirs.

#

A date's been set for the double mastectomy. Now to tell the family. She tells Daren first, receiving the response she was expecting, knowing that he wouldn't be a support. Then it's the kids. It's much easier over the phone with Esi than in real life with Rey and Zeb. The kids are good, though naturally they're concerned for their mum, especially Zeb, whose friend was Alice's daughter. Zeb believes, as most kids do, that if something happens to one person then it will happen to everyone else in the same situation.

Ana reminds them that she's beaten cancer twice before. That many people survive cancer. That she's strong, she will survive.

In the week leading up to the operation, things bubble and overflow more than normal between her and Daren. Can she really have this operation with all the friction and shit at home? She doesn't think so.

One night, she simply asks, "Do you want to end this?"

"Yes," Daren replies, leaving in the morning.

Weirdly enough, she's relieved, feeling she can now breathe. She arranges for Mardi to come and stay with the kids while she's in hospital. Giana will cook food and Layla will take her to the hospital. Rey also wants to come to the hospital, to be present for their mum. Just days before the operation, while she's sitting in the humid air of the sauna, her mind wanders, and tears roll down her cheeks. When she gets out, she feels the need to write, to record this moment for herself, for her kids, for others.

I sit, sweat slowly building upon my body, as my eyes wander down taking in my lumps and bumps, trying to visualise the image that will be before me days from now. Hesitantly I cup them, first one and then the other, feeling the weight of them, their sexuality, their feminine statement. Feeling the hatred, I used to carry for them.

I feel the pain of them being twisted and pulled, leered at, laughed at, shamed, admired. For so many years I wanted them gone. I didn't want to be reminded that I was a weak female whose body was only there for others to use and abuse. Over time, my mindset changed as I healed and grew, and I began to love the shape they created. And, I admit, the allure they had and the control they seemed to have over others at times. I could look in the mirror and admire their roundness, their ability to still display such feminine beauty, and they were mine.

Now as I sit, the sweat mounting as I try to cleanse my body, I cleanse my mind and soul too. That cleanse brings the emptiness, the awareness that very soon I'll look very different. I'll no longer hold form, the form so dictated to us by society, how I, a woman, should look. No, I will look apart. I will be different. And I'm sure in my difference I will have others avert their eyes. I too will avert my eyes. Not because of my difference, but because of what I lost, after only recently finding the joy and honour of having them.

I gently pull each to the side, trying ever so hard to visualise what I will look like. You would think this would be easy for me as

I'm such a visual person, but I'm struggling. The tears running down my cheeks are not helping.

I sit back, trying to absorb what will be. I try to clear my mind, try to convince myself that there is some higher good in all of this. My soul knows this, but my ego says, "Why? when will it stop?"

I'm missing many body parts, most hidden from view. This will be harder to hide. It's right there in your face. In the field of view of all I interact with. I'm sure most will try to divert their line of sight, not wanting to feel like they're prying. I don't know if I will too when I stand before the mirror or see my reflection in a shop window. I don't know at all how I'll be, I've never had to deal with this before. I hope to hold my head high, walking with honour and strength gathered from all those who have come before me and walked this walk.

I could have things looking like 'normal', but my body and mind don't do intruders well. To wear this, like a badge of honour, is my wish. To be strong, to show my kids that there's so much more to me, to her, to every female than what they look like. I gather my innerness, my faith and my me-ness, having walked a path twisted and rugged, smooth, and enjoyable, forever changing, with me changing along the way. I know the path keeps going, as too must I. I'm clearing the Karma, as a friend puts it.

#

Giana listens as she reads aloud, and responds with, "Let's do a plaster cast of your breasts."

How good is that? Such insightful, caring, supportive friends. Materials are bought, clothes stripped, cold plaster laid. All the while she is giving thanks for her breasts, for them nourishing her kids, for the joy she's found in them, for the love she has for them, knowing she's going to paint the cast, in time. The cast is so beautiful, her eyes leak. The simple act of giving from the heart that Giana did in that moment, the nurturing of body and soul, the acceptance that everything changes, it's all such an overwhelming experience.

#

Melisa's heard Ana's words too. There on the table in today's session is a lump of playdough, with glitter as a side dish. She's so touched, so overwhelmed by that simple gesture.

"Playdough's great. It allows you to create and then destroy, then rebuild again. Add in the majikality of glitter and you have perfection."

Now what to create and then destroy?

They talk about the victim impact statement that needs to be compiled. Melisa's unsure how Ana's going to be able to say all that she wishes. She's worried that the document may not accurately reflect all the impacts the abuse has had on her. They talk about the doctor's supporting statement, made even now, years on. Reading that the abuse, that what she holds within her, is so easily visible to those that have eyes to see, is too much. It makes everything so much more real.

The significance of this operation has been going around and around in her mind. She makes up a hospital sanity kit with items she feels will be supportive in her healing. There are crystal cards, homeopathic pillions, poo balls, coconut milk, chai, the Tao of Pooh, runes, and of course, her much-loved Shiva lingam.

The night before the operation provides such wonder, an aurora lighting the sky. Ana thinks that watching the sunrise from kunanyi/ Mt Wellington before the operation is the next logical thing to do. Without too much nagging, Rey, Layla and Ana drive to the top of the mountain and watch the sunshine its rays of warmth over the town. For her, it's huge. A special way to experience the start of a new day, on a day that she truly feels wouldn't worry her if it was her last.

#

They walk from the car park to the hospital. As they cross the bridge between the carpark and hospital, Layla stops and looks down at the passing traffic. Then she looks at Ana.

"I dare you."

Ana looks down at the passing cars, replying, "Nope."

"I double dare you."

No other words are spoken, yet they can read each other's minds. A double dare is not something that you can simply walk away from, so Ana turns and fully faces the window. She lifts her top, exposing her breasts to the passing cars, all the while laughing and laughing.

"If the police come looking, they won't find any boobs on me."

Rey's trying to dissolve into the floor as they text Layla's kid saying that their mothers have gone mad.

"Been mad a long time now."

Before the operation, a dye's injected to see whether the cancer has spread to the lymph nodes. Ana's handed a sheet with exercises outlined on it, "To help move the dye around".

As Layla's a yoga teacher they offer to lead the exercises. They stand facing one another in the waiting room, Rey questioning their presence here with their mother's madness, and Layla leads.

"Breast in ... and ... breast out."

Ana loses it. Right there in the waiting room.

Others are looking, wondering how someone in that space could possibly find anything to laugh about.

"Did you hear what you just said?"

"Nooooo, what?" comes the reply.

"You said breast instead of breathe."

Ana takes a big gasp of breath between the giggles of laughter. Layla's laughter joins the chorus of sound. It's good to laugh, always, especially when things are shit.

Chapter 16

Acceptance of new

Kimberly has intervened. Ana's feeling so blessed, she has a female surgeon and by the looks of it an all-female theatre staff team too, except one male. But he's ok, he's going to Antarctica, so he needs to know how to perform this operation if it's needed. Lucia often visits Antarctica, as well as many other women, so Ana feels comfortable with his presence.

The surgeon asks if she intends to have reconstructive surgery. "Nope."

The very thought of something not of her stuck in her body, in such a vulnerable space, with no ability to remove it at any given time ... Nope, not her ... Not going to happen.

"Ok, but I'll leave some extra skin in case you change your mind." The surgeon is obviously oblivious to Ana's steadfastness.

She has full faith in her surgeon, truly not caring if she never wakes up. She has an acceptance of death, of life's ending. If this is her time, then so be it.

Giana comes to visit that night. Some clarity is obtained as the anaesthesia starts to leave Ana's body. Giana's face reflects concern that possibly Ana doesn't look too good, especially when Ana states she'll be leaving in the morning. The only thing keeping her there is the blasted catheter. Though this time, having learnt from the last operation, she sends it much love, allowing her body to let it go, knowing that her body will take over.

There are drugs waiting, heavy, addictive drugs that she wants no part of. The nurses are very surprised. Especially by her request that they remove the OxyContin completely from the room. She wants no part in this kind of medication, confident the two Panadols alongside

Arnica and Hypericum are all she'll need to get through the night, no problems. She's trusting, knowing the benefits of homeopathics and how well her body responds to them. Her chest hurts, that's for sure, but it isn't anything major. Trying to shake off the anaesthetic, trying to pull herself back in, that's the hardest part.

Morning comes, and Zeb arrives bearing flowers. Mardi's dropped Zeb off, they were so wanting to see their mum.

"I'm coming home."

Zeb simply raises their eyebrows, knowing better than to question their mum's determination.

Ana feels for her kids. She knows they're scared, they're angry. Their whole world has been turned upside down in a matter of weeks. Their family's no more; still a family but different. Their mum's having major surgery. Dealing with cancer. It's a lot for anyone to absorb, let alone kids.

She leaves hospital after the surgeon has done the morning rounds, telling them she's right to go home, that she has others looking after her, that she's ok to leave. Simple. The surgeon sees the determination, the longing in her eyes, and makes no objection, instead agreeing that she can indeed leave if she so wishes. It's wonderful having Mardi waiting at home, meals being delivered and prepared with so much love from Giana. It's like having sister wives, only without the annoying male. The constant calls and drop ins of support from so many friends move her to tears of overwhelming emotion.

Mardi keeps thanking Ana.

"Thanking me? Why? It's I who should be thanking you."

"No, no, no," Mardi shakes their head. "Thank you for being my voice and the voice of so many others unable for so many reasons to share their stories. Thank you."

They hug as tears stream down their faces. Mardi keeps saying how strong Ana is, how brave Ana is. She doesn't feel it though. She feels weak, a nothing.

Oh, why do we have to be kindred souls over such shit?

She's able to move, kind of, enough for her to head out chasing the next night. An aurora's forecast and some wonderful chasing friends are picking her up so they can all enjoy the majikality. The physical pains worth the mental joy she gets from sitting under the night sky.

And what a night it is. Calm, starry reflections, some red aurora, good company, friendship, what more can anyone ask for?

#

He's there again, Jack. He's seemingly all over her social media posts. There's definitely a connection, one she's still unable to find. Does it really matter though? She thinks not. One day she may meet him, one day.

The thing that makes Jack attractive is his photography. His photos speak to her. She sees such a depth of his soul in each and every one of them. Most importantly, he too loves trees and rocks and stars and aurora chasing. That's enough of a reason for a connection, though part of her is scared to be present for someone else. She was hurt a lot more than she realised at the time by her marriage to Daren dissolving. And now she's trying to get her head around someone seeing her like this, with no boobs and a big scar. She's not ready for that. After all, it's only been two weeks since the operation.

#

A plea offer has been submitted. It isn't sent to Ana though; it's sent to Melisa. Did they really think Melisa would be able to convince her to accept it? Fucking idiots.

POS:
- is willing to plead to a representative charge(s) of Indecent Act / Indecent Assault consisting of inappropriate touching on a number of occasions
- will not plead to any allegations of sexual penetration
- will not plead to any allegations from before he turned 14 years of age
- will not plead to any allegations involving threats

This throws her.

"Touching", is that what POS calls it? Like fuck it was touching. Touching by a cock, yes. Like, what the fuck? She's so mad.

Naturally, she rejects the plea. He can go to hell, burn in hell, rot in hell. She's super angry now. This pain adds to the physical pain of the operation.

"Why the fuck won't it all just stop?"

#

Dreaming happens, no surprises there. She's in what appears to be a shopping centre. There's this young teenage boy standing near the wall to her right. She looks at him in recognition, saying to herself, "I know him."

He approaches. He puts his arm around Ana, asking, "Did you see that, did you feel that?"

He points to a young lady walking towards and then away from them.

"I know you from a dream I had last week," she tells him.

"But did you feel that?"

She did. She'd felt the force of such negative energy coming towards her, it was overwhelming and all-consuming. She'd began to feel paralysed, then started reciting The Lord's Prayer and the intensity had immediately diminished.

Next, she's lying down in her real bed feeling a presence next to her as though someone's laying their head on her shoulder. It feels so real that she turns to her right, kissing the head she feels is there. She's unable to make sense of this dream. Who is this boy? And more importantly, who is the lady with the strong negative energy? She has no idea.

#

A drumming and healing meditation are just what's needed. She's so grateful to have found her Spiritual family in Tasmania. Part of the workshop involves a ritual. She's to write down seven wishes for the year ahead:

1. *My own home*
2. *Completion of karma*
3. *Peace within*
4. *Growth*
5. *Conscious expansion*
6. *Evolution of self*
7. *Harmony and unity.*

Too much?

Chapter 17

Pondering – the simple act of being

Things are still undetermined with all the legal crap, though apparently the judge has set aside some time early in the new year, in the event it does actually make it to court. The question is, would Ana prefer to go there, to that space that holds him? Or would she prefer a video link, so she can stay here in the space that oh so beautifully holds her? This requires great pondering.

Pondering is a new thing, a new way of being. In the past, she would react without thought, simply as a defence mechanism. Now, since connecting with Jack, she's learnt pondering and quite likes it. She's grateful for the opportunity it provides to remove herself from an immediate response. Instead, it allows quiet reflective time to think. So that's what she does now – she ponders deeply.

She keeps switching between wanting to be present to have her voice heard and being like, "No fucking way does she want to be in the same space as him."

Instead of deciding, she feels herself melt bit by bit into the earth, becoming a nothingness. It's all too much.

There's too much going on. She just wants to curl up into a ball, to roll down a very big, steep hill, going so fast that when she crashes at the bottom, she'll explode into a trillion atoms and become that which she originally was, circling her planet Zaphron among its gravitational rings. A simple atom. A simple existence.

Making decisions, like this one, it's not her thing. It involves way too much brain space, space she'd rather dedicate to things that bring her joy. Thankfully art and exhibitions come to invade her thoughts, taking her away.

The *Minds Do Matter* exhibition is happening again. She decides to enter two pieces: *Inspire* and *Free from the Past*. She includes her story with the latter, wanting others to see her story and the story of so many others.

During the opening, three different men approach her, saying how much they admire her strength, how grateful they are that she has spoken out. They all have leaking eyes; she's so overwhelmed with their openness.

#

When she arrives home, there's snow on kunanyi/Mt Wellington. Wondrous divine white goodness. As it's a weekday and there are not many people around, she gets to sit on top of the mountain all by herself. The silence is deafening, the untouched snow like a majik carpet laid out just for her. She relishes the fifteen minutes of total absorption in wonder, in silence, before it is punctured by the arrival of others.

#

Her scar is already looking amazing, healing beautifully as her mind gets used to the reflection in the mirror, her new physicality, her newness in the place of a relationship. She's not sure if it's real or imagined that some people look at her weirdly, more so than normal.

Together with the local butcher she shares a laugh, "I'll have two breasts please," leaving others in the shop wondering what's so funny. Support groups have never been her thing, they are not spaces she finds helpful, though she thought she'd give the breast cancer one a go, you never know. The stories in the support group are heart-wrenching, leaving her feeling so blessed that she didn't need further treatment.

It was a blessing she'd decided to fully remove both breasts. Her surgeon informed her after the operation that they would have had to remove both anyway, as the cancer was far more widespread than they'd originally thought. That in actual fact, if left untreated, the cancer would have escaped the milk ducts, resulting in Stage 4 breast cancer. Ana would have been dead within six months. That was a lot to take in.

One lady in the support group had already undergone ten operations in their reconstructive process, and things still weren't right. Ana was so grateful she hadn't chosen that path. She would have ripped out the implants, unable to live with a foreign item in her body.

As much as she hadn't wanted to be there, it was good for her to hear the stories, to see the faces, to feel the pain of so many others on this path. One lady shared how she'd ended up stuck beneath the bed trying to retrieve some keys. She'd twisted her body to accommodate the new implants, ending up with an implant on either side of the base beam, unable to move, to squash, to manipulate the implants to allow her to change position. Thankfully, her phone was within reach, and she managed to call for help. That feeling of helplessness, of being trapped, would have done Ana's head in.

There was a story from another lady about walking though the bush. They were trying to pass trees but were unable to do so comfortably. Implants don't move, they don't allow shape shifting, they simply are, they hold their form, always.

That night, Mother Nature once again steps in to clear her mind, to cleanse her soul. It's one of the most incredible aurora displays she's seen to date. It truly is a gift to witness such wonder.

#

Negativity literally destroys her. Her body crumbles. So, she leaves, escaping to silence, feeling the need to physically escape the negativity within her home. She understands that the kids are angry and upset, but please, oh please, can they stop directing it at her? She can't carry this now. She's still there in all the shit, with all that's happening, she's still there.

Into the car go Big Dog and Little Dog, camera equipment and her. She's hoping for an aurora, but she doesn't really care. As long as she can see a star, she can breathe.

#

Ana's given an opportunity for a road trip. A friend has bought a house up the coast and wants Ana to take some pics. So with Layla, she heads there for some sunshine and joy.

Walking on the beach, they discover amazing sand sculptures simply placed upon the sand as though straight out of an Austin Powers movie, they catch rainbows, count seagulls playing in the blowhole spray, listen to the waves crashing. She's ever so grateful for friendship, appreciating the space and allowing it to simply hold them.

#

Returning home, she contacts the Office of Public Prosecutions (OPP). The lady seems nice. Apparently, a committal has been listed for the 12th March. Her solicitor will need to speak to her.

"That's wonderful," she says as the anxiety rises. She realises that she needs to make sure she has space around her when talking to them. The OPP explain that there is some complexity around the finer details of the case concerning some of the charges. This makes no sense; this is why she so needs Melisa. The OPP also want to explain the committal process, which is good. They suggest that she has a support person with her during or after the conversation, as they're aware it may bring up things for her.

"No shit."

A letter comes from the OPP explaining what a committal is all about. Explaining with written words, what was heard in her last phone conversation with them. She takes it to read with Melisa, hoping for greater clarity than what her mind is currently capable of delivering.

"The committal hearing is where the lawyer for the accused has called you to court to ask you questions (cross-examine you) about what's in your police statement. It's also a preliminary hearing for the magistrate to read and hear the evidence and decide whether there's enough evidence for the accused to be committed for trial in the County Court.

"If there is enough evidence, the trial will occur later in the year or early the next. (It's a pain how long everything takes with court; they are all booked up.) We will know the trial date, if he's committed for trial, the day after the committal.

"Does this make sense? Court can be a daunting, confusing, and emotional process, so if there are any other questions, concerns, uncertainties, etc., please ask."

Certainly, that's a lot to try and make sense of.

Melisa's patient, allowing time for her response to sink in, making sure there's some kind of clarity in Ana's mind, that it sits better within her being, before she says goodbye. She wants to make sure Ana's state of mind is ok.

Apparently, she needs legal representation for the Victims of Crime component of her case. The fact that the hearings will be held in Victoria makes getting representation even harder than it already is. Finally, a firm accepts her case, leaving her hoping this will at least take the frustration and confusion out of that aspect. A meeting is held with the OPP as they explain more about the charges and the committal process. Ana's really happy. Her legal team's all female, as is her court-appointed support person. Things are sitting a bit better within her.

Mother Nature holds Ana as she grapples with all of this. The space simply allowing her to be, to sit in silence, to breathe.

#

Mardi and Ana sit, reflecting on their pasts, the impacts of what has happened and how differently they each have been affected. They seem to be doing a lot of that lately. They discuss the different directions their lives have taken, Mardi saying they truly believe their husband saved them from following a similar path to Ana's. Mardi's very grateful to him, all the while continuously thanking Ana. Mardi does that a lot, saying how Ana's their voice; that they don't have the strength to do what Ana is doing. After hearing as many stories of abuse as she has, and listening to the current lives and relationships, Ana believes that:

1) Those who were abused as a child by someone Ana refers to as a "peer" (as in, not an adult) seem to really struggle with relationships with peers, especially intimate ones, when they are older. Most continue the abusive environment into adult life, feeling unworthy, feeling "less than". Therefore, they find themselves, more often than not, in violent relationships, time and time again. They are seemingly not equipped with the ability to find healthy people to be around (as opposed to unhealthy). She guesses that's because the first intimate peer relationships they had were dysfunctional, were abusive. She knows that she has a lot of work ahead before she'll be comfortable trusting herself in a romantic relationship again.

2) Those, like Mardi and Layla, who were abused by an adult, an elder, have ended up in relatively healthy adult peer relationships that have lasted for decades. They give thanks to their partners for the paths they've trod.

This leaves Ana feeling as though someone should do more research into this and possibly offer some constructive healing learning to those abused by peers. Maybe one day.

It's not surprising that she dreams that night – violent abusive sex. Lots of it, and it's everywhere.

#

Jack seems to be in her life more. He just sort of came to be. They go out at night to sit under the stars, she in person, and he on her phone, as he teaches her about the constellations, sharing the story that led him to be in that space.

Ana believes that everyone who sits under the stars has a story behind their presence in the dark. Most are there due to the need to survive. They are searching for a space of solitude and quiet, a space to simply be, without judgement. Most of the people whom she's met have mental health issues. This space, the stars, the quiet, are so much better than any medication. Together, yet separate, she and Jack form a friendship built on common histories and love for the Universe. It helps to get her out.

Sometimes she feels so overwhelmed by shit it leaves her with no energy to move.

Then Jack calls, "Come on we're going."

Unable to say no to Jack, out she goes. She's always grateful.

#

It's time for another bone density scan. She's really interested in knowing the results of this one; her back has been like crap. She's feeling the deterioration in it, let's see what the scan says.

To say she's shocked is an understatement. She wasn't expecting good news, but she certainly wasn't expecting things to be quite this bad. Her BMD is down 16.3% in two years. It should have gone down less than 1% in that time period. Her spine has aged sixteen times more than normal. That's not good. But it certainly explains the pain.

#

The victim impact statement is weighing heavily on her. She's not sure why. A walk-up kunanyi/Mt Wellington in the fresh clean air is what's needed to bring some clarity. The statement is her opportunity to speak her story – not just the legal factual side, but all the implications that have resulted as a direct impact from the childhood abuse. She wants her story told; for others to hear it. She believes deep down that by speaking out, saying her truth, it will help others. Maybe they'll find the strength to follow the legal path too, or maybe they'll simply find the strength to share their story with others. Maybe it will bring awareness to those who haven't been abused, possibly bringing an understanding of the behaviours and coping mechanisms many use.

Apparently, her statement will be heard if he pleads guilty or if the jury find him guilty.

#

Before the mastectomy, before the ending of her relationship with Daren, Ana had said yes to helping with a local inaugural art event. Now, however, she regrets it. Not because she doesn't want to be part of it; she does. But she's sore, it still hurts to move, lift, and stretch her body. Her mind and soul are sore too.

It saddens her seeing other couples having fun. She doesn't miss Daren, but she does miss having someone walking by her side, especially now. It makes it hard to focus.

What she really needs is quiet and rest, not being surrounded by strangers for a two-day event, part of which is a night photographic workshop she promised to hold.

By the time the workshop starts, it's the last thing she feels like doing. But she made a commitment, so she'll follow through. At least it's dark. People can't see the pain on her face, though maybe they can hear it in her voice. The group are amazing, full of enthusiasm and wonder. A young lad is with his papa, showing such excitement over the Universe. "I remember seeing the stars through my camera for the first time too," she reflects to the participants.

Then to top it off, there's some bioluminescence in the waves. Once again Mother Nature delivers.

#

One afternoon after school, Zeb and Ana head to the east coast for what turns out to be an unimaginable night. There's bioluminescence everywhere, turning the water an electric blue. Zeb's transfixed by the wonder, as is Ana. It's like a majikal world has been created through something that reflects a negative reaction in the environment. She has such mixed emotions, wanting to protect the environment, yet finding so much joy in its imbalance. Together they stand. The only sounds coming from them are sounds of pure joy. This is so much more educational than sitting in a classroom, not to mention the memory that the two of them will always have.

#

It's weird. She's seemingly strong; that's how most perceive her. Yet sometimes she feels as though she could simply melt to become a sobbing, blubbering mess.

Sitting with Melisa, she discusses all that's been going on with life, the legal crap, the Universe, letting it all empty, all she's held in these past months. She asks Melisa, "Could you please contact the police about the impending committal?"

There are still unanswered questions that are causing anxiety. She's also still not 100% sure if she'll go to Melbourne.

"Can I make a decision the day before?"

Melisa says they'll talk to the police about this.

She just doesn't know if she's really strong enough to be present in the same space as him. Part of her wants to show her strength by physically being present, but the other part of her wants to run and run and just keep running.

It's been over two and a half years now since she started this. It's exhausting, and there's honestly no end in sight. The thing she finds the most difficult is the waiting – waiting to hear back from the police, waiting to hear from the court, waiting to be able to see someone for support. That's the hardest wait – when you need to see someone, you need to see them now, not in two to eight weeks' time. But you have to wait until there's an available appointment. It would be great if there was like a legal therapist, one person you could deal with during the whole process, someone who knows the legalities and physiological processes and effects of childhood abuse. It's different from other abuse and really needs to be supported differently too.

Chapter 18

Jack

It's time to meet Jack, in person. A few weeks earlier, she'd been aurora chasing, Jack by her side, in her pocket, close to her heart, on the rocks beneath her feet as she changed lenses, between her lips, her teeth holding ever so gently to the phone as she snapped happily away. The Lady Aurora dancing, the wonder of majikality before her, the nocturnal animals going about their business, the sounds of waves rippling over the sand. No one else in the space – just her and Jack. She gives thanks for all that was.

That night seemed to last forever. With each word spoken and unspoken between them she could feel herself falling more deeply in love with this man, a person whom she'd never met, yet felt she'd known for ever. There was such a strong connection between the two of them that travelled back through time. At the beginning of the Universe, not only was its infinite magnitude created, but also the connection between Jack and Ana began.

Things will change now, they will know one another's physicality, as they're about to meet in person like real people do. Ana's super excited, nervous, scared, overwhelmed, afraid, all mixed up. She feels that meeting may be a tad overwhelming, so she ponders the perfect place to meet. It must be a place where she feels safe, comfortable, at home. A place with lots of space around it. She decides to meet under the big divine old cork oak tree in the local botanical gardens.

She loves this tree with its far-reaching, gently curving canopy. She feels hugged by Mother Nature when she sits under it. The connection will help ground her, and she hopes Jack will appreciate the space too.

It's such a gorgeous spring day, and so many flowers add to the colour palette. She arrives early. She knows the gardens rather well, and walks some of her favourite spaces, feeling her feet on the wetted grass, listening to the bird song, watching all the insects flying around. Taking a deep breath (and repeating) numerous times.

She feels her body shaking. Is it nerves or excitement? She's not too sure.

Suddenly, self-doubt and self-hatred come into her mind. Will Jack like her in the flesh? Will he think she's stupid? Fat? Ugly? A waste of space? Will he wish he'd never started talking to her, let alone driven three hours to see her?

Now she's really shaking. She wants to run, to hide, to climb the big cork oak tree. But she can't. She's made a commitment. She'll hold herself to it, she'll be accountable for all her actions, for all her choices. She'll be present. As present as she can be.

If he's not the person he appears to be over the phone, or if she doesn't feel right, or if she can see contempt or dislike for her on his face, then she can simply leave.

She knows this but she also knows that she won't leave. She always believes, in the moment, that she doesn't have a choice. How weird is that?

Ana sees him arrive. She knows it's him. She can sense his he-ness in the way he walks, the way he suddenly stops, something having caught his attention, his head slightly turning upward. He looks toward the tree, checking the map, hoping he's in the right place. He can't see Ana. She isn't present, she's hiding, thinking to herself that maybe it would be better if she stays hidden. But she knows she can't; she has to go and meet him.

Jack stands, the sun on his back, looking across the lawn to the convict wall. It's an impressive architectural statement constructed back in the 1830's by the then superintendent of the gardens, who believed such a wall would help keep the grasshoppers out. And some think *Ana's* crazy.

She comes from behind, using plants to hide her as she works her way under the tree. Jack's oblivious to her presence in his space.

She walks around the side of the tree, jumping out in front of him, seeing the surprised look on his face. Is that good surprise or disappointment surprise, she wonders. She knows she loves him the moment he smiles. She takes in the shape of his face, the colour of his eyes, the lumps of his nose, the line of his teeth, the taste of his lips. They hug and, without any thought, kiss. Such a deep kiss. A kiss of remembrance, of connection, of true love.

Since then, she's found more joy in her life. And even though Jack isn't always there with her physically, he's ever present with her emotionally. As their relationship grows with the sharing and connection of likes, values, beliefs, she feels more comfortable within herself in his presence.

#

The thought of telling him what's going on doesn't leave her mind. To be able to share this weight with a male whom she feels, hopes, believes will be there for her adds to the feeling of love she has for him. One night, under the stars, as Jack's showing her the constellation of Scorpius, she feels it's time. She knows her behaviour can be weird, that others don't understand why she behaves in certain ways, why she says such random things or simply isn't present with them. She wants to honour what she feels growing between them, so taking a big deep breath, she speaks.

Jack remains quiet the whole time, looking Ana in the eye, never wavering, never appearing as though his love for her is in any way changed by the words rushing out of her mouth. When she's finished, he simply takes her in his big bear-like embrace, brushing away her hair that's become caught in the wetness rolling down her cheeks.

She feels herself collapse against him, sobbing the deep sobs of profound grief. Jack remains silent, waiting for her to break the silence, simply accepting who she is. It seems like hours before she moves. When she does, she reluctantly detaches herself from Jack's embrace. Looking at him, she asks, "Do you still love me?"

Jack just shakes his head. "Why would I not? I love you more and am so grateful you felt safe enough to share such a horrific time in your life. I'm super proud of you and honoured to know you."

Sobs once again escape her being, Jack's words, his actions, the love so obviously displayed in his eyes, is more than she ever dreamt possible. In that moment, life seems perfect, complete, an ok space to be present in.

Chapter 19

Reflecting with gratitude

One day there's a moment of memory; a good memory from when she was little. She had a flatsy doll. She loved that doll. She used it as a bookmark. She was fascinated by the difference between herself and the doll. She would run her hand along the naked torso, wondering why they had no breasts, no nipples like all the other dolls, like all the other people. Now, she realises that she too is a flatsy doll. She needs to get herself one. Then there can be something else that looks like her.

#

It's the end of another year. A year where so much has changed, good and bad. A year she feels the need to reflect upon, giving gratitude for all that is.

I'm eternally grateful for each of my three kids. Their strength of character, their resilience in the face of extreme adversity, their ability to stand apart from the masses, to follow what's in their hearts even when the cost is quite high. The love and support they offer one another and all those they encounter. I'm grateful to be called mum, MOTHER.

As I entered this year, the third year of legal proceedings against my childhood abuser, I am so grateful there is a judicial system that allows me the opportunity to start the proceedings. I'm grateful for the support and guidance from the legal and social services that I'm finding along the way. For their presence, their understanding and, best of all, the words: "I believe you".

I'm grateful that through this totally cruel process I have such incredible friends walking alongside me. Without their love and support I truly may have lost my mind.

And now as I enter the fourth year, I do so with greater strength, gained by knowing that I'm not alone on this journey.

I'm grateful to those who have shared their story with me. I know how precious that is and I'm truly humbled by their strength. I'm grateful for the 15 years of marriage. For the great times and the raising of my kids. I know I grew astronomically in that time and know I am far from the person who started that journey.

I'm grateful I got to truly love, appreciate and take ownership of my breasts before they were removed. I'm grateful for my female surgeon and a near all-female theatre staff. That was pretty special. I'm soooo grateful that no further treatment is required.

I'm eternally grateful for the kinship shown over this year. For the unity of women, especially the strength we have as a whole. It's beyond measure, it touches my very core and is helping me become a better person.

I'm so grateful for the amazing opportunities that have been presented to me over this year: to take part in the Bob Brown arts collective, to journey deep into the pristine wilderness, to walk on sacred ground, and to be present in a majikal world. I'm so grateful to sit under the night sky as the planets align, with a complete stranger whom I now call friend. I'm grateful for the many times spent in freshly fallen snow, to bask in its wonderment of shhh-y-ness and majikality.

I'm eternally grateful for the many, many, many nights spent under the stars, in awe of their beauty. Then to have an aurora dance, making it ever so majikal. This has truly saved my sanity, my life. I'm so grateful for the experience of witnessing the truly stunning beauty that is a bioluminescence bloom. And I'm grateful to learn that even though it's visually amazing, it actually means there's a negative imbalance within nature. Sharing that with Zeb was true bliss.

I'm grateful that I had the strength to hold a solo exhibition that was successful.

I'm soooo, soooo, soooo grateful to my friends who have held me, hugged me, cried with me and laughed with me. The ones I've known for years, and the ones I've just met, near and far. They have made it all ok, and for that I'm eternally grateful.

I'm grateful that through all of this I am a changed being.

To all, may the new year be full of laughter, peace, love and growth.

#

As the new year begins, she finds herself pondering on how she believes the abuse has affected and still affects her physically, mentally, and emotionally. She hopes to gain some clarity, some awareness, truly believing that once there's an awareness thing can never stay the same. Change will and does happen; healing transpires.

Some of the effects she feels her childhood abuse has had on her are:
- Continuous nightmares
- Unexplained medical conditions
- Chronic PTSD and anxiety
- She doesn't believe she has a choice, ever, with men and sex
- Inability to work properly since having kids through fear of this happening to them
- Never feeling safe
- Constant fear of being found – feeling there is nowhere to hide
- Fear of being abused again
- Fear of passing fears onto kids
- Social anxiety – feeling "less than"
- Agoraphobia
- Fear and intimidation by others who are older
- Freaking out when certain names or looks appear in her space
- Lack of trust in others

- Finding it hard to form and maintain relationships
- Alcohol abuse
- Suicide attempts
- The belief that she had no right to say "NO", leading to her being a sexually promiscuous teenager
- Graves' disease diagnosed one year after starting therapy for the abuse
- Constant stomach problems
- Constant headaches
- Cracked teeth from clenching and grinding them
- Always moving, never feeling safe. She has moved 23 times in 30 years.
- Trust and betrayal issues
- Low self esteem
- Depression
- Insomnia
- Fear of being killed
- Becoming a control freak
- Fear
- Fear when making love, feeling vulnerable
- Fear of success
- Fear that anyone can violate her space at any given moment and there's nothing she can do about it
- Lots of anger
- Dissociation in most life situations

And Ana's core beliefs:
- She's too fat
- She's stupid
- She's no good at anything
- She's a liar, she makes up stories
- She should never have been born
- She has no right to feel good
- She can't win

- She will always fuck up
- She's judgemental
- She's pathetic
- She's useless
- She doesn't deserve any good
- She should feel guilty about everything
- She's a tart, a slut, a prostitute
- She's not worthy
- She has no right to voice her opinion.
- She is never right
- She deserves shit

Now let's look and see what good things she believes have come from the abuse:
- An ability to look within
- An ability to see things others can't necessarily see
- A sixth sense to see that others have been abused
- An ability to provide a space for others, for kindred souls, to share their stories
- A great imagination
- The ability to dissociate in any given situation, which, yes, can be very unhealthy but can also be a wonderful form of self-preservation in a healthy way
- Belief in the importance of gratitude
- The ability to always see some positive, no matter what the situation
- A deep love and appreciation for Mother Nature
- An appreciation for silence
- A creative, different edge to art interpretation
- A quirky personality
- A strong sense of justice
- Strength
- A deep faith in Spirit
- A great ability to be able to astral travel

It's not all bad. The positive things that have come out of it are what make Ana who she is today, and she kinda mostly really likes that person. So, in one way, she's grateful for all that has happened to her, the good and the bad, as it's all made her who she is today.

Chapter 20

I am safe

The committal's only a month away. She's still undecided as to whether she'll actually go, whether she can be in the same room as him. There also isn't confirmation on exactly what costs the police will cover. None of this is helping the stress levels.

On the outside, to those unknowing, Ana appears calm and together, but that's just a façade. On the inside, she's a mess, crumbling and crumbling fast, like a three-day-old cookie between a child's sticky fingers.

The police believe there's a high chance of conviction and that if Ana is physically present, the chance is even higher. This is all so wrong. Why will it carry more weight if she is there? You would have thought the opposite.

This whole thing, the whole legal process, feels so much more supportive of the accused than the victim. POS' lawyers are trying to discredit her truth, saying she told some therapist she made the whole thing up.

"Like, sure I did. Why then would I include other people in my made-up story? And why then would those made-up people give statements supporting my made-up story? Fuck off."

She's so mad. It's a joke. POS is such a gutless piece of shit. Why won't he simply hold himself accountable? Why won't he say, "Yes, I did all those horrible things to Ana, I'm sorry, I will accept the punishment of the court."

Why isn't he a man enough to do that? Fucking piece of shit.

She didn't know, no one had ever told her, but apparently, her body reacts when she's talking about the abuse. She becomes tense, and there are twitches in her face and neck. It leaves her wondering,

"If I have these physical representations happening in my body, then how could I have possibly made any of this up? Does my body know how to lie for me too?"

Kimberly suggests seeing POS as an animal while he's on the stand.

"No. I love animals, all animals, and I never want to have any animal associated with him."

Instead, she decides to visualise him as a piece of shit. It seems much more of an accurate representation. She's feeling more positive about going, about being physically present, though there's still two weeks to go. The flight's booked, the accommodation is sorted, now all that needs to happen is for her to get on the plane.

She discusses with Melisa how she can work towards changing the laws concerning historical childhood sexual abuse cases, to try and make it more supportive of the victim than the abuser. Melisa passes on some possible contacts. When all of this is over, maybe she'll still have some strength left to go down that path.

Having to read over her statement AGAIN really fucks with her head. It makes her stress so much. Do they not realise that every time she reads it with her own eyes, her words, her story, she's back there again and again and again reliving everything that happened.

But she has to read it, just so she gets it right.

Of course it's right. It's her fucking story. It's her truth. FUCK IT.

She's reminded that she'll be in control the whole time; that at any point she can ask for a break. It's all well and good to know that, but it's another thing to actually believe she has the right to say, "No. Stop. Enough. No more." This she knows she'll struggle with.

She contacts the OPP to ask them if its ok if she doesn't go over her statement anymore.

"Sure. The morning of the committal is ok."

So why then have you been drumming it into me "Read your statement, read your statement"?

#

On top of all the impending committal crap, her family life is in turmoil. It's understandable, but still, it's so hard. She's already dealing with all her own past crap and now having to deal with present crap as well. Zeb's so angry, blaming her for the marriage ending, saying how much of a bitch she is, and that it's no wonder dad left. Like, seriously, if only Zeb knew the truth. But they're a kid and it's not their story to carry. One day they may forgive her or have a greater insight into the reality, until then, their words cut and crush her.

She arrives home to Rey saying that Zeb's afraid of her. She feels herself sink onto the cold, comforting kitchen lino. Is she hearing correctly? Is she someone to be afraid of? Is she someone she doesn't even know, let alone remember? Are things so fucked that this could happen?

"Oh, please world, just swallow me whole."

#

An unexpected phone call from the police leaves Ana absent for days. That, combined with having to reread the statement, just intensifies everything. Why wouldn't you leave yourself with all this happening?

It's really weird, but in these moments of complete overwhelm, when a contradicting emotion expresses, it can push her over the edge. When a friend shows compassion, something she doesn't feel worthy of, it leaves her unable to sleep, unable to cope with everyday activities. She simply cries and cries, feeling so alone.

How can an act of kindness make one feel so miserable? Well, when you feel so completely worthless, less than nothing, a touch, a smile, a kind tone can be too much niceness to bear. She truly believes she doesn't deserve anything good, not when she's immersed in such deep stinking, putrid shit.

#

It's time for a distraction. Thankfully Layla's started *Yoga on the Lawn*, it's the perfect place, on the grass with trees as neighbours. She gives herself some time out, feeling weird, trying to get her body positioned in all these unfamiliar, sometimes uncomfortable poses. Even though it hurts, she can feel the good, the releasing within her being.

Layla's explaining that Yoga Nidra, whatever that is, is actually really good for PTSD. The best part is that you simply lie there. Ok, she's in.

It's good. It keeps her present, pulls her back into her body. Now, when she's unable to sleep, she plays the recording from Layla, listening to Layla's soothing tones, visually connecting with her body parts. And with the added help of a cookie, the creepy crawlies that have been having a party under her skin settle long enough for sleep to arrive.

Sleep deprivation is the worst. She doesn't feel she can do another night of it.

Instead of focusing on shit, Layla and Ana head to Mt Field to walk in the alpine healing energy, embracing and relishing the cold summer winds. The silence is so welcome, the space inviting. They give thanks.

#

How much time does she really want to spend in Melbourne? And where? One minute it's this plan, then something will happen, and another plan is formed. She isn't able to settle on anything definite. Maybe that's because, deep within her soul, Ana knows she won't go. She knows she really truly doesn't want to be in the same space as him.

Eight days to go.

#

She discovers a fun fact while visiting the knife shop.

"Cocker Spaniel hair is the worst; the hair migrates to your nipples," says the sales lady.

"Phew, thank God I don't have to worry about that," she replies, wiping her hands down her flattened chest, bringing emphasis to the lack of breasts, let alone nipples. The sales lady notices, together they laugh, as the man behind looks on perplexed at such weird behaviour in a knife shop.

Chapter 21

Dolphins

It's a good day. Big Dog and Little Dog are happy. They've had two walks. Tomorrow's session with Melisa may change that, this is why we just breathe and repeat.

The visit to Melisa is interesting. Ana knows she has majorly disconnected, due to an email that arrived that morning from the police. Reading it she felt herself floating further and further away, hating the power the legal associations have over her.

During the session with Melisa, she feels herself floating even further away, seemingly to another Universe. Now wouldn't that be good. It's a weird but welcoming feeling, kind of being like superman, able to simply shoot off somewhere, anywhere that's not here.

There are times through this whole process that she's felt extremely strong, knowing she's faced some really trying times over her life, that she's always managed to get herself through them. But this – this Ana feels may finally be the thing that breaks her. She's unable to handle negativity, words, tones, behaviours, they immediately cause her to leave. She's unable to tolerate it from anyone. Instead, she tries to surround herself with positive supportive people, those who are real and don't buy into all the negative bullshit. Lille is one of those friends.

Lille was there when Zeb was born, when Jason was a complete prick, when Esi went to live with their dad, when Ana broke down on the back steps and cried the deep gasps of enormous grief. Lille was there comforting, supporting, helping, and years on, Lille is still there, comforting, supporting, helping.

The best part is that Lille's so far away. She's not physically in her space. This allows complete openness and rawness, a safe space to be in. At times it's a great way to connect but it's also not a good way to bring her back into her body. It allows for disassociation through physical absence.

#

That's it. It's done and dusted. She's not going to Melbourne.

There's only five days until the committal, but she simply can't do it. A video link up is organised at the Hobart Magistrates Court. She doesn't care if it reduces the chances of a conviction. She's simply unable to physically make herself be present. The thought of having to be in the same room as POS, having to inconvenience friends to be there to support her, being away from friends, from home, from Big Dog and Little Dog especially, it's destroying her soul. It's doing her head in.

How her physical absence can change her story is beyond her comprehension. What part of trauma do these people not understand? Why should she have to go back to the space where it happened? Why must she be in a room with the person who did this to her? For fuck's sake! It's so fucked up.

Why isn't the court process happening here? Here where she lives, where finally, for the first time in her life she's found a safe place to be.

Upon reflection though she's grateful it isn't. She doesn't want her love of this space tainted by his foulness.

She's simply not feeling strong enough to put herself through the journey, believing that there will be nothing left, that she will have broken off and floated away into a trillion different pieces, unable to pull herself back together.

There seems to be so much anger in her. Anger towards POS, anger towards the rest of his pathetic gang – the Bowman brothers, Donna, the elders who chose to turn a blind eye and keep up appearances rather than to help a young child. So yes, she's angry. Fucking angry! Rightfully so.

She wonders why no one ever asked her, as a child or teenager, why she was behaving the way she was, why she was doing the things she was. But then again, would she have had the strength to tell? Possibly not.

She did tell, once, when she was about 14 years old. She told someone she thought was her friend. Turns out, this girl was in love with POS, so they told him instead. Telling resulted in Ana being threatened again, with the hiss of "I'll kill you" ringing in her ears. For a long, long, long, long time after that, she didn't trust people, especially females. How could she? One had stood there, laughing as things were done to her, things that should never be done to any child ever, ever. Then to have another girl betray her, empowering her abuser. Like fuck, she's going to trust another female. It wasn't until her own female offspring came along that she was able to start forming healthy, supportive, functional relationships with females.

#

A summary of charges arrives to be read. Inhale, exhale. *"Indecent and unlawful assault of a girl and sexual relations."*

There it is, written in black and white, written down forever for the world to see. Eat shit and die, POS.

The Supreme Court is where the committal's happening. That sounds so dramatic, so important. Is it really that important? Nah, she's just a nobody with a pathetic story, boohoo. What happens in that space will dictate whether there's enough evidence to go to trial. At any point throughout this whole process, he has the power to stop it. He can simply take accountability.

"I am guilty," he could say.

But nope, no such words cross his lips. Instead, each time she deals with the police, with the court, or has to reread her statement, she's retraumatised.

It's worse in one way, being an adult reliving it. As a child, she wasn't aware and didn't understand what was happening, what was being done to her. Now, as an adult, she has an adult's perspective, an adult's understanding, an adult's knowledge of how truly fucked it all was. In one way this is worse, knowing what happened to you as a child, that no one did anything to stop it, that you did nothing to stop it. That's a pretty heavy load to carry.

#

As a child, Ana would read and read, allowing the places within the books to offer her some kind of sanctuary. Once again, she's finding herself turning the pages of her favourite Enid Blyton and A. A. Milne books, loving being present up in the Faraway Tree, smiling at the antics of Pooh and Piglet, giving thanks for all that they gave her back then and still do now.

At night, the Universe provides a space of sanity – clear skies, a stunning Milky Way, and the Lady Aurora dancing. She feels so much gratitude. The next day, while she's walking along the local beach, some dolphins come, bringing their energy of the breath, of life, reminding her that amid all of this shit, she still needs to breathe and repeat.

#

There's a Skype session with the legal team; Ana asks Melisa to be present, realising how much she misses through dissociating. When anyone talks about the abuse, a word or a phrase can be a trigger, sending her to another space, far, far away. Having Melisa there, their ears, their physicality, helps.

The committal is in three days. Her anxiety levels are naturally rising. Her crystals and oracle cards are chosen, even her outfit with the materials she likes touching, the textures that give her comfort – smooth satin, voluptuous velvet, flip flops on her feet for quick release, so that she's able to place her bare feet on the ground.

Layla's coming to court, though they aren't allowed inside. Instead, as the wonderful friend they are, they will wait in the gardens for as long as it takes for Ana to reappear. Layla's staying the night, then Giana's staying the next one. She's so blessed to have the friends she does. Kimberly advises her not to drive for the three days before the committal and she knows she shouldn't. She knows it's not safe for her or anyone else – she leaves her body way too easily at the moment. Instead, she walks or catches the bus, remaining anonymous amongst the other passengers; she likes it that way.

The day before the committal there's yet another Skype session. She doesn't want to be there, to go over her story again. It's still the same story she told them four years ago. It's still the same story she told a friend when she was 24 years old. It's the same story she shared with that girl when she was 14. It's still the same story that's haunted her through her teenage life. It's still the same story that creates so many nightmares in her sleep. It hasn't changed. It's still the fucking same. So why the FUCK does she once again have to speak it?

She knows she's totally not present, why would she be? Her emotions are overwhelming, her body reacting to words, phrases, tones. She just wants silence, no noise, there's too much noise in her head. She just wants everything to stop, to be still, to be fucking quiet. But still, they speak. But still, they make noise. Still, they expect something from her.

Yet she has nothing, she is nothing, just an empty shell waiting to be thrown away, discarded, forgotten.

But she's started this. She must finish it.

Maybe tomorrow will be the finish. Maybe the judge will decide that there isn't enough evidence to go to trial. Tomorrow she'll know, tomorrow she will breathe again ... possibly.

#

The legal team try and explain what will happen during the committal. How possibly POS may be in sight. Should that happen, they'll put up a screen. They try to convince Ana that she's in control. That in any moment she can stop things. That if she doesn't understand a question, she should ask them to repeat it until she does. If she doesn't know the answer to a question, to say so, not try and make up an answer.

The whole time she's laughing as though she's in control. Yeah, right.

Ana's gone, she knows it. The voices are muffled, the images slightly hazy. She breathes and repeats, reminding herself that she's safe.

He may be seen by her, by her eyes. She knows she'll see him long before her eyes do, she'll sense his energy, she'll smell his stench, she'll shudder with his force.

There's still no guarantee that Melisa's allowed into the room. How is that fair? She needs Melisa there, physically, for her, with her. She needs to see she's not alone in this.

Her crystals are coming though, even if she has to hide them in her knickers.

Chapter 22

Magpie – right and wrong – necessity in both

It's time, thankfully Melisa's already there. Layla hands over the care of Ana like the father of a bride does, entrusting the health and well-being of his most precious item to the care of another. It's such a touching moment, and one she wishes she was more present for. They sit in the waiting room until the video link is working.

There's some problem at the other end, so time seems to stop. The room gets smaller, her heart beats faster and faster, she just wants this to be over.

The cold bare courtroom lacks any form of comfort. Thankfully, Melisa's there, on a chair in the back corner, away from view of the video but still present. Ana sits at the desk, takes her shoes off to feel the earth under her feet, lays a green tourmaline, rose quartz and three Archangel cards, Archangel Michael, Quan Yin and Wild Woman, on the floor beneath the desk. In her lap, hidden in her clenched fist, is a Shiva lingam, the cool smooth surface of this crystal helping to keep her a little bit present.

Next to the copy of her statement, a photograph lies on the desk. It's placed with no understanding of its impact on Ana. It's Ana as a child, she's wearing the overalls made for her by Mother Blobfish, the overalls she so vividly remembers wearing the first time it happened. She sees herself walk up the driveway, looking down at her clothes, seeing those stripes. That's how she always knew how old she was when it first began.

She doesn't want to look at the screen on the wall. She can hear voices, the familiar voices of her legal team, and the unfamiliar voices of his. Glancing up, she sees the person she believes to be his lawyer, looking as sleazy and creepy as POS himself.

It's his voice that's making her cringe. She glances back at Melisa, grateful for their presence. Movement on the screen grabs her attention. She looks from beneath her eyebrows and quickly looks away, her whole body's shaking.

Melisa notices, asking calmly and gently, "What's happened? Has he arrived? Did you see him?"

"Yes," she says, pointing to the screen.

She doesn't want to look, to possibly see him. She doesn't want to see any part of him ever, ever again. Something is done and he's removed from any possible sighting, but she knows he's there. His putridness is now all over the screen.

She focuses on her toes, squishing into the softness of the carpet, visualising them sinking deeply into Mother Earth, her fingers and toes brush over the crystals and the cards. She's grateful for their energies.

Questions are being asked. The voices seem muffled. She wonders if it's a technical issue or simply her floating further into a safe abyss. She doesn't understand their questions; that happens lots in normal life. She's dyslexic, so she often doesn't understand the way some people phrase things; this is one of these times. She clutches the cold, hard, heavy Shiva tighter, her knuckles turning white. She wishes she could propel it towards him, strike him hard, bring him to his knees. She wants to scream at them all, at the screen, at the vacant air in this cold claustrophobic room.

"WHAT PART DO YOU NOT UNDERSTAND? HE RAPED ME, REPEATEDLY, FOR SIX YEARS. WHAT PART DO YOU NOT FUCKING GET?"

Instead, she keeps those words in her head, trying hard to focus, to listen, to answer. Here is the last place she wants to be. She'd rather run as far, far away as possible, or find a pub somewhere and get shitfaced, or smash things, preferably his head. But she does none of those things. Instead, she remains seated, physically present, mentally, emotionally, spiritually absent. Answering what she can, not answering when she can't. Not hearing words, only noises.

She repeatedly turns to Melisa, wanting them to have a majik wand, to wave that wand over her and make all of this just poof into a cloud of majikality and simply disappear. Oh, why did she ever think she was strong enough to do this, to stand in court, to think she has a voice, to think that voice will be heard? Such a fucking mess. There are all these questions being fired at her, about the place where it happened. They want her to describe it, the entrance to it blah blah. She can do that, she knows it off by heart, it's been etched into her soul. She knows they're trying to trip her up. The place won't be the same anymore if it's even still standing, but she knows what it looked like then, the colour of it inside and out, the flooring, the décor. She sees it all like it was yesterday. But she doesn't want to go back in there.

POS' lawyer just keeps at it, asking her to describe basically every step she took as a child leading up to her entering the space where those things were done. She feels sort of present until she's asked to go around the side of the building and in the back door.

That's it, she's shot off past Sirius. There's no way she can stay in her body as she describes all she sees before her, her memories as vivid as real life.

Ana can still see the dust particles dancing in the sunbeams in the workshop air, she can feel the sawdust between her her-ness. Oh, why, oh why, do they want her to go in there again? A place she swore she'd never ever return to. Yet here she is and it's real, she even has those blasted overalls on. She wants to rip them off, rip him off, rip his skin off, layer by layer, to watch him bleed and squirm with pain. She wants him to hurt like he hurt her.

They are really trying to catch her up. To get her to say something different from what's in her statement. She knows that won't happen. This is her story. She's lived it for the last forty-plus years. It's part of her, so yes, she knows it.

The judge asks POS how he pleads.
"Not guilty"

It's over. People get up and leave. There are lots of voices still audible. Wanting them all to stop, she picks up the remote, turning it off, not caring if they've finished with her, she's done.

With Melisa by her side, they walk outside, taking in deep breaths of the wondrous fresh, crisp air Hobart offers. Layla's there, waiting, loving. Together they walk silently around the garden, taking in the healing colour of green, laying exhausted bodies upon its goodness. They decide a snorkel is in order. A way to try and bring her back into her body, to cleanse all the sticky stinky yuck of court, of abuse, from her being. They stick their heads under the water, becoming absorbed in all the wonders unseen by most. Much like her soul, she thinks, like her tainted being – no one can see it, but it's there, hidden beneath the facade she puts on, the clothes she wears, the smile upon her face. Nothing can ever hide the truth though for those willing to look, to see, to hear. Like a fish swimming in the big ocean of life, she chooses to focus on the wonder outside of her, not the crap inside.

#

While she's at the beach, her phone rings. It's her legal team; they ask her what happened in the court room.

"Was there a technical issue?"

"No, I just couldn't remain in that space any longer."

"It's ok. We have good news for you; it's going to trial. The judge feels there's enough evidence."

She feels herself collapsing. Is she hearing right? It's going to trial. She is believed. She is heard. Her pain is real. She is real. Holy fuck!

She and Layla jump for joy, oblivious to the strange looks from the passing school kids. Then they jump back in the water.

Ana contacts Melisa, thanking them so much for being there with her, letting Melisa know that it's going to court, that the trial will be toward the end of the year. For now, she wants to try and be normal, to forget about all the legal stuff and simply live a little. May she get back to Melisa closer to the trial? Receive her support once again?

"Of course."

It's been so all consuming, so soul wrenching. Taking its toll physically, emotionally, mentally. It's changed her, her family, her very core ... again.

What happened as a child changed her. Reliving it as an adult has changed her. Only this time, instead of the actions of another disempowering her, she has found the strength, amid all the angst of life, to give herself a voice.

She wishes the trial was tomorrow, wishes it was all over. The end of the year seems so far away and, like the legal team said, anything could happen. He could plead guilty between now and then. The date could be moved because of courtroom politics. Anything. It's really hard trying to live when your life seems to be hanging by a thread. The ending of this chapter, the most influential one in her life, is dictated by the words and actions of another.

Chapter 23

Space – an endless commodity, a necessity

Mother Nature's solace provides much need sanity. It comes from walking, snorkelling, sitting, tree climbing, anything that allows Ana to be in that space, to breathe and repeat. It clears her mind as well as her body. It clears her soul, allowing space for thoughts to form, for emotions to be released.

#

When there's quiet, when there's no one else around, her mind can wander to some deep questions, to some deep pondering on why this absolute shit that happened to her, can and does still happen today.

I'm struggling to comprehend the ignorance around childhood abuse that still is commonplace in today's society. It is never, ever ok. It is never, ever normal. It is never, ever the survivor's fault.

I hate the word victim. If you have been through this then you are a survivor, another word I don't like. I think we should all be called legends. You are still here, they did not beat you.

No form of childhood abuse is any less than another, certainly none is better. All forms are wrong, so very wrong. There are no excuses, there are no excuses for the actions that the perpetrator chooses to enforce on another. I'm sick of hearing, "Well what do you think happened to so-and-so for them to do what they did?" Personally, I don't give a flying fuck. They did it, they chose to do it, what more is there to it?

Instead of people trying to normalise this and find some kind of weird justification in the actions of the perpetrator, stop and think. None of supporting that soul, who through absolutely no fault of their own, was fundamentally changed forever, from the being they were, to someone they had no choice in becoming. We seem to focus so much energy on the perpetrator, on them getting the opportunity for reform, on forgiving them, on trying somehow in screwed-up minds to justify their behaviour. I ask why?

Instead, next time you see a child or adult displaying some inappropriate or confronting behaviour, stop and ask them if there's anything they'd like to share? If they don't want to share, that's ok, but stop judging and condemning behaviours in many who have been abused, and then trying to justify such horrific behaviour in perpetrators. To me that just doesn't make sense.

And please, please, never ever tell a person who's been abused that they need to forgive those who abused them, that they need to get over it. What a load of crock. I don't forgive mine, and I have no intention of ever doing so. It doesn't make me a bad person, it doesn't mean I will go to hell, I doesn't mean my life will never be fulfilling. If someone chooses to forgive another, for anything, that's their choice, not something that should be pushed upon them.

From where I stand the only way such horrific actions towards children, that STILL happen today, can be stopped, is by people standing up, saying, "No. This is not ok." By a child saying, "No. This may be your normal, but I don't want it to be my normal anymore."

It takes incredible strength to stand and allow yourself a voice. Most times you will lose family and friends. Even though, at the time, this will hurt and cut ever so deep, there are wonderful people out there who will fill those spots left by those no-longer conducive to your wellbeing.

I'm asking all of you to please stop and show some genuine compassion and acceptance of anyone you know who has the strength to be that voice. To the kid down the street who is running amuck, you know the one, who lives in that house where you hear all the yelling. To the young adult, struggling with memories of abuse trigged by their recent journey into sexual relationships. To the parent trying their darnedest to make sure the cycle of abuse stops with them, even if it means doing it alone.

I'm not saying to hate the perpetrators (though I do hate mine) after all, they too are human, but from where I sit, the survivor is *minimised and forgotten, less of a priority in our thoughts, in our legal system. My friends have filled the void left empty by absent family. Without them, I would be struggling to let my voice be heard. I have to speak up, I have to follow my path. It mightn't be everyone or anyone else's path, but then again, my story doesn't belong to anyone else, it belongs to ME.*

She sits under the stars that night, more to catch her breath than anything else. And as she looks into the depths of the Universe, a shooting star appears, leading to reflections on the similarities between that and all the incredibly strong, determined, persistent, brightly shining people she's honoured to call friends. Which then naturally leads her to Jack.

She must ring him. She hasn't spoken to him since the committal. Hopefully, she can see him again soon. She knows, deep in her soul, that she and Jack can never actually be. That there are forces keeping them apart. She has no control over any of that, like she has no control over how incredibly deeply she feels for him.

Jack reaches a depth within her soul that even she didn't know was there. Even knowing there's no chance, she can't help feeling the way she does. So now she sits with tears upon her cheeks, pain in her heart, a heaviness upon her soul, wondering what she's supposed to do?

She yearns for him, for his tone. Yet more than anything, she yearns for his presence, his physicality to be here next to hers.

How could she be so stupid? She wishes she knew. It's not her, it's her soul. Her soul sings in his presence and is silent in his absence.

"But you know he can never be yours," a voice speaks. "Yes, I see, but my eyes are blind."

Thankfully Mother Nature provides respite from Ana's troubled mind. She eats breakfast at 4:30am, before finally climbing into bed after the best night of aurora chasing ever.

#

Through the simple action of being present in a space that offers so much, an incredible number of amazing experiences have been laid at Ana's feet. She has such a love of nature, a desire to protect it as the unique and powerful space that it is, and for others to be able to experience its wonder. She is humbled when, through her love of, and joy in, these spaces, her art is acknowledged. And through her art she is able to promote and protect those spaces.

Back on the trip to the Tarkine, she had come across a burnt-out tree standing so strong and centred in what seemed like a circle of other trees giving praise to the central elder one. The scene captured a very Spiritual representation of Mother Nature. She titled the photo, *Grandmother Tree*. It became the banner photo for the *Ten Days on the Island* festival, then continued its journey to the Wilderness Gallery at Cradle Mountain as part of the *Extreme* exhibition. She has to pinch herself when she thinks of that.

Something shifted when she visited the Tarkine. It changed her in a way she can't even begin to explain. It moved her soul; it brought joy back into her life. Naturally, she paints, symbolising that, finding solace in the meditative process of dotting, feeling comfortable doing so, unable to create when she doesn't.

This place, this space she calls home, the space amongst the vastness, creates peace within her soul, leaving her complete and whole. In each moment she spends connected to all that is around her, she can feel pieces of herself coming back home, another piece of her jigsaw puzzle falling into place. With every breath there is a realisation that this is where she belongs. She knows this. Her soul knows this. Her heart knows this. This island has captivated her being, it has opened her heart, and it's called back the joy that has been so long absent in her world.

Chapter 24

Is suicide an option?

Sometimes you should ignore your hunches. Nah, that's crap. Though she does wish she'd timed this hunch a little better. She's grateful it's come now, and not a month ago when the court shit was happening.

Going on a hunch, she has looked through the private belongings of Zeb, finding some drugs. Like, seriously? She thought she'd taught her kids about drugs. About what they do to you, and to those you love. Obviously, it didn't sink in.

She told them all that if they ever did drugs underage, when she was responsible for them, she'd call the police. Yep, she'll call the police on her own kids.

So, she does.

Zeb's out with Daren. When they arrive back, she tries to talk to Daren, to explain what's happening, that the police are going to come and talk to Zeb.

The police come and soon they're all seated around the dining table. The police are fantastic, explaining the process, the line that drug taking may follow, possibly ending in jail or death.

There's a female and male officer, both offering their perspectives of drug taking. Zeb sits there the looking ever so sorry.

When the police have gone, she asks, "Why? Why did you feel the need to take drugs?" Not that she wanted an answer now, but she wanted them to spend some time thinking about it. In her mind, understanding Zeb's reasoning may provide greater insight into what they're possibly feeling right now. She knows they're angry – the family's split, their mum's had cancer, life's different – but what's their reason? That's what she'd like to know.

Zeb comes back saying, "I took the drugs because I don't have any early memories of when we were a family with all of us at home together. I thought taking drugs would give those memories back."

"And did it?"

"Nope, it didn't. So I don't see the need to take drugs again and haven't since."

Zeb's being is crumbling from the weight of disappointing their mum. Ana gets that, gets their reasoning. Zeb owns their actions, at school the next day, they tell the year coordinator what they've done. The year coordinator rings Ana and commends her on raising such a fine young person. She breathes, grateful in that moment, feeling as though she's done something right as a parent.

#

What's the best thing to do when you have thoughts of ending your life? Take a personality test, hoping it may provide some insights into why your head is so fucked up. It comes back as ENFP.

"Only 7% of the population are as screwed up as you." Hmm.

It is, however, extremely accurate. So, she reads it again and again.

And yes, she has those moments when she's suicidal. Then she takes a breath, and she sits under the stars, hugs a tree, jumps in the water.

#

What's better than snorkelling? Snorkelling around rocks that are over 250 million years old. Such joy. Though getting seasick underwater is an interesting experience. The movement of the tide combined with the flow of the seaweed all leads to the feeling of motion sickness. The water pushing her one way, the seaweed moving another.

What's better than to dive under the water? To go to a place that takes you away from all the crap, a place that offers such wonder to your eyes. When her body breaks through the water's surface, she feels everything washing away. She becomes lighter, more able to breathe.

She needs those spaces, those moments away from real

life. #

The kids seem to be playing tag team. Each one putting crap on her. It's easy when there's only one person present to cop all the shit, only one person present to blame. She gets that, but it doesn't stop the deep hurt she's feeling. One day they may know the truth, until then she keeps pretending.

It's Esi's birthday. She needs to be present for them, to be up, to sound ok. But she's not ok. There's too much going on in her external world, and she feels so overwhelmed. There are teenagers committing suicide, teenagers staying in her home for safety, teenagers being abused by their partners. There's abuse everywhere. She really wants some time away from that energy, but she can't turn her back on someone in an abusive situation no matter what. So, she remains present for them, for her kids, hoping that soon things will settle.

All that's going on, however, sets flashbacks racing across her eyes. Reminders of her own abusive past. No wonder her brain feels like it's going to explode. It's hard to talk to people when she's like this. It's hard to be physically present. So instead, she talks with her trusted and treasured friend so far away, telling Lille how she's so confused, overwhelmed, afraid, for life, for humanity, not seemingly able to get past today, the line becoming finer and finer.

Chapter 25

Divine intervention

Sometimes she has little or no control over what she does, rationality doesn't seem to be a factor, only survival. She's just had one of those moments. A pivotal moment, probably the most impactful one to date. She spent the night messaging Lille, grateful for the connection and even more grateful for the lack of physicality, feeling she wouldn't be able to do that which is foremost in her mind if someone was in her space, demanding her to be present.

You see, she so wants to die. She wants to end it all, the legal shit, the family shit, the physical pain shit. The only way she feels she can do that, in this moment, is to take her own life.

She's often reflected on those who commit suicide. Her Gran had. She hated Gran for years after, she was so angry that they would leave her. She hated Gran until, as an adult, she visited her friend Asia in a mental health unit. Then she saw the harsh reality of those spaces. It was horrific, and it was at least thirty years after Gran had been in one. When she left, she sat in the car offering an apology to Gran, saying she could now understand why. From then on, she's had a different opinion of those who choose to take their own lives, seeing them as incredibly strong. Not weak at all.

So, here she is, deciding to do the same. The thought of her kids, of Big Dog and Little Dog, her amazing friends, the life she has, the joy that's only recently come back into her world, none of that outweighs the load she feels, carrying all of who she is.

She has an image in her mind's eye of how and where she'll do it. She'll drive to the Tasman Bridge, climb over the railing, and fall into the cold bracing water. It's a place she feels at home in, safe in. She's not afraid of heights, so she figures that is a good option.

Also, neither the kids nor her friends will find her body. Instead that task will befall some random stranger or the water police.

The only thing that's clear in her mind is that she must leave; she can't stay where she is. The negativity, the tones, the overwhelming heavy burden of trying to stay afloat, is too much, instead she wants to give in to the call of death.

Lille must have sensed something in Ana's unspoken words. She stays up all night talking to her, listening, reassuring, agreeing with the fuckedness of the world.

#

Ana waits until the kids had gone to school before coming out of her room. She goes downstairs, and packs away her treasures into boxes, the things that matter to her, the things she feels are *her*. Her crystals, her books, her paintings and art supplies, her camera equipment. She wants them packed away, hidden from other eyes. With the wrapping of each treasure, a memory arises. The reason why she had that crystal, that book, why she'd created that work of art. The tears slide silently down her cheeks until they too fall to the ground, along with her hopes and dreams of a happy life. Big Dog and Little Dog sit there silently, watching, aware, alert. They know something is up. They are so attuned to her, so aware of her body language, her tones, her outspokenness. They don't leave her side. She looks at them every now and then, asking them not to plead with their eyes.

"You'll be better off without me."

They don't believe her.

As the packing takes shape, the boxes pile up. She takes the full ones into the garage, tucking them away in the dark, hiding them as though hiding herself. She must go, she knows she must. But can she? How can she be one of those mothers who leaves their kids? She'd always thought so badly of mothers who commit suicide, wondering how anyone could leave their kids. It's something she's never been able to get her head around, yet here she is leaving hers.

Will it be for good? So many things can go wrong. She really should jump in the dark, unseen. Now it's light, possibly someone will try and stop her, or call the police. They would not see the pain she carries within her soul. She doesn't want anyone else in control of her life. He has controlled her life for over forty years. She's had enough. She simply wants to be free, free to be herself.

Just as she's finishing, Daren comes into her house. How dare he? He has no right to enter her home. She's furious. And in that moment, her focus shifts from her impending demise to the confrontation she knows is about to happen. She hates the negativity in Daren, and he's bought it into her space without asking.

Daren obviously sees the packed boxes and Ana standing there with leaking eyes. Instead of offering comfort, he lashes out, "What the fuck are you doing? You can't just leave. What about the kids?" He's yelling and angry, which only makes her want to leave even more. She can hear Daren's tone, see his body language, but the words are muffled. She's once again left the building. She keeps doing what she was doing before he so rudely entered her space.

Daren's trying to get in her way, trying to get her to look at him, asking Ana if she wants him back.

"FUCK OFF!"

No way in hell does she want him anywhere near her.

"Maybe we could make a go of it. I can help."

She wants to scream at him, to hit him, to smash him. Doesn't he realise that he's part of why she's in this state now? He hasn't supported her, he hasn't supported the kids, instead simply choosing to live a new life. That's all good – she wants nothing to do with him. But the kids, he just left them. So why the fuck is he here now in her space? Just like POS suddenly appearing in her space those years ago. What's the Universe trying to tell her? She really doesn't care. All she wants in this moment is to go, to disappear, to never have to
deal with him or any of them ever again.

Daren's going on and on and on about the kids, so she asks, "Why don't you come and look after them then? Haven't you always said they were like your own?"

She knows they'll be all right. They're smart kids. Resilient. And she has friends, she knows her friends will always be there for her kids, even if she isn't. They'll be angry with her, sure. Upset. Hurt. But she can't carry their stuff at the moment, she doesn't even have room for her own.

She tries to walk out the door. To where? She isn't too sure. Just anywhere, away from him, away from the house, away from her life. She'll have to find somewhere to simply be until dark time comes.

She pushes past Daren. Past the words still falling from his angry mouth. She calls Big Dog and Little Dog and puts them in the car.

All the while he's yelling, "What about the kids? You can't just abandon them."

"Like hell, I can't. It's either them or me, and right in this moment I need to think about me."

She rings Esi as she drives away. Esi, like Lille is thousands of kilometres away so it's safe to tell them her truth. Well, not all the truth, just parts that hopefully Esi can deal with.

She tells them she can't keep doing this. That she feels the kids with their anger, Daren's anger, the legal stuff, her memories, her operation, all of it has finally broken her. She's no longer strong, she's no longer this person that others see. She's ever so damaged, and whether she can be repaired is still undecided.

As she's talking with so much love and guilt in her heart, she looks over at Big Dog and Little Dog. How can she leave them? She cans see the love in their eyes. They seem to know the pain she's experiencing. She can't leave them.

She says goodbye to Esi, wondering if it will be the last time.

Pointing the car south she rings Layla, "Can I ... Would it be possible ... if I could come for a few days?"

Layla asks nothing, simply replying, "Yes."

None of this was anything she'd ever even remotely thought about, but it happened. Amid a whirlwind of tears, sadness, and despair, she'd left. But she'd chosen self-preservation over self-destruction.

She wonders why; the answer lying in the months and years of inner and outer turmoil, in the random acts taken by others and self, in events beyond and within her control. The past has created the Ana of today, fate, karma, bad luck, good luck, Spiritual intervention, all this has made her who she is. She trusts that no matter how totally overwhelming and dark a black hole can be, there is always, always the tiniest glimmer of light waiting for you to focus on it, leading you along an untrodden path. As the car heads south, it seems Mother Nature's reflecting Ana's tormented soul. A storm gathers energy with each passing kilometre.

She loves a good storm, loves the brashness of the wind, the raw force as it reclaims its space.

As she approaches Assay Cove, she pulls over, wanting to place herself within the raw energy. She stands on the edge of the jetty, allowing the wind to take away all the negativities stuck to her soul, watching the waves smash against any surface they can find. The clouds create patterns and images just for her. She feels Spirit, her crown tingling, tears leaking from her eyes. She can feel their presence, there are so many, their energy makes her heat up. She spreads her arms wide, opening herself up to all that is the brutal raw honesty of Spirit and Mother Nature.

Suddenly a rainbow forms right in front of her. It's a sign. She deeply believes that it's Spirit saying that things will be ok, that she just needs to remember to breathe. She knows that Spirit has her back, today, and always.

She stands for what seems like a lifetime as the storm passes on to another in need. Back in the car, she feels ever so grateful, and continues her journey south.

Layla's waiting. There are still no words, no questioning as to why Ana's there. They simply provide a space, and a quiet one at that. They know she'll talk, explain, share, when she's able. Right now, all she needs is a cup of chai and a hug.

#

In time, as words form, Ana opens up, exposing her vulnerability, her shame, her guilt at doing what she's just done. She feels guilty about leaving her kids. She truly is a shit parent.

Layla listens, saying nothing, simply acknowledging they've heard. After Ana falls silent and takes in some clean fresh bush air, Layla speaks.

"You are not a failure, a bad person, a shit parent. You saved yourself. In doing so, you will teach your kids how they can save themselves should that moment ever arise for them. I don't want to hear one more word against yourself. They will be ok, they will survive. They will get through this, and maybe this will be the wakeup call they need to start treating you right."

Simple.

Oh, how grateful she is. She has the most amazing friends ever. She feels she must have done something right at some time in this life or a past to have these divine souls here, present with her now in all the crap.

As the day turns to dark time, Mother Nature knows exactly what's needed to get Ana through the night, some colour in the sky with a touch of dancing thrown in.

There's a cute little jetty near Layla's, it's perfect for sitting alone in the quiet, watching all that's before her.

Her attention is focused on the wonder in the sky, and she fails to pay attention to her belongings and drops her glasses, sending them to the bottom of the sea. She grabs the torch, thankful it's low tide, and without looking past where the glasses are or even thinking, she lunges over the side, whacking her chest on something in the process. After retrieving the glasses, she then gets back to photographing the aurora.

Then it hits. The pain, it's like a sledgehammer across her chest. Someone hitting her harder and harder with each breath. But she so doesn't want to go, the aurora's incredible, she's being given a gift, she wants to stay and embrace it.

After about another hour she gives in, the pain is beyond ok.

"Fuck, life sucks without your natural bumper bar."

The force of the impact was right on her scar and boy does it hurt.

In the morning, alive and still present on this earth she returns to the scene of the crime, wondering exactly what it was that has caused this pain. This pain in her body that's reflecting the pain she feels deep in her soul. The insurmountable grief, the inability to breathe deeply, the pain, the sorrow, the blaming of self for such stupidity. There it is. It wasn't her being stupid or careless. It's a 4-inch by 4-inch chunk of wood looking ever so innocent, put there to stop people stepping over the edge of the jetty. They obviously never thought of anyone throwing themselves over the jetty.

At least there's a valid reason for the pain, which only intensified overnight.

Layla's like, "You must go to a doctor." "Nah, it will be all right."

In one way, she's grateful for the physical pain, it's something that can be seen and understood. It makes a cover for the pain she's feeling inside, the pain not seen by others, not understood by most.

Chapter 26

Being present

The police make contact. Does Ana oppose POS' legal team obtaining a report from her psychologist?

"Nope." She knows she has nothing to hide.

She sits pondering. Wondering what it was that triggered her during and after the committal. What it is that has kept her absent from her being for so long? She wonders what it was that added to the accumulation of crap that led her to leave home.

There seem to be these memories, distant ones. She can sense them tucked into the far recesses of her mind. Part of her wants to see them, to know them, but part of her is afraid of seeing. The good thing is, at the moment she doesn't seem to have the key to unlock that door. Over the years she's had dreams in which she's being told, by whom she doesn't know, that there's things she hasn't remembered, but that she will one day. After each dream, she wakes saying she doesn't think she wants to remember. What she does remember is bad enough. If there's other stuff, it must be worse, and possibly she can't deal with it and may never be able to, and that's ok.

There's a presence in that void between remembering and not. Its Mrs Bowman. The hidden something is to do with them. She's just not sure what it is.

After a few days at Layla's, Giana arrives, offering a space in their home to Ana for as long as needed. Naturally Big Dog and Little Dog are welcome. Giana and their husband are about to travel for a month so she can have the home all to herself to rest and find some peace within her world.

She finds herself sitting with Big Dog, Little Dog and Giana's puppies all gathered around, keeping her safe, offering a shield of protection and love. The birds sing their morning song, happy to be alive. The sun is warm upon her exposed body, offering its healing powers to her deepest core.

She loves the sun but not the heat, preferring the cold, the snow. The beautiful pure white snow, its freshness untouched by humans, embraced by nature. Divinity at its best. She feels it's time for a trip back to Mt Field and hopes it's cold enough for snow. She wants to stand on top of the mountain and scream and cry and give thanks. Yes, that's what she must do.

The "ding, ding" of the phone signals a message. It's trying to distract her. Does she succumb to its allure? She doesn't know who it's from, certain it's either Layla or Jack. But which one?

Her curiosity's always great. Can she resist and remain focused on the wonders of nature around her? She doubts it.

It's Jack.

"Oh Jack, how I miss you. How I wish you were here with me. You seem to get me, to see me, to understand me. Oh Jack, how I love you."

The wanting falls on no ears.

Maybe one day.

In the meantime, they keep texting, seeing one another whenever Jack drives the truck into town. Then they either sit under the stars, if he can stay overnight, or walk amid the wisdom of the aged old trees on the island.

No matter what they do, or for how long they do it, they are so connected, so comfortable with each other. So comfortable with being in one another's space. These moments bring so much joy to her damaged and fragile heart.

The sun's causing beads of sweat to form on her body. It's autumn, but the weather's so strange. The sounds of Mother Nature mix with man-made sounds creating a symphony of notes, the track of life. Ever changing, ever cycling, different tones, different levels, different pitches. She tries to remove herself, to leave only nature.

\#

The pain in Ana's chest hasn't let up. It's been nearly two weeks. The worst part from that night is that the photos she loaded into her computer at Layla's have gone. Vanished, never to reappear. It's like the show in the sky was just for her.

Maybe a visit to the doctor is needed, but she hates the doctors. They never seem to listen to what she says. She's pretty in tune with her body, acutely aware of any changes or irregularities. But when she tries to explain her *her*-ness to them, they simply offer a prescription. She doesn't want drugs, but ouch, this hurts. An x-ray is ordered but there's not much visible. Ummmm, like sure, is this pain all made up too?

Mardi invites Ana to a Tai Chi class in the local hall. As she's waiting, a lady sits down. Turning to talk to the stranger, she flinches. The lady notices, introduces themself as Mia, a friend of Lucia's, and asks if they may place their hands on Ana's chest.

Ana remembers Lucia saying that Mia is a Bowen therapist. Ahhh, so them wanting to place their hands on her chest is just normal.

She can feel the warmth coming from Mia's hands, she can feel the energy, the presence, the comfort in this stranger being within her space.

Mia removes their hands and tells Ana that she should come see them for a treatment. Why not? Having some bodywork may just be what's needed. It's not often she meets practitioners who she feels safe to let into her space, but Mia feels ok. Mia feels safe.

#

She reflects back to a time when she was a young adult. People would ask what she was on, as they wanted some too. She was high on life. She was filled with joy. She'd survived six years of childhood abuse, she'd survived her teenage years (though not entirely functionally), she'd survived nearly dying at the age of nineteen when given a dose of morphine and having a horrific reaction, she'd survived being told at the age of twenty that she had cancer with a 50/50 probability of losing her leg, yet she was still filled with joy.

She wasn't resentful. She wasn't angry with the world. She wasn't questioning "Why me?" Well not for longer than a brief moment anyway. She was living her life as best as she could, doing things that brought her joy.

Upon reflection, it wasn't a life of joy, it was more a life of avoidance. She didn't want to think about what POS had done to her. She didn't realise at that time that all the things she was doing were reactions to what had been done to her. She was living on the edge, accountable to no one and loving it, she was alive … simple.

Then something changed. She walked into another life, a life that so many seem to desire, becoming a wife and very shortly thereafter, a mother. This was a tough struggle. She found mothering exceptionally confronting and demanding, and so claustrophobic. She was now responsible for someone other than herself. She couldn't continue with those risk-taking activities. She had to be responsible.

With responsibility for another came fear, fear of them being abused, fear of her not being able to protect them, fear of her fucking them up. She felt like her whole being had been invaded. Not only was she not her anymore, but she also had no personal space. Those who may have been abused can possibly relate to the need for personal space and how the constant presence of a kid can be too much.

At the time, she had no idea why she was reacting the way she was, that it was because of her childhood that she was struggling with what she was. She had a husband, she had a beautiful wondrous kid, yet bit by bit she felt her joy fading.

Things happened, life changed, two more kids appeared, and she found herself in another relationship where even more of her joy was literally knocked out. Still, she didn't become bitter. She was angry at times, angry for her kids, for the losses they were having to deal with.

Yet another relationship, and still no long-lasting joy.

#

It's weird being in someone else's home by yourself. She remembers the last time she lived alone, near on thirty years ago, before she'd become a mum, before the memories had taken over. The memories restarted back then, because Mother Blobfish had begged Ana to let POS stay in her flat.

"NOOOOO, I don't want him in my home," Ana had pleaded just as strongly. Mother Blobfish had paid no attention.

Apparently, his fiancée, who he referred to as Chook (the pet's name he had for Ana when she was young, that alone was super creepy) had ended the relationship and now he needed a place to stay.

Two days later, he was there when Ana got home. She did not know how he got into her flat, and assumed Mother Blobfish let him in. More importantly, she did not know why she was the one who had to provide a roof over his head. Like, how was that her responsibility? Was he family after all? Was he an uncle, a cousin, a half-sibling from one of her parent's previous marriages? No one's ever clarified that for her, but it would explain the huge family divide that was created when Ana told her parents about what he'd done to her.

All she remembers is him being in her space for a month. She was drunk a lot that month. Lying awake at night, a baseball bat in her hand, waiting, wanting him to come in, to try it on. Then she could smash his head in. She'd have a reason, an excuse to kill the motherfucker. She'd cut off his piece of shit and ram it down his throat. "See how you like that." Then she'd kill him with vigour, with glee, with hatred, with contempt, with joy. All that would remain would be splashes of blood and grizzly bits. She'd throw them out the window to the feral cats, watching with fascination as they'd sniff, unsure of the contents, knowing there's something foul about the energy coming from the food before them. But hunger would soon overcome their caution. They'd devour the food, pausing only when finished, feeling the weight of the energy they now carried.

Upon reflection, she realised she must dispose of him in another way, so as not to pass on any of his foulness to innocent beings. She must burn it, release it, send it back to Mother Earth; to have it transform into good as only they have the power to do.

That was a time in her life she'd tried to keep locked away. It's all such a blur. Possibly due to the amount of alcohol, or the fact it's buried so deep. Maybe one day she'll have an answer. Maybe the Universe was trying to get her attention, get her to talk about, heal from, charge him for all that he did to her. She wasn't ready then, just like she wasn't ready when the serial rapist sat outside her share house, cutting her clothes (and only hers) on the clothesline, repeatedly cutting the telephone line until Telecom Australia refused to repair it, the police saying there was nothing they could do until he physically hurt her. Or the time when her neighbour tried to run her over one afternoon as she was walking along the country road. Or the time when Jason was so abusive she thought he'd snapped her femur after he Muay Thai kicked her. Or the time he smashed her head against the brick pillar. Or the time Jason described in detail how he was going to kill her and eat her in front of the kids, and then laugh everyday as he sat in jail, not caring, as she'd be dead and that was all he wanted. Or the time Jason sat in the lounge completely off his tree, loaded rifle in hand, waiting for the dog to come home so he could shoot it, unaware of, or simply not caring about the two kids sleeping in rooms on either side, Ana lay awake all night with heightened senses, asking the angels to keep the kids in their beds, to keep them safe. Or the time when Jason hit her in the chest, hard enough to stop her breathing, after she'd told him she had to go to hospital.

None of those times had she been ready, able, strong enough to do this, to do what she is now doing. No wonder she's had a breakdown. Fuck, when thinking about it, reflecting on her life, sometimes she's amazed that's she's still here, that she's still sort of functions, that she's sorta kinda normal.

She needs to remind herself sometimes that she's actually a legend.

#

Random writing is happening. She's learned over the years to simply let the words flow, to not try and control them. Just to accept whatever is given.

Breathe and know that you are free. Free at last to fully flourish and expand, allowing light to flow fluidly within and without, encompassing all of life, all of love. Allow the heart to be open for only pure unconditional love to pass through its chambers. In doing so you are freeing all who come before and all who will follow.

The path is long, the time seemingly reaching to infinity and beyond. There is a start point, but you must go back, way back to where it all began. Before this life or the ten before that. It doesn't matter if you can't find it. Just know it's there. Acknowledge and thank it for all the lessons learned, stemming from the original act, that original moment that has become so many, so vast, so deep. Release and know that all is as it should be. That healing is transpiring as you write these very words. Know that we are always here for you, surrounding you, uplifting you, holding you, allowing you to be all that you deserve.

You wait, you'll see a new you. What a gift it will be to you and to all. Stand tall, walk with grace, with confidence, with strength, in the knowledge of all those who came before and come after. Walk with love in your heart, love in your eyes, love in your words, love in your actions, love in your thoughts. Watch the world, your world, evolve around and within you. The light has never died. It's maybe dimmed but it's always there, it's gaining in power, each moment of each day, of each breath. It's happening, it's evolving, it's real. So, let it be, trust, have faith, believe in self. Trust that all will be known at all times. Spirit has your back, now and forever.

Chapter 27

Raven – majik, sitting in silence

There's something about her timing or lack of it. She seems to find new passions at inappropriate times. Like aurora chasing when heading into a solar minimum, snorkelling in autumn, astronomy in summer when it's not dark time until like 10 or 11pm. Aurora chasing allowed an excuse to remove herself from her family. The space to sit in silence, to be humbled, to breathe amid the anguish of legal shit, family shit, life shit. Snorkelling has done the same, it's a space she can breathe, the beauty underwater once again humbling her, the brashness bringing her back into her body. A good wetsuit helps sustain her body warmth in the colder water, allowing her to stay present for longer.

#

Ana's always kept a journal, always recorded her dreams, her wishes, her life, believing one day she'll write a book, possibly to help others who also have walked this path. As she's going back through some old journals trying to find an extract from Spirit, she's unable to find it. Instead, she finds her desire to write such a book.

"Maybe when all of this is over."

It's weird how over the last three years, the years that have been seemingly endless with so much going on, she's not written much. The act of repeating on paper that which is happening in her reality has been too much. Instead, she has written random notes, random dream recordings, random poems. Poems are an easy way to express intense feelings, they're short, less words, more removed. That's what's needed these days, more removal from reality.

#

When Giana returns from their trip, they throw this perspective out there:

"You are overdue 16 ½ months long service leave, 9 years total annual leave, god knows how many sick days. You are overworked, overloaded, undervalued, underappreciated. Having a breakdown is just the natural progression."

Ana so loves her friends. She needs to learn to take better care of herself, allow proper "her" time, and that means this time and space away from the kids. Just Big Dog and Little Dog and a space to breathe.

There's a raven in the distance calling out its song. Will another answer? Sure, they will. Birds are like that, they communicate. They don't dictate like humans tend to. Life is complicated enough without adding to it.

A raven responds to the original call. Soon the air fills with an orchestra of tunes, floating, the wind lifting and carrying the tones, adding its own depth, varying the density with gusts, changes in intensity, gentle, firm, gentle, soft, ever-changing, ever evolving. Simply going with the flow.

Big Dog and Little Dog are here; they keep her here. They are her sanity, her saviours. The younger one, Little Dog, offers comfort, sitting on her lap, warming her body, its love enveloping her soul. "When you feel like life's pulling you in different directions it probably is," she laughs to herself. The irony in the statement is reflected in the four dog leads all stemming from one wrist, all going in different directions, much like how she feels.

#

When she finally allows someone into her space, allowing them to touch her body, heal her body, she's so grateful. The session with Mia is incredible, it's like her body knows Mia, trusts Mia, and in doing so, responds amazingly to their touch. Her body gurgles and ouches as Mia moves and manipulates, releasing parts of her that she feels have been trapped for eons.

Mia says they've never seen a body as traumatised as Ana's. "Finally," she thinks, "someone sees my truth." Needing more of this, she books another session. Apparently, Mia thinks Ana's second rib has rolled over, like a venetian blind. Instead of it lying flat alongside the others it's rotated on an angle. No wonder there's pain.

It leaves her wondering what would have happened if she hadn't seen Mia. Would her rib have remained like that? Unseen by an x-ray but certainly not unfelt by her. Would her body in its infinite wisdom of adjusting so many times to changes, eventually adjust to this too? Would the pain eventually subside, adding another body deformity to the list?

#

A police officer arrives at the door just as the sun's setting. She knew they were coming, but that didn't lessen the impact it has within her physicality. She needs to remind herself that she's safe. This place, her new home, is safe. Big Dog and Little Dog are with her. The police officer's a lovely empathetic soul, so much so that she finds herself telling the officer about her recent breakdown, about leaving the kids, her home. It feels like she's sharing with an old friend. But the officer has a job to do. They are there to serve papers. She's being subpoenaed to appear in court for the trial.

Even though this is good, she feels like the accused, like the guilty one. The word subpoena always feels like a guilty word, never associated with an innocent party.

The subpoena states that Ana needs to be physically present in court. It seems she will have to travel to Victoria no matter how she feels about it. The committal had been harsh enough, so harsh it led her to being here, in her friend's home. She can't imagine what the trial will do to her.

#

It's that time of year again, thankfully, time to head to the Tarkine to be amongst like-minded souls, to sit amid the silence of nature in its true raw form.

Her friend Astrid from Melbourne is coming, along with Danika, both welcome and much needed distractions. Astrid arrives a few days early, so naturally Ana shares this place she loves. They visit Mona, the coolest museum ever, jumping on the trampoline like little kids, the simple joys. They eat ice cream on what was once the port where the whaling ships pulled in, the crew would jump ashore and spend their time in brothels and pubs, right where Astrid and Ana enjoy the taste sensations of cold gelato, letting it run down their faces, life's simplicity, perfect.

Naturally snorkelling's on the cards at the Tarkine. How much they see is beside the point, to be in the wild west water, currents that must travel three quarters of the way around the world without touching land, ahhhh that's joy. That's embracing the rawness of Mother Nature.

Obviously, Astrid and Danika join in, having no intention of letting Ana have all the fun. There's some huge kelp moving in the most amazing rock pool. It's on the point of a point. Huge, jagged rocks covered in vibrant orange lichen create the perfect space to submerge oneself. The smash of the waves against the rocks creates bubble patterns below and on the surface. They're mesmerising.

She floats, letting the current, the waves move her whichever way they go. The huge ribbons of kelp perform a dance for her to enjoy, reminding her of the ballet performances she would go to as a child with school. She loved the ballet, the strength in it, the grace, the tones. Now nature's providing all of that for her. She could have stayed there forever.

Even though they're back in the same areas around the Tarkine, they manage to visit some new places, one of which she claims as her new favourite. It's a random find, they're meant to be on the beach learning some indigenous history, but she doesn't feel right about it. She doesn't feel as though she should walk on that land. So she doesn't, instead sitting in her car, embracing the alone time.

When the other two come back, they head for a spot along the way that drew their attention. How could it not? It is bright green ground with charcoaled trees from last year's fires. The contrast is amazing. The sounds of frogs provide some wonderful background tones to soothe their souls. Ana's waiting, hoping that Shrek, or Jack (at times they'd pretend he's Shrek, and she's Princess Fiona living in a fairy-tale) hoping either version would appear from the swamp. Unfortunately, he doesn't, but that doesn't stop her from becoming completely immersed in the wonder.

It's another incredible time away. A chance to reconnect, to breathe the freshest air in the world, to simply be. Each time she returns to this special space, to the Tarkine, the space she feels such a deep connection to, she feels as though she's come home.

#

Big Dog and Little Dog are waiting, well snoring, really, back at Giana's place. The rain muffles all other sounds, welcoming her home. For the Tarkine exhibition this year she doesn't have time nor the brain space to create anything that she feels will encapsulate her experience, instead she decides to try to create an image by combining photos of her favourite places. Technology, specially designing, is not one of her strong suits. Basically, she's hopeless. She wonders why she thought this would be easier than painting a picture, but she's started now. She has an idea in her head; she just needs to get that idea into a tangible form.

After hours and hours, and lots of frustration and learning, she feels happy with the result, titling it A Few of my Favourite Things. She sends it off to the printers and jumps into bed.

The next morning, she goes back to the computer, wondering if perhaps she could improve things. Obviously, she can. The question is, will she? Can she be bothered?

Divine intervention steps in. Her creation, all those hours of learning, are completely absent from her computer, from her external HD, from everything except the file sent to the printers.

This can't be happening! Like, seriously, what's going on? Not only has that creation disappeared, but so too have lots of other works of art, her vibrational images, lots of her photos, creations from years ago, writings. It feels in that moment that the Universe is wiping her slate clean. Looking at it that way she can accept that this is what it is, even though she doesn't understand why. She learned years ago to never question but to simply accept that Spirit always, always knows what's for her highest good.

She wants to cry. She does cry, big deep grieving sobs. She feels as though some of her soul has been thrown out. But some of those parts she wanted to keep, she's proud of her creations. Thank fuck, at least she has the final draft of this latest one anyway. She can't change anything, as the layers of work aren't there, only the printable image. The computer must spend the next month undergoing reconstructive surgery with no guarantee that all will be recovered.

Breathe ... and repeat.

The print comes back looking awesome. She's so excited. A friend frames it perfectly, with just one day until opening night.

\#

She never feels at home at openings, especially if she has anything on show. She just doesn't like being exposed, being seen through her creations. She feels so vulnerable, she simply wants to hide in the corner and not talk to anyone. She wonders why she's there in the first place.

Thankfully, her kids and some of her friends come to support her, to support the cause. She's trying to see where her photo's been hung, scanning the huge space full of people, both familiar and unknown. She sees it, it's hanging on a wall under a light, people are looking at it. She doesn't know what to do. It seems everyone's excited.

She lets her friends carry her along to her creation, and she nearly faints. There's a red dot by her name. Someone, some random stranger, has bought her creation, finding joy in something that she, Ana Suci, created.

She has to pinch herself. All her friends and the kids are so

excited. It's pretty special selling on opening night, especially among so many other incredibly talented artist and photographers. One of the organisers walks past and congratulates her. She feels seen, validated.

Chapter 28

Blobfish nurturing

In last night's dream there's something to do with legal stuff. She dreams that the trial has been moved to July. How fantastic would that be? That's only two months away.

The bliss of wishing this is so doesn't last, as a letter arrives. The trial of Patrick O'Shanesy is commencing in the Melbourne County Court on Monday 30th November. The accused is pleading not guilty to the charges.

Where can she go from this? How can she move past seeing those words? Pleading not guilty. Like fuck he's not guilty. She knows. He knows. Others know. Why the fuck can't he just say "guilty" and end this torture?

After the complete dissociation that resulted in Ana leaving home, she wants to make sure that she'll have people she knows, loves and trusts in the court room with her. Is that possible? It's a "Yes" from the OPP.

She wants to get that organised, even though it's still months away. She needs to have it clear in her mind that others will be there for her. Naturally, Astrid and Olivia say yes. They offer spaces and themselves for as long as is needed. Olivia even puts in a request for time off work, so they know they'll be free. Such a blessing.

Jack says he'll be there, he'll go on the plane with her, he'll stay with her, hold her hand, hug her, hold her, hear her, see her.

An email arrives asking if she'd rather be present via video link up? She has no idea what's going on. She'd been told that it simply wasn't an option, that her physical presence was required. She's just spent the last four months agonising over whether she'll be able to deal with being there. She'd managed to get it all to sit somehow sort of comfortable within her, and now there's an option … fuck.

It's such a complex process to have to organise her brain around something she knows will trigger her. It takes a huge amount of brain space to do so and doesn't leave room for much else. So, when this option is offered, she can feel her brain melting.

#

People really don't get what it's like to be so overloaded with PTSD that the simple act of buying food, let alone preparing it, is so hard. Many times, Ana finds herself walking into the fruit and veggie shop only to stand, stunned, overwhelmed, by everything around her, unable to get it together enough to buy food, to organise a meal. She becomes robotic, picking up familiar shapes, colours that are in familiar spaces, without any conscious thought as to what she's actually doing. It's a major drama if the shop decides to move anything. She just collapses, her brain just doesn't have the space or energy to file the new information, so she simply goes without. Tuna and rice are a common dinner. Not much thought required, nor cooking skills. She used to be and probably still is a good cook. She just can't get it together enough to be one at the moment.

She eats alone most days. First cooking the rice. That's easy – ½ cup of rice, one cup of water, put lid on, bring to boil, simmer for 10 minutes. Perfect. Then open small can of tuna, tip onto rice, add mayonnaise and pickled ginger, maybe some carrot and cucumber if the brain can manage it. Then eat all in the saucepan. Even moving it to another bowl is beyond the brain's capabilities. Breakfast is porridge, much the same process, lunch a toasted cheese and spinach sandwich.

#

Negativity really plays havoc with her being, her physicality, her soul. The other night Daren called. She doesn't know why, as all he said was how much the kids hate her, how much they love whichever woman he's dating right now, how the kids tell him he's such a great dad, how they never want to see her again.

She doesn't know why, but she never hangs up on him. It's never an option that crosses her mind during any of the calls. Only afterwards, when she's left crumbling, feeling like absolute crap, hating herself, wishing that bridge was just there so that she could jump off it, that's when she thinks she should have hung up. But she never does, she listens to his words, hating his tone, hating him.

Thankfully, it's time for another session with Mia. She knows her body's not good, she's feeling it respond to Daren's words, to her kids' anger, to her own self-loathing. Mia feels it too, saying her body's as restricted as it was the first time she visited. Holy fuck, really?

Not only is all of her shit displaying in her physicality but a visit to the GP for an updated mental health plan reveals a new mental health diagnosis: adjustment disorder.

A person with an adjustment disorder/stress response syndrome develops emotional and/or behavioural symptoms as a reaction to a stressful event. These symptoms generally begin within three months of the event and rarely last for longer than six months after the event or situation has ended. In an adjustment disorder, the reaction to the stressor is greater than what is typical or expected for the situation or event. In addition, the symptoms may cause problems with a person's ability to function; for example, the person may be have trouble with sleep, work, or studying.

She questions the words, "The reaction to the stressor is greater than what is typical or expected for the situation or event." Did whoever write this bullshit ever have to deal with childhood sexual abuse? She thinks not.

Feeling somewhat insane, she decides to display that by jumping into the very cold winter water. But oh, how her body thanks her. She feels all the crap, all the negativity, all the words of others wash away as her mind turns to the wonder before her.

A message from the OPP is waiting on her phone when she climbs, shivering, from the water.

"It is preferable that you physically attend court. You can have a video link from the room next to the court, so you don't have to be physically in the same room as him."

She knows this will make no difference. Her soul will sense his putrid energy, she will be breathing the same air as him, smelling the same scents, she will be there with him with or without a wall separating them.

She's thrown, all over again. She jumps back into the water.

#

For the first time since Mother Blobfish died, she feels them around. She asks why they're there? Why now? And believes she hears the reply, "I'm sorry".

She hopes they are; they should be. She hopes it's not just her mind playing tricks on her. Believing that Mother Blobfish really is sorry.

Chapter 29

Unique – unlike anything

Other people, especially those who, thankfully, haven't experienced trauma, really don't understand how it affects someone when they say, "Oh, we'll get back to you with confirmation about this issue." An issue that, whether they know it or not, is causing you untold anguish. It's just not acceptable.

After being informed that she'll find out a couple of weeks before the trial whether she can be in the video room next door or if she needs to actually be in the same room as him, she's like, "No I need to know now, not immediately beforehand. I need to sort all this stuff in my head, to have it all in places that I can somehow manage".

Sorting it in her head isn't something that just happens. It can take from days to weeks, or even longer, to have it comfortable within.

\#

Sometimes you simply need to stop, to take in the moment, to embrace what Mother Nature is offering you. So, one morning she stops the car, knowing she'll be late, knowing they'll understand. The light on the water as the sun rises over the River Derwent, combined with the early morning mist, is not to be missed.

The turning of the fagus is happening. It's quite simply a place to soothe one's soul. She heads there even though the forecast isn't the best. She doesn't care. She needs to stand on Mt Field with the cold snow air rushing around her body, taking away all the stuck energy, cleansing her soul as she breathes in all the wonder before her. The colours of the fagus against the snow … it's purely sublime. That's why she goes, that's why she's present in such rawness.

#

There's a nude swim every winter solstice. It's occasionally crossed her mind that this is something to be part of, but then the anxiety of being totally exposed overwhelms her, leaving her just hearing the stories year after year. This year's different though, this year she has no boobs, she has no partner, she only has one private body part to cover. She can do this.

Registering, she prepares her mind for the exposure, for being present amongst others. The cold water doesn't worry her, it's the eyes of others that does. As the day approaches, her mind's doing terrible things.

"People will stare, people will turn away, avoid looking at your deformity, looking at you. They will laugh behind your back, smirk to your face. Like, who do you think you are? Seriously?"

The morning of the swim, as thousands gather, baring their bodies, laughing, she lies in bed, shivering, hating herself, her weakness. Wanting to escape her mind, her inner judgement, she jumps into the water by herself. The winter cold brings such clarity to the underwater world. The wonders she sees are so worth it, especially the amazing eleven-armed sea star nestled amongst the bright colours of weeds. Such beauty, such an escape.

#

A laughing group. Who would have thought? Such a great idea. She's been invited along by Lucia and was a bit reluctant at first. Does she really want to be meeting new people? Especially people who are happy? The first thing she notices is that the facilitator has no breasts.

OMG, this is amazing! They are the first person she's meet who, like her, has chosen to stay in their new raw, authentic form. "So that's what I look like? What I feel like?"

The group's fantastic. It feels so good to laugh, to let go, to allow her body to be at peace. There are so many ways to laugh, who knew? Her favourite's the snort. Jack snorts when he laughs, his belly wobbling; it's one of the many reasons she loves him.

It's strange hugging a woman who doesn't have boobs. Now she sees why men like hugging women. Their boobs feel so soft and comforting. It makes her sad knowing she will never again hold that form. Then she blinks, reminding herself how grateful she is to be alive.

#

Just when life is sort of, kind of liveable, when things are sort of, kind of in a place where she can sort of, kind of breathe, a phone call from the hospital in Queensland comes. Father Bullshark's been admitted, along with Mitria. Both have apparently lost awareness of who they are. Someone needs to be present and act on their behalf, they need to be placed in an aged care facility.

Like fuck. Shit. Fuck. No way.

A trip to Queensland's needed, there's no other option, but she doesn't really want them here, not Father Bullshark anyway, she loves Mitria but can live the rest of her life without having to deal with him. It seems the Universe is conspiring, trying to keep her in her past. It's either leave them up there, putting way too much responsibility on Esi, or bring them here, which requires her presence. Going back has never been a thing for her. She doesn't go back to relationships, places, friendships. If they end, they end for a reason. Why? Why would she go back? To the house? To her kids? To Daren? To the negativity? Back to how things were. She doesn't want that; it so wasn't working for her. Instead, she wants to live in a place of positivity, of peace, of joy, of minimal conflict. A space she can feel hugging her every time she comes down the driveway. That's what she wants. The constant self-criticisms running around her head, the constant repetition of "You're such a bad mother" are silenced by her longing for peace.

She's only been back to Queensland twice since leaving. She doesn't like going back … anywhere. But now, she must. To clear, clean, pack and comfort all.

It's hard for Esi, they have a great relationship with their grandpa. It's hard for Esi to say goodbye, knowing it's the last time. Tears fall upon their cheeks. Ana so wants to be there for Esi, but instead she must jump on the plane with her parents and bring them back into her space.

Some much-needed respite under the night sky awaits. Such a stunning aurora. No-one else around, just her and Spirit. She's so grateful to be home, to be in the places that make her happy to be alive.

\#

Trauma affects your brain, affects the performance of the simplest of tasks, tasks that you've performed millions of times. Your brain can suddenly cease to be able to turn the key in the ignition, buy food, wash hair, drive a car. It can be and is really scary at times. She's feeling the pinch of a brain so overloaded with trauma that she decides to try and write a passage, so that others may possibly understand what's going on in her head.

An analogy of my brain

Average brain:
Green light – go
Red light – stop

Traumatised brain:

Green light – oh do I go? Are you sure I'm meant to go? If I go, won't I get sideswiped by that car? Does green mean go? Oh no! Now there's cars coming at me! That car is going to hit me. You're sure green means go? Cars turning, they're going to hit me. You're sure green means go? Is it really safe? Ohhh.

Red light – umm sure I'm meant to stop, yes? But if I stop, won't the car behind me crash into me? Am I meant to stop? What if red really means go? Now I don't know what I'm meant to do. Leave body. Phew. Honk, honk. Oops back in body, foot to floor. Was that light green?

Chapter 30

The unsustainability of opposing emotions

It's just friggin fucked. She's a complete mess again. How many times can her heart break before it stops altogether? She just wants to be free of trauma. She's unable to carry it anymore.

When she's in nature, feelings of freedom, joy and wonderment fill her. Gratitude for Mother Nature embraces her soul. Yet when interacting with her family she holds nothing but sadness, dismay and complete and utter despair. The guilt's overwhelming. The disappointment that's there is such crap, darkening her soul. Her eyes leak with hot water.

She feels so empty, so nothing, when trying to define herself as a parent. It's a label she's always struggled with, doesn't feeling worthy of, feels has never fitted her.

Yesterday, the family pretended to be happy for Zeb's birthday. She'd never felt so uncomfortable, just wanting to curl up and roll down the mountain, it was horrible. But instead, she remained present, putting a smile on her face, all the while crumbling inside. Afterwards, she walked with Esi around the rose garden, discussing the meaning of life and everything, walking and talking. The phone rang; it was the police. She stopped, unable to talk on the phone and walk at the same time. Esi looked at her weirdly, questioning why she had stopped.

After she hung up, Esi was like, "What's going on, Mum? You used to be able to multitask so brilliantly."

She thought for a moment.

"I just can't seem to do it anymore."

"Nah, I know what it is. Why woman can multitask and why men are crap at it."

This should be good.

"Woman's breasts, that's where the multi-tasking tool is. You don't have them anymore, so you can't multitask. Simple."

A big grin crossed Esi's face. Ana grinned in reply.

"Yep, you're probably right."

#

Is it bad to remove yourself from the environment that's destroying your soul? She feels like there is two of her: one who loves nature, her friends, who's grateful for all the love she has in her life. The other? The other's constantly battling to stay alive, to keep her head above water. She's drowning, unseen by most. She wants to run back home to her soul space. Which of the beings is going to win? Is this the unknown point? The moment that determines whether she lives or dies?

Maybe she should try it out. Maybe in her dream the reason why court is over in July is not that POS is dead, but that she will be? If she is to die, she can live with that, knowing that all is as it's meant to be. Part of her will be relieved, all the crap will stop. For her, anyway. What happens to those left is out of her control; it is as it's meant to be.

#

Being around negative people, even if it's family, is just way too much at the moment. She takes Zeb and Mitria to the farmers' market. Both of them are in negative moods, criticising everything. At least Mitria has an excuse. She was diagnosed with early onset dementia when they arrived here.

"Why don't you two go get a coffee and wait for over there me?" she says, quickly heading in the opposite direction, gulping big breaths of fresh air.

After such crap, a snorkel is in order. She needs to wash away the morning's negativities. It's the end of winter but the water's still cold. She likes it like that. It shocks her back into her body, for the moment.

#

Later that night the phone rings. It's an old friend of Father Bullshark. She remembers them from her childhood, from the drunken parties her parents used to have, from the food the children weren't allowed to touch. She can still hear the vulgarity spoken so openly amongst those older, the smells, the leers, the completely inappropriate comments being directed at her, a child, from those who should never speak such shit to someone so young.

Ana's back there in her childhood home, surround by the smells of alcohol and smoke, of cheap and nasty perfume, by the sounds of voices too high, voices that should be shushed, by people who make her want to hide. The lady is speaking, they're asking about Father Bullshark, but she can't hear them. The memory noise is too loud. She hangs up, shaking.

During the night, waking for the toilet, she finds she can't walk properly. She's unable to stand straight, she's leaning to the left. She walks herself along the walls, hoping they'll keep her upright. She's unable to straighten herself. It's the same in the morning only worse. It's like she has major vertigo. When she tries to get out of bed, she nearly faints, collapsing back into its safety, feeling blackness engulf her.

#

She hates who she becomes before, during and after being present in any way, shape or form with Father Bullshark. It zaps her of joy, leaving her feeling empty and vile. Fuck it. He's such an arse. So fucking negative, so fucking verbally abusive to Mitria and now to the nursing home staff too. She's embarrassed every visit. Ashamed of him, feeling guilty for his behaviour.

She talks to the staff about how she's feeling, explaining what it does to her when she's in his presence. They can see how it affects her – she's crying, her whole body's shaking. They're wonderful and supportive, advising her not to come in, that they will take care of him. That's their job.

But what about Mitria? They'll look after her, making sure Father Bullshark isn't too abusive. She's so grateful, she really can't go anywhere near him. His presence makes her want to vomit, to smash him, to harm him.

#

Thankfully a new obsession appears, allowing her to remove herself from the earth, literally: rock climbing. It's so much fun, hanging there by a thread so to speak, high above everyone, untouchable.

It's also a great activity to do with Zeb, it's non-confrontational, but they have to work together. They compete to get to the top first, and its fun, even when Zeb gently and lovingly drops her a bit too fast whilst belaying. It doesn't matter, they're together, they're communicating, she's feeling good.

#

While she's on a walk through some pretty spring countryside, the phone rings. It's the legal person. They want to ask questions. She asks if they can please put it all in an email and send it, knowing she's only hearing every third word, only understanding every fifth. But they don't listen or hear. They just keep talking. At no point does she feel or even have the thought to hang up. Instead, she holds on to the phone, taking one step after the other, all the while feeling her body crumbling.

Thankfully, a session with Mia helps reset the damage done. Mia comments that Ana's body is in really bad shape. She knows it's true, she can feel it. She felt it happening yesterday while on the phone. She's crushed. It just shows how detrimental her past is, even in her present.

#

Ana seriously doesn't know how she'd be, or if she'd even still be here on this earth, if she didn't live where she does. The availability and accessibility of Mother Nature and all it provides truly is her life saver.

She takes a drive to Mt Field, following the morning mist and frost. It's pure majik to watch the light change as the sun rises, melting the frost drops. It allows her space and time to breathe. The icicles along the roadside require photographic attention, as do the blue mykes interspersed around them, the most majikal fungi seen to date. When the wonders of nature are absent, and the brashness of life replaces its beauty, she wonders if she should throw in the towel on this whole legal process. But then, what would the last three and a half years have been for? Is it that simple to just walk away from all the personal evolution, the family changes, the body changes? Nope. Can't do it. So she keeps going. Keeps breathing and repeating.

Giana reminds her how far she's come. She acknowledges the strength she's found along the way. That even though she's still vulnerable, in speaking out, in telling her story, she's already helped so many others.

"Remember that this isn't only about you, it's about so much more." Giana hugs Ana tightly, hoping to take on some of the load.

Chapter 31

Breathe and repeat

An interesting and enlightening conversation happens as Ana and her friend Oscar, whom she met through an adventure group, walk from one side of River Derwent to the other. She has to cross the Tasman Bridge, the one she'd planned to jump off that night not so long ago.

She opens up to Oscar, telling them her story, her wishes that night, her desires to end her life, right here, where they now walked. Oscar shares their own story as Ana stands, leaning over the side thinking about what could have been. She wonders if her body would have smashed against the concrete force of the water, or whether she would have died of a heart attack before entering the coldness. Oscar says how early one morning driving across the bridge they saw a young lady trying to climb the rail. There was no traffic, so Oscar stopped the car and walked over to the young lady, gently asking them questions, commenting on the wonders of the sun rising, the warmth it would bring their soul. The young lady turned, seeing Oscar just before their second leg found its way over the ledge. Oscar's voice made the young lady stop, bringing a moment of clarity to their seemingly out-of-control world. Oscar asked if they'd like to sit and talk, they nodded as they removed themself from the ledge and walk slowly towards Oscar, seeing their big welcoming smile, feeling safe in their presence. Oscar knew emergency services would be on their way, they monitor the bridge constantly. Together Oscar and the young lady sat watching the sunrise in silence until help arrived. As Oscar shares, Ana realises that her choice, her actions, may have had an impact on some innocent passer-by just like her good friend. She hears the pain in their tone as they retell the story, tears welling as they remember the young lady, safe by their side. They are grateful they couldn't sleep that night.

She says sorry to Oscar, sorry that they had to experience that. She thanks them for being there and apologises for herself possibly causing trauma to another. They continue their walk to the other side, along the rock cliffs, walking to the edge of one outcrop, wanting to see the water, the seaweed. She's absent from her being, from the space, from awareness, and her feet slip out beneath her on the weed covered rocks. She falls extremely hard on her bum, the impact sending her head back, whiplash-like, her body shuddering with the force. Oscar calls out, asking if she's all right.

"Fuck that must have hurt."

He holds out a hand to help her up. They sit for a while, as good a spot as any to have lunch.

Ana reflects on the metaphysical message in her fall, today she fell onto her back, her past, after walking across the bridge where she was going to jump off, to end her life. That day she left her home instead of ending her life. She'd fallen then too, but that time on her front, on her chest. It pulled her up, it gave her pain, it made everything real. Now she's fallen on her back, the past, it hurts to be back there, in that space, which is so true. Instead, she needs to focus on the present, to absorb the wonders before her, not reflect on the horrors of her past.

In the process, she realises the need to grieve. To grieve for what was and will never be. To grieve for the her that felt so totally alone that taking her own life seemed the only viable option. To grieve for the space, she didn't allow herself to feel, for the hatred so present in her heart. It needs to be gone. She hears a voice in her mind:

"Life's a journey and each day we walk it. Each step leaving its mark for those who follow, carving a path for those who lead. Each moment has great meaning, great love, great joy. Remember this always."

#

Friendships truly are sacred, appearing in many forms for various lengths of time. Each one a treasure, bringing untold awareness, strength, creativity, passion and love into a life. She's more aware than ever of the friendships in her life, constantly giving thanks for the friends she has, for their openness in sharing and caring, their beauty inside and out. She feels truly blessed to be surrounded, enveloped by such divine souls.

And then there's Jack, Jack who's ever present, ever him. They grab whatever moments they can, mostly sitting under the stars. Jack knows so much about astronomy he's always happy to help Ana learn and explore the Universe. If only they could build a spaceship and return to the stars, oh such bliss.

The astronomical names, like the botanical names for the fungi, are something she struggles with. So, she creates her own astronomical vocabulary that makes so much more sense. First up, instead of Eta Carinae, she calls it *the pinkie purply twirly thingy*. (Because it actually does twirl. If you stand still on a clear dark night, you can see it moving.) The large and small Magellanic clouds, which are both dwarf galaxies, she calls *the large and small magenellicaia clouds*. Magellanic is one of the many words her tongue struggles to embrace. The Jewel Box becomes *such a pretty thingy*. The Southern Cross becomes *the flag thingy*. Sirius, the *all so shiny thingy*, the brightest star in our night-sky vision. Three stars to the right, five galaxies past, is her home planet of Zaphron. Rho Ophiuchus in the constellation of Scorpius, that becomes *the spidery thingy*. Orion's nebula is t*he purpley explosion flame thingy*, which is so pretty in a telescope. The Pleiades or seven sisters she calls *the things that spark ever so brightly*.

One clear night while heading home after aurora chasing, as she comes up over a rise, she catches a glimpse of the Andromeda galaxy, a mere 2.5 million light years away, set to collide with the Milky Way, Earth's galaxy, in about five-plus billion years, to create a new night-time landscape and naturally a new earthscape too. That's if earth even exists then. How cool will that be, she wonders.

Being under the stars, learning about their size, their distance from planet earth, is humbling and ever so life giving.

#

It's the end of July. She's still present, the legal proceedings are still happening, she doesn't understand what her earlier dream was saying. "It will be all over June/July." What was it referring to? She checks back in with Melisa, feeling the need to reconnect, even though the trial's still months away.

POS' lawyers have proposed another plea of guilty to indecent assault. Like fuck! She replies with a big, "NO."

She dreams that night. Lots of baby whales all swimming close to her, right in front of her. It reminds her of a dream she had many, many years ago of a whale. Only that time, there were two whales, and she was using them like water skis to ride into the sunset. That dream recall is so vivid, so present in the now. Whales can signify that everything will be ok. This was so true in her past dream, so she gives thanks to Spirit, hoping that it will be now too.

#

Volunteering is something she's been doing for the last thirty years, ever since she first had cancer, wanting to give back to the hospital that treated her so well. Over the years she's volunteered in many different places in varying roles. Now it seems that she's found her dream role – being a pirate on an incredible, divine wooden boat called Lady Nelson.

Zeb's most upset that all those years ago she didn't lose her leg, cause then now she'd be like a real pirate complete with missing leg. But nope, she has both her legs, enabling her to power up the shrouds to the main topgallant, her most favourite spot alongside the outer jib, standing on the very end point of the bowsprit suspended above the water. Such freedom.

How she loves being on the water, learning what seems like a new language and skills, building up her physical body. She needs that right now. She feels so weak inside that she needs her physicality to be strong, super strong, to protect her, to hold her. So, pirating, along with some seventy kilometres of walking a week, helps her body grow firm, and her mind to find peace.

She can sail as much as she likes and ends up often spending half the week on the water, up the mast, stinking of sweat when she gets home. Exhausted, but ever so happy. The climbing's good, it stretches her body, her chest, opening and expanding the scar tissue. She feels it pull each time she reaches up and grabs hold of a rope, pulling herself, her whole bodyweight up and over the futtocks. She feels the stretch, the release, the gratitude from her body. When she's handing or setting the sails, sometimes she's even lifted off the deck.

She's a lightweight at the moment. She knows she's lost weight, a fair bit. She sees it in the eyes of her friends when they hug her, hears it in her kids' tone when they ask if she's ok. She's lost nearly 15 kg since her hysterectomy over three years ago. Stress does that to her. She's healing so amazingly well though. The mastectomy scar's reducing weekly, leaving what she calls side boobs from the skin left there by the surgeon. She's not too keen on them, hoping that over time they'll reduce, but still ever so grateful for the amazing healing her body can achieve after having dealt with and still dealing with so much.

At first being with people, with strangers within the small confines of the boat, puts pressure on her mind, her being. But the bracing sea air combined with climbing to the heights away from the deck, away from the passengers, away from being present on earth, allows compromise of self. So she stays, learning and growing with each interaction, with each uncomfortable moment.

It's so good for her physicality, she doesn't want to lose it, her biceps are remembering their form held over a youth spent butterfly swimming and then as a bar attendant lifting all those glass trays. It isn't long before they're larger than Zeb's, oh how she relishes that.

In fact, her body becomes so toned she can now pop her pecks, just like a body builder. What a great source of embarrassment for the kids.

At least they can all laugh about it.

#

As the night's clear she heads to a good local dark sky viewing space to observe the sky through a friend's telescope. It totally blows her mind. She's able to see five of the moons of Jupiter align, then the many stunning and ever so pretty colours of the Jewel Box, leaving her truly feeling blessed and humbled. She believes in God/Spirit, believing with all her soul that there's a force greater than herself. A force so divine that, if tapped into, it can provide your world with all you desire, for your highest good. It's something she lives by.

Her faith in Spirit is immovable, her acceptance of Spirit is solid, having seen and experienced too much in her life to not believe. She believes in angels, having seen, felt and heard them. She believes that we all have choices in every moment of every day, choices that can fundamentally shape our existence. Many times, she's found herself so overwhelmed in a moment that she's chosen to deny the simple fact that she does have a choice, instead choosing to hand over accountability to all number of things, people, life.

She knows now that she and she alone is accountable for her world, for how she sees her world and who she allows into it. Some choose to be surrounded by people they know aren't the right sort of energy for them, whose presence compromises their own them-ness. They may be rich, they may be powerful, they may be influential, they may be physically beautiful, yet their souls simply don't fit comfortably. Some choose to work in an environment that they know crushes their soul, destroys their essence. Why? Because it pays good money, because they get acknowledgement, because, because, because. Ana chooses to remove herself from that, choosing to honour herself even if that means not having much. She's happy and free.

Chapter 32

Life's complexities

The legal system, its wording, its logic, plays havoc with her more literal brain. When it comes to compensation, they say they'll pay for a family holiday but not the purchasing of a campervan, something that's less expensive, something she'd embrace, find peace in, a van she could use time after time, and which would be so much more in alignment with her as a person. The solitude, the spontaneity, she'd love that. A stupid family holiday, pre-booked, surrounded by strangers with no peace, organised to fit into their stereotypical image of what a normal person would want, is something she would so hate. So fucking stupid.

She's been told to ask for more than what's she expecting in compensation, so as not to be too disappointed. How about they just give her what she asks for? Up to a certain amount, of course. Now that would make a lot more sense.

It certainly doesn't help her sense of self-worth, this questioning, this rejecting of the things that bring her joy. She asks for some photographic equipment. Photography being an activity, whether above or below water, that has most definitely saved her soul over the past three years.

After some research she comes up with this wish list:

- Sony A&R11 $3900
- Sigma 35mm f1.4 ART $989
- Nikon 105mm f1.4E: $2990
- Nikon 24-70mm f2.8G ED: $2700
- Nikon 24-70mm f2.8E VR: $2990

- Olympus TG5 $649
- Nikon 70-200mm f2.8E FL VR: $3400
- Lowepro Protactic 350AW backpack $350
- Skywatcher Black Diamond 12" Collapsible Dobsonian Telescope $2399

Total: $20,367.

She's not feeling confident about any compensation, it's not why she's doing this. But sure, anything would be great.

They ask her to list the loss of wages resulting from the assault, relevant to income at the time of the assault. Like how is that even relevant in her case? She was six to twelve years old. She was not even working back then. But once she had kids, once she clearly remembered her past, relieving it daily, that affected her ability to bring in an income, yet when she asks for clarification around this, she's told that in her case she cannot claim loss of income.

It seems all she really can do is possibly have her victim impact statement read out in court, if she's lucky, if he pleads guilty or is found guilty. If not, then she won't even be able to do that. The whole process seems so very wrong, leaning towards making things comfortable for POS, making sure he doesn't feel hard done by, making sure he feels that he's not a bad person. Like, fuck off.

#

It's really interesting, amazing and frightening how much stress plays havoc with her brain. She takes a trip with Rey to the dentist, the same dentist they've been going to for the last five years, yet she's unable to find it. It's like someone has picked up the building and moved it. It isn't in the space she remembers.

In the end she stops to look it up. She's only a street away, yet it may as well have been a trillion miles. Her brain's so fried. New and old information is just not being retained. Of course, not being able to perform such a simple task only adds to the brain-fried-ness.

#

Without forethought, her hand once again goes up. This time she's dobbed herself in to perform at a live poetry reading to promote the Tarkine. She's written a few poems reflecting on the impact that the space has on her soul, and she feels they're good enough to share with others. She's forgetting that sharing with others in this instance means standing and speaking in front of strangers. And that hopefully the strangers will be listening. She becomes less and less sure of herself.

Thankfully, her friend Matilda's visiting. Matilda teaches her that it's not so much about speaking the words but delivering the story by *being* the words ... argh. So, for two hours prior to the performance, they practise and practise, which is actually good. It leaves her feeling a lot more confident ... until she's before the crowd.

Others have already spoken, they speak with such passion, such poise. She's nervous, but she made a promise, so she walks onto the stage. She knows she's detached, naturally. She hears her words, seeing herself from a distance, watching like a member of the audience.

My senses are awakened as I sit amongst the silence that is
  sacred space

My eyes listen to the colours before me as drops of dew melt,

embracing the dawn

My ears smell the earth as I tread upon her hallowed ground.

My skin hears the rustle of the wind as the leaves sway to her
  rhythm

My soul senses the beauty in that which is unseen

I breathe in gratitude for a gift such as this

My eyes fill as emotions of pure joy overwhelm me

I look to the heavens, I give thanks to Spirit

I start to question, then I clear my mind

I count the stars, I'm here for a while

She takes a big deep breath before delivering the last line, imagining herself in the space that warms her soul. Feeling she has honoured all, she exits the stage, unable to look up. Instead, she keeps her head down, hurrying back to her seat amid the applause.

#

In the process of life and family, Rey's decided they'd like to live with their mum again. As much as she'd love this, she's hesitant, still completely unsure of sharing her space with another, of being a mother again, of having to be present, of dealing with negativity. Maybe it is time for her to be a mum again, maybe this isn't about her, but about Rey and their needs. She uses all means of rationality, trying to get the idea to sit within her space comfortably.

Looking for a home is a challenge; rentals are scarce and expensive. She investigates public housing as an option. It's so humiliating, she shouldn't be in that space, that need, how did her life get here? It takes her back many, many years ago to when she was single with three young kids, barely managing to keep her head above water, eating only three tablespoons of food for her evening meal so that her kids had enough. It was Christmas time, she had no gifts, no decorations or special food. Swallowing her pride, she found herself visiting the local Lifeline shop asking for and accepting handouts of food and presents for the kids, going home exhausted, deflated, ashamed and grateful.

That turned out to be a wonderful Christmas. Her neighbours were amazing. They went into the house Christmas Eve when she'd taken the kids to Father Bullshark and Mitria's for dinner. The neighbours put out the presents from Lifeline along with gifts from themselves. When they all got home, the kids were blown away. Santa had remembered them. Even Esi who was eleven at the time was stumped.

The power of majik.

She's feeling the humiliation now again. Wondering why? How? Wondering when it will stop, this roller coaster of life she continuously finds herself on. This self-pitying won't get her anywhere, she knows that. She knows she needs to be accountable for herself, her life, where she is in life at any given moment. But sometimes she just wants to crumble.

Acquiring public housing won't be easy either. Ana has special needs when it comes to where she lives. Obviously, she needs to feel safe, to have privacy from passing eyes. She needs space for Big Dog and Little Dog. There must be no smell of tobacco. The setting must be relatively free of noise, especially loud aggressive noises. This is why she loves where she lives at the moment. She feels safe, it's quiet, there's no one that smokes nearby, the loudest noises are children playing or the neighbour learning the trumpet, which she loves no matter how bad they sound.

She's put on the list; it's now a waiting game. Will her number ever come up? In the meantime, she needs to think of alternative options and she wishes she didn't. There's so much going on. Her brain's unable to find any space to deal with this. But deal with it, she must.

#

She finds some respite in the form of wildlife animal rescue training, enabling some peace as she sits, something which she finds so difficult, learning all about the amazing wildlife around her space. She learns how to care for injured animals, how to contact others for more assistance.

At lunch time, she walks around the sanctuary, watching and listening to the rescued animals as they heal in a safe space. There's too much roadkill in Tasmania; she's never seen so much. She wants to be able to save even one animal if she can.

They're taught how to compile and keep a rescue pack in their car: a pillowcase, gloves, a towel or blanket. They're taught where and how to look for babies in pouches, how to cover and move injured animals. She feels the need to save others, knowing what it's like to hurt.

While Ana is cooking dinner that night, Gianna reads from a children's book. It's such a simple gift and it brings so much joy to Ana's scorched soul. It doesn't, however, help to bring her back into herself. She knows she's disconnected. When she looks in the mirror whilst cleaning her teeth, she sees herself disappearing, becoming littler and littler. She struggles to sense herself when looking in a mirror, instead seeing, sensing a stranger. She's often confused when someone mentions something she has on, or something about how she looks, her hair, her smile. She doesn't feel as though they belong to her.

Chapter 33

Gifts abound

Ana can hardly believe it, she's at her first artist in residency in one of the most spectacular spaces on this planet, Cradle Mountain. She applied a few months ago, meaning to come then, but she had to postpone because of Father Bullshark and Mitria moving. Yet she's here now, amongst all the beauty. It's surreal. She's staying in the gallery, stunning works of art invading her eyes, soothing her soul. The late and great photographer Peter Dombrovskis has a whole room dedicated to his work. It's incredible seeing the images on the walls, then walking in the same spaces outside in the wintery wonderland.

Wandering through the gallery she comes to a sign. *Extreme.* Holy crap, she'd forgotten all about the exhibition from the *Ten Days on the Island* festival. It's still on display, which means her photo should be in that room.

At first, she's slightly dubious about entering, allowing only her head and one eye to peek around the corner. She sees photos from some of the most respected landscape photographers, those she admires. And then there, in between her two most favourite, is her photo, *Grandmother Tree*. Is this real? Like, seriously? She's so disbelieving. She can see herself in the description of the photo, she can read her words. Yet she feels as though they are the words and image of a stranger.

The first evening meal is laid on the table. The aroma of roast cauliflower soup invading her nostrils, the first spoonful touching her taste buds. Tears well up, and she wonders how with all the crap that's present in her life, the crap that has been her life, she's so blessed, so gifted to now be in this majikal space, eating this divine food that she didn't prepare and doesn't need to clean away. She feels forever grateful, feeling like she's in a fairy-tale, wondering what's going to happen next.

Snow happens next, with a side show of aurora for good measure. Can you believe that?

Lucia has loaned her some warm Antarctic gear so she can sit under the stars, in the cold. In her infinite wisdom and rush to capture an aurora over the lake with snow-capped mountains, she puts the overalls on first, then adds another four layers, feeling confident that she'll be warm enough, not thinking past that. She just wants to be out there. The wind's ferocious, moving the tripod around, challenging her photographic skills. She's not easily defeated. She doesn't care if they aren't clear pics. She, Ana Suci is here, at a world-famous natural space, under the night sky, with the aurora dancing, snow-capped mountains surrounding the lake. Does anything else really matter?

Well, something else *does* matter, the need to have a wee. Normally, this isn't an issue. Bush wees are part of a joy-filled life. But as it's below zero and she has four layers she needs to take off to access her overalls, having a wee doesn't seem a viable nor a likely option. Thankfully, motherhood prepares one well for holding on. So hold on she does until she can no longer.

Oh the joys of aimless wanderings and ponderings in new snow-covered spaces. Such beauty surrounding and enveloping her being, soothing her soul. She lets her feet direct and her soul choose the space to wander, leading to so many gifts, such beauty, such silence.

Along one walk, a snow gum appears to be asking for Ana to stop and behold its beauty, asking to be hugged. She loves hugging trees, loves feeling their strength, their grounding. If she listens silently, she can hear their wisdom. Standing, hugging the tree, tears once again run down her cheeks. She's crying lots in this space.

As she hugs and cries, she asks Spirit what this is all about. Will the legal stuff be ok?

She lets the silence engulf her, waiting patiently for a response. It may come in a variety of ways – an animal appearing, the call of a bird tickling her ears, a sound coming from the mountains, a scent, a feeling, a word, an image. She waits, feeling the grounding energy of the gum, its wisdom, its knowing.

Then she hears the words, "Everything will be ok, the legal process will be in your favour."

Simple, yet so life giving.

The snow flurries circle, gently settling upon her being, adding to the majikality of the moment. She's in shock. Overcome with gratitude. In awe of all that Mother Nature and Spirit are offering to support her.

#

One day she walks and walks, up and up. She's looking at a high space, wishing to get there, to sit up top, to look at all the wonder below. It's prehistoric in appearance. The silence is deafening, yet so welcome to her hypersensitive ears.

Ana sits, trying to grasp the totality of life, of her life, of her journey, of the ending of this chapter anyway. A rainbow appears over the lake that's formed from Permian and Triassic times, originating as glaciers thousands of years ago. Solid chunks of dolerite or congealed basalt lava have transformed the area over the last two million years. In a moment of pondering, of self-reflection, she thinks about the ages of the magnificence before her, acknowledging that she's but a mere blip in the history of Mother Earth, and even less in the history of the Universe.

#

It's the last night, she's wishing for fresh snow. She wants to try and capture some snow, tree, and star wonder. Spirit hears, and as dark time blankets the space, so does snow. Fresh white goodness.

Dark time driving is slow going anywhere in Tasmania, especially so in somewhere this remote. There are so many night-time creatures enjoying the space. The slow crawl along the road allows her time to look and see what's being offered around each corner. She stops by a walkway with trees and Sirius shining brightly through the clouds. It's cold though, bitterly cold. At least this time she has her overalls on the top, no way she's going to make that mistake twice. The clouds take over the night sky, so she moves ahead to a place that may possibly be ok. She parks the car, taking out the camera, proceeding to take some pics in different directions, the snow falling around and on her.

Even in what some might call ridiculous conditions, she's in her element, loving the rawness of this space, the shhh-y-ness created by the snow and dark time, the beauty of it all. Such a gift.

She points the camera west and checks the back of the camera. "Yep. That's the shot."

The core of the Milky Way is lying low, perfectly positioned between two eucalyptus gums, the snow-covered button grass lit up by the car's headlights. She's unable to imagine anything more stunning. She takes a few shots, happy and ever so grateful, packs everything up, jumps in the car, and heads back to the gallery and into bed, the smile on her face only just conveying the joy in her heart.

#

The last morning arrives with last night's snow still fresh on the mountains. She heads to the lake, knowing she's missed sunrise but still hoping to get a touch of golden hour colour. It's incredibly pretty driving along the snow-laden road, without a soul in sight. The sun's rising over her left shoulder, its rays offering warmth to the frozen ground. The lake's before her, it's mind-blowingly stunning. The only footprints have been left by the local Bennett's wallabies. The silence is so welcome, the air, life giving.

"What an incredible experience this whole week's been, I'm ever so grateful," she breathes as she places her hands together in silent prayer. The long seven-hour drive home is worth every minute. She discovers a stunning waterfall along the way and finds the biggest plate fungi she's ever seen.

It starts snowing. She's whooping with joy, singing, crying. Coming over a rise there lies some flat land, blue water, and a rainbow, leaving her knowing in that moment that everything will be ok. Simple.

#

She's back to seeing Melisa regularly. The trial is only a few months away. How she's missed Melisa's input, their presence. She explains to Melisa about her breakdown and the path since, it's been that long since they last sat and shared. Ana speaks of her inner journey, the pain, the self-realisations, the peace, the joy, the finding of space that simply lets her be, the tuning in more to her body, listening to its needs, removing herself whenever necessary from whoever, no matter what.

She shares that every time she must go back to her old home where Daren and kids are living, she feels physically sick. Big Dog and Little Dog won't even leave the car. The space seems to have been overcome with negativity, leaving her mentally, emotionally, and physically empty.

She shares how she feels like two different people. When she's out under the stars, in the bush, up a mountain, in the water, with Big Dog and Little Dog, she wants to live, to be present, to embrace all of life's wonders. Then there's the other self, the one who wants to kill herself when she must be present in the "real world", when she has to deal with negativity, simply no longer wanting to be here, the pain's way too great, the cost seemingly too high. Death appears as a much better option.

There doesn't seem to be any neutral ground. It's one or the other. Which one will win?

She explains how being under the stars or under water brings peace, grounding her. How snorkelling brings her back into her body, the initial shock of the cold water upon her exposed skin awakening her senses. How standing on the bow of Lady Nelson lets her breathe, how the salty sea spray tastes so welcoming upon her skin, the sound of the water against the hull silencing the screams in her thoughts.

How being around Father Bullshark makes her want to kill herself or him, the negativity of his tone, his appalling behaviour to others leaves her skin crawling; he's such an arsehole.

Chapter 34

Stubbornness – a strength, a weakness

As much as no contact with the police is a good thing, the uncertainty, the not knowing, plays havoc with her mind. She wonders if it's really going to trial on the date that's been set. Will they make up some excuse? Prolong it further? Or will POS have the balls to be accountable and have it all over before then? So many unknown, uncontrollable factors, creating so much uncertainty within her soul. She can feel like someone else is dictating her life. Like she's completely powerless. But she's not. She has a voice; she just needs to use it.

She's angry. Why hasn't POS admitted his guilt? It's not just her story, but the story of others. Others who for whatever reason are choosing to remain silent. But she knows them. She's seen them, been told of them.

But she needs to accept that she's in this alone. After all, it was her choice to do this, this legal shit. To speak out. To give herself a voice – give others a voice through her story. To disrupt and destroy her family, herself. This is all her choice, her doing. She needs to stand firm in her decisions no matter how hard. She knows, she has faith, that only good can come from it. Whether she wins (such a stupid word in this instance) the legal stuff or not, Ana knows she'll be a better person because of it all. She can already feel the changes within. She hears them in the words spoken by her friends, in the looks in her kids' eyes sometimes. As though they don't know the person standing before them.

So yes, she's angry. Angry at others for not having the strength to tell their stories. And at him, POS, for doing this to her in the first place. And mad at herself for thinking she could even possibly get through it all. Like, how fucking dumb is she? There's nothing she can do now.

Well, there is. She could pull the pin. But what good would that do? Absolutely nothing. So instead, she breathes ... and repeats, taking one step at a time.

Her old stubborn part won't let anyone too close, instead she believes she can do this pretty much alone. Revealing as little as possible about what's really going on inside her. Not wanting to involve anyone else in this mess, this shit, this crap. Thankfully though, her more mature self knows that she can't do it alone. That she needs support. That she needs a hand to hold, a body to embrace, a shoulder to sob on, a space to scream into.

None of this stops the overwhelming desire at times to end her life, to simply leave this earthly plane. But then either Big Dog or Little Dog will sense those feelings within her and will come and nudge under her hand, making her touch them, feel them, hear them, know that they are there for her, demanding attention. She can't leave them. She loves them. She is ever so grateful for their presence, their love, accepting that if the time should come when sitting beneath the stars doesn't make her feel any better, then that will be the point in her life, her pivotal moment, to end it. For her, there will no longer be any meaning in her existence.

Somehow, she's sort of managed to get the victim impact statement into some kind of order. It's so hard, when rereading all the pieces of her puzzle, to see where some fit, and where others are still missing. The seemingly never-ending effects of the abuse. It's so overwhelming.

Thank god for the water.

#

The body pains, where and why they occur, is a story of how minds and bodies are so linked, of why metaphysics resonates so completely with her. She wants to scream at those around, as they appear oblivious to her truth – the fact that she feels like she's crumbling, like her body has no support, no strength, no structure. Having to speak is huge, often leaving feelings of vulnerability, doubt, insecurity.

Her ribs are once again sore, feeling as though there's something going straight through her chest and out her back, an image from an earlier memory recalled: Mother Blobfish pierces an arrow through Ana's back, killing her instantly. It hurts, really hurts, both the physical and the emotional, the betrayal, the hatred Mother Blobfish must have had for Ana in that life, and seemingly in this one too.

In a session Mia explains that somehow her shoulder joint is off centre. She's dislocated a bone in her hand and pulled the muscle that runs along the collar bone. There's a spot – on her chest near the scar line, on the right, close to the sternum. Mia's hand pressing on that spot hurts, like really hurts. Her eyes begin to leak. The pain's unbearable. So deep, yet she has no idea why. She shares her past-life image with Mia who replies, "Oh, betrayal".

Yes, that's it. Betrayal. She's feeling betrayed by the legal system, by her family, by life.

#

Pirating, as well as being a space to escape to, is a newfound obsession. The adrenaline rushes, the challenge of being present for others and having to interact with them, combined with the new language of the sea and the physicality of sailing a tall ship, keeps her mind and body busy focusing on something filled with joy. It's amazing how quickly her muscle mass is forming. It's like her body has memory from many years ago when she'd do over four hundred sit ups a day, bench pressing decent weights too, all while trying to give up smoking. She needs her body to be strong. Her mind feels weak. She needs the physical strength to be able to be present at the trial, to be able to stand strong. Pirating's good for that. The wind on her face. Climbing the mast to the highest point. Looking down on life from her dissociated view. Though this time, she's present, very present. She needs to be, for her safety and everyone else's.

Lady Nelson is filled with males. Mainly older, like father or big brother figures. They're nice men, gentle souls, they help teach and encourage her. She loves listening to their stories about their wives, how much they love them, it gives her hope that one day she too may find someone to connect with like that.

One of the guys who is always sailing with her is a Patrick. At first, Ana's like, "What the fuck are you doing to me Universe?" Then, standing back, she realises that perhaps instead of the Universe trying to upset her, it's in fact showing her that not all men named Patrick are horrible, cruel people. In fact, they can be kind, supportive and helpful, just like this Patrick. Together they spend many hours on the water, Patrick teaching, mentoring, explaining, guiding, sometimes frustrated at her use of the word "thingy" for any and everything, her brain too fried to remember the correct terminology.

#

She's been invited to apply for the *Fisher's Ghost Art Award.* Not reading all the details is one of her shortfalls – only ever reading the first two lines of a letter. If nothing of interest is revealed within that space, then she doesn't feel the need to continue. Anyway, all she read was blah blah blah, art award Campbelltown blah blah blah applications closing 5th August blah blah blah.

Without reading the fine print, she makes up her mind to enter a piece, wanting to make a triptych of her breast cast, depicting her journey from abuse to the operation, and what got her through to the present as a flat-chested person trying to fill her life with joy. She doesn't want to use the original cast. That's hers, will always remain hers. It carries the energy, the pain, the loss. It's Ana in her most raw, vulnerable state. So instead, she uses that to mould two new casts, and then Gianna helps make a cast of the new Ana. It's so much fun and just as healing as the first time. She's beginning to love her new form, the shape she now holds. She knows others are still challenged, but that's theirs to carry, not hers.

She wants the first new cast to be symbolic of the abuse, so it's dark, focusing on being entwined in the web of life. There's a tree as the major point of reference in her original cast that she wants to use in the triptych too. She loves trees – they saved her as a child, providing a space to climb. And now as an adult, they give a space to hug and connect with. She wants the last cast to display the peace she's somehow managed to find, so the tree changes somewhat, becoming more symbolic of all that is. The simplicity of the art reflecting the simplicity now present in her life.

She sends an invitation to her good friend and fellow aurora chaser Noah and his partner, asking if they'll come to the opening night. She likes them both, enjoying the dark time she spends with Noah, under the stars, watching the sky dance before their eyes.

So, she's initially upset when she gets the reply, "Sorry, too far to go for one night."

"What? Its only up the road ... a little bit."

Noah sends a map. All she reads, once again missing all the details, is "Campbelltown".

"Yes, what's your point?"

"Looooook, it's not even here, it's like miles and miles and miles away, like overnight and then another overnight and then another overnight to get there."

"What?" she's confused.

Now she reads the finer details. Noah's right, holy shit. Now she must work out some way of getting her art transported to this faraway place near Sydney with only three days left before the competition.

Thankfully Gianna's husband comes up with a really good way of mounting the casts. The hard part's finding a courier that will transport art without it costing a fortune. Apparently, it's a high-risk item, who knew?

A courier's found, her treasures boxed, and she sends them away. She's sad in one way that she won't see them on display or possibly ever again, but she's learned a lesson: Read all the information.

#

We don't do normal. She doesn't anyway. She teaches her kids to dare to be different, to not confirm to the masses, to not become subjected to peer group pressure. She needs to practise what she preaches, which many will say she does exceptionally well. Normal would be one of the last words anyone would use to describe her; she likes it that way. Though sometimes, fitting in and blending with the crowd seems like a viable option. But that isn't her. Even in her darkest hours she still feels it's important to honour who she really is. So, she does. She stands out from others, whether that be in her dress sense, her unique and somewhat quirky way of combining colours and textures, her wild and untameable hair, or her gregarious nature. She simply is Ana.

#

Tiredness. Lack of sleep's common among aurora chasers. Sometimes she just wishes the Universe would give her a night off. After all, she could say no. But can she? Really? Nope. Noahs on the phone hounding her, there's yet another aurora forecast, the third this week. He'll pick her up in twenty.

"Oh, fuck it, you only live once, right? Well, in this life anyway." She drags her weary and not-rested body into some warm clothes, making a thermos of chai, packing her bag, waiting for Noah. In the morning, she's so grateful she has the friends she does, who don't listen when she says "Nooooo I'm too tired" and instead drag her out to be present under such wonder. The sky crystal clear, the Milky Way sparkling with all its five thousand-plus stars visible to the naked eye, the aurora dancing across the sky, as waves of bright blue bioluminescence flash in the waves, a picket fence forming as the aurora changes shape. Like seriously, how can anyone be present under such wonder and not be humbled?

#

There are some funny moments in life, moments that bring you back to simple-ness. One morning, she bent down, toilet paper in hand, expecting to pick up what she believed was a present left behind by either Big Dog or Little Dog only to discover that it was actually a Tektite crystal (helps to open and clear lower chakras, assists one to remain present in body while open to higher consciousness), or what she refers to as alien poo. The laughter escapes her being, echoing throughout the home.

#

Sometimes being stubborn, refusing to give in to the limitations dictated by others, pays off. Just short of a her 52nd birthday, she goes snowboarding for the very first time up on Mt Field with Danika. It's love at first contact. It's so much fun! She spends more time laughing and falling than actually going down the mountain. She doesn't care; she's filled with joy, surrounded by white shhh-y-ness, laughing and laughing till she falls badly. Ouch, she felt that one, she's fallen right on her ribs. She knows the pain; it's a now familiar pain. She's hurt her ribs and curses the fact that she's finally found a need for breasts when hers are gone. Fuck, shit, bum, the pain's pretty bad, but that doesn't stop her. Once again, she's off, sliding down her most favourite mountain, hearing the yells of encouragement from Danika, "Life should always be like this!" When the pain becomes too much, they walk the hour trek back to the car, not caring. She's had one of the best days of her life, defying all those doctors, those experts, with their limiting beliefs, "Fuck them all."

She had a very informative session with Mia after the snowboarding adventure. Diagnosis: two popped ribs, a popped humerus, and whiplash. Thankfully at least she was wearing a helmet. Totally impressive. She's been told to rest up for a few days, something she struggles with especially now as the images, the fear, all become too much. She'd much rather be out walking in Nature, but she can't. Instead, she decides to play around with some images, trying to improve her very limited Photoshop skills, wanting to combine her loves, her joy spaces into the one photo. She has all these ideas, these concepts. She just needs the skills to be able to do it. After hours of learning, she manages to produce a feeling of peace. Combining two spaces: Mt Field covered in white shhh-y-ness, with a moonlit aurora. For Ana at least, those spaces bring joy.

#

In a session with Melisa, they talk about grounding and dissociating methods. She feels herself leaving, quicker and further as the court date looms closer. Each time, it's harder to pull herself back in, knowing she needs to be present now, to stay present till after. It hurts so much though, the pain's overwhelming, the sadness, the anger, the frustration all becoming too much. So, she leaves, she runs away in her mind, it's safer there, safer than here anyway. She feels that possibly having a look inside the courtroom in Hobart will help give her a mental picture of what it may be like in Melbourne. They discuss some other coping strategies, coming up with the following:

Before court: inMelbourne
Being with supportive friends
Going to parks and the beach
Sitting under the stars
Going to galleries
Walking around parts of Melbourne that have good memories

During court
Hankies with familiar, comforting smells on them
Crystals ... Yes, she knows she'll get them into the court room, no matter what.
Having bare feet on the floor, if possible.
Touching a chair ... cold surfaces
Textured clothing
Crystal necklaces

After court
Go on Puffing Billy
Head to a beach if possible, walk in the waves, cleanse the soul
Have friends around

#

The thing she's looking forward to when all of this is over is some more EMDR sessions. She clearly remembers the impact from some sessions over twenty years ago. It worked so well that she now can't remember exactly who it was that shoved their penis in her mouth at the same time someone else shoved their penis where no penis should go in someone so young – the reason the others, Otto and Donny Bowman, can't be charged. How fucked is that? It's like, by trying to heal from some of the trauma, so wanting to bite that penis off, she's compromised possible accountability for that penis owner. It just doesn't make sense. Which is why she's decided: no sessions till after the trial. She needs to display her raw form in court, not the slightly healed form. Does that make sense?

#

Not exactly the birthday she'd hoped for. She wants to head out, dive under the water, hike a mountain, climb a tree. Instead, she's meeting Melisa out the front of the Hobart Supreme Court.

Melisa's arranged for a very kind and gentle man to show them around. As they're led into the court room, she just can't seem to get herself inside the space. It's like there's this negative energy shield stopping her. She uses Melisa's body as a buffer between her and the energy, feeling so bad that she's putting Melisa in that space. But she can't help it, she can't handle the feeling. It's like he's here. It's like she's in Melbourne. Her body's shaking. She's left the building.

The lovely court man notices Ana's unease and leads them into the waiting room, talking about the court system, answering any questions she has, like, "Can I simply leave?" "Can it be made so I don't have to see or hear him?" "Can I kill him? Is that ok?"

Everything's fuzzy, muffled. It's so fucked. This isn't even the court that's she's supposed to be present in with him, yet she can't even be present here, in this court, which is so far removed from the impending reality. Even though the whole process takes less than thirty minutes, it feels like a lifetime's passed. She needs to get out of there, unable to take another breath in that space. She's grateful that such beautiful green, lush grass awaits her soon-to-be-bare feet – lovely grounding energy.

Melisa presents Ana with a birthday present, a pile of plain white plates, for her to write on and then smash the crap out of after the trial. Such a thoughtful, appropriate gift that she's overwhelmed. She talks with Melisa, calming herself, breathing. Then she heads out for a snorkel, the brash water bringing her back in, washing away all the negativity she feels clinging to her every cell. The trial day's looming ever closer, causing more and more anxiety within, making it all more real. Is she ready? She doesn't think so … fuck.

Chapter 35

Strength – physically, mentally

All these amazing, wondrous experiences keep appearing, reminding her of the joys of living, reminding Ana that she's worthy. Somehow amongst all the many incredibly talented artists who submitted work for the *Fisher's Ghost Art Award*, her piece, *Sacred Space* is a finalist. It will be displayed in Sydney. How incredible is that? It's weird though, the art pieces had to be submitted without any stories. She hopes she's been able to tell her story with respect and honour through her creation.

#

She needs to get her body super strong. It needs to be in peak condition, stronger, faster, than ever before. She looks fit, others comment, but she doesn't feel it. She needs to be able to crush him in one hand, to see him crumble before her, just like how she's been feeling all these years.

The constant body pain is a daily reminder of the pain she feels within, unseen by any. The pain keeps it real, keeps her feeling, keeps her motivated.

The legal team are trying hard to convince her that her physical presence in court will carry a lot more weight than if the jury sees her via a video link. She's unable to understand this, and hates feeling pressured into being in the same room as him. Honestly, she doesn't know if she'll physically be able to. The vomit that she's so long suppressed could quite easily and understandably erupt, spewing forth from her being, hopefully spewing all over him. The process seems more centred around making things comfortable for him, about making sure he's ok. Like, what the fuck? Why is his comfort even a thing worth considering?

Melisa and Ana sit, talking, going over the trial, the process. Ana's anxiety rises, but she doesn't really have the brain space to deal with any of that right now. Her clothing reflects a doesn't-give-a-crap attitude. It's drab and colourless. So unusual for her. So different from her normal daily colours.

Melisa suggests two sessions after the trial. Part of Ana wants to keep seeing Melisa forever and ever, they're like a sanity space, a calm space, a safe space.

"Do I really have to give you up?" she screams in her mind, knowing she does, knowing that unfortunately there are so many others out there who too share stories like hers. When the fuck is it going to stop? There's a Skype session with the OPP in Melisa's office. Ana knows she's already left before they all enter the room. They want to go over her statement, pretend to ask questions they feel the other side will ask, but Ana can't, she never wants to see those words, read that statement, ever again. So, she doesn't, she leaves her body, leaves the room, jumps in her car and drives.

Not a good option. She only narrowly avoids an accident, which in one way brings her back into her body. She really should have left the car there and taken the bus home, but in the moment, she doesn't think of that, can't think of that. So instead, she drives, knowing she's completely absent from her body.

#

Something's happened at the family home; she has had to move back there so much sooner than she'd planned. She's not ready to be present for the kids again, to be a mum, to be a person. The trial is in a matter of weeks. She just wants to breathe but feels totally unable. Instead of focusing on self-care measures, she's busy packing up her divine little home, her sanity cave at Gianna's, the space she loves with all her heart, and moving back to that house. She needs to reclaim it, to cleanse it, to rearrange it. It's her space now.

How she's going to financially afford that house is beyond her in this moment, but she must be able, otherwise Spirit wouldn't have sent her back. She reminds herself to have faith, to trust that all will be well. She's struggling to get her head around how all of this happened, how she's suddenly thrown back as quickly as she left. She doesn't want to be there. She wants, no, she *needs* to be alone. But she doesn't have a choice. She's a mum.

She knows she's stronger than when she left seven months earlier, but in that time she's become very sensitive to two major triggers – negativity and tones. Now she has to be present with two moody teenagers. Go figure.

Too many changes. She wants the world to stop moving, to stay still for a moment, for a space, for a breath. She feels like she's drowning, with the only life raft being herself. But she feels as though she's full of holes, that the air will simply spurt out everywhere as she sinks slowly to the darkest depths.

She used to love changes, rearranging the furniture, moving to a new house, changing friends, towns, cars, clothes. But now, she can't deal with change, has no brain space for change, instead she wishes for the simple pleasure of a monotone existence.

Oscar and Felix, another friend met through the walking group (they're just like the TV Oscar and Felix, *The Odd Couple*, so different yet so alike) help move her back to the house. She nicknames them the "two grumpy old men", suggesting it as a name for their new removal business.

They're not really grumpy, they are wonderful friends and super funny. They lift, take away, put down, re-arrange the furniture for the third time, as Ana walks around, drumming and smudging, the intent of what she'd like in her space always present in her heart. It's exciting on that level, to create a nurturing, safe space.

#

Trees have always brought joy and comfort. They have always been safe spaces. So, when she sees there's a recreational tree-climbing group in the local area, she climbs. It's super cool, climbing trees as an adult, not getting told off. She's never understood why tree climbing became such a dangerous activity, believing instead that tree climbing skills are a vital part to anyone's learnings. She loves climbing to the highest heights, even higher than on the Lady Nelson, to look below, to sit in the canopy, to be present with the birds, to embrace the silence of wind amongst the leaves. Oh, such joy.

Whenever the chance arrives, she climbs. Either trees or the masts on Lady Nelson. It's her go-to space, climbing higher and higher until there is no more. So high that everything looks so little, reflecting how everything feels when she's detached.

Patrick often sails with her, as do the same couple of women. As the trial gets closer, she shares what's happening for her. She feels herself leaving sometimes while on the boat, and she knows that's not good. She needs to learn to step back when she's stepped out.

The other crew are fantastic, ever so supportive, such kindred souls upon the water, leaving her finding much solace onboard Lady Nelson. At times it can be hard though, mentally having to get used to allowing others into her personal space, to listen to the directions from another, something she's not keen on. Some of the people she finds more challenging, just different personalities, different tones. Sometimes she leaks unseen tears behind sunglasses, sometimes, when she thinks of giving up, she reminds herself how good it is for her physicality, her soul, and her mind most of the time. How these moments of conflict may in actual fact be teaching her more than she realises.

#

It's the last session with Melisa before the trial. They head to the kids' room, the perfect space. Melisa even has glitter playdough waiting. Ana loves the feel of the playdough, the tactileness of it, the pliability of it, the way she can transform it as they speak, creating anything she wants, and then, in the next breath, destroy it, crushing it, distorting it. Then rebuilding it.

Melisa explains that a new law's being passed, a law that will allow her to tell her whole story in court. Currently. only the parts of the story directly linked to the charges are allowed to be spoken. It makes no sense, as there's so much more to her story, to anyone's story, than the crime. There's a whole lifetime of story that deserves a space to be heard. Hopefully now her story will be heard.

There're only two charges left from the original eleven, the others having been dismissed basically because she can't be 100% sure on dates and her exact age. It does her head in. Like, how is she meant to remember dates, times, exact ages. She was a fucking child! They seem to forget that minor fact. It all works well for him, for POS, but gives Ana even more determination to have him found guilty on the remaining two.

She shares with Melisa how she's been writing her life story. That she thought when she turned forty that would be the end, then when she turned fifty it still didn't feel right, Melisa asks if she feels that the time is coming to end her story.

"I guess my story will end when I die, but different chapters can end along the way. I truly hope that after court, when things have settled, when life becomes more 'normal', when there's space in my head, then maybe this chapter can end."

Melisa suggests that Ana takes herself as a child into the courtroom. "What? To be present with him?"

Her whole body's reacting negatively to this idea, shrinking in upon itself, trying to find a space to hide … away from him.

How can she possibly put herself as a child, back anywhere near him? Yet she knows she must, feeling it deep within her soul, knowing by her reaction that this is something she must do, but how? She doesn't feel connected to her child self. If she's scared going to court, then her child self is petrified. She knows she has to be the voice for her child self, but it's hard, she has no idea what her child voice sounds like, it's been silenced for so long.

She shares with Melisa how she still holds shame about what happened, that she didn't stick up for herself, that she didn't scream and shout, that she didn't tell him to stop. But he was so much bigger and scarier and older, his words echoing for all time, "Tell anyone and I'll kill you." She believed him then, part of her still believes him. He's mean. He's cruel.

She remembers seeing him hanging with his gang, an ice-cream container lid in one hand. POS lit the lid, the plastic melting and dripping, dripping onto the ants nests he stood over, dominating, hurting. Even back then she knew he was a cruel, evil, horrible person, and hoped the ants would bite him, again and again and again. She thinks it's ironic that he'd chosen ants to dominate, ants, she knows, carry special energy. They are super strong. They reflect cooperation, collaboration and community, everything POS lacks. She's arranged a session with Kimberly for after the trial, over the phone while she's in Melbourne. This is so fucked, it should be in person, but she won't be in her home space, she won't be surrounded by all the things that bring her joy. No, instead she'll be present in a space that she's has only returned to twice over the last thirty years. There's a reason why she doesn't go back. Yet soon she will. She really has no choice.

#

Reclaiming her space is at least something different to focus on. She's furnished the bottom part of the house, hoping it reflects peace and tranquility, her books and crystals taking pride of place. She likes the feel of it, it welcomes her when she enters, holds her while she's present. Eating on the balcony is one of her joys, looking across the River Derwent through the many varied trees, listening to the bird calls, inhaling the flower scents.

While eating dinner a week before the trial, she feels a great sense of peace come over her, leaving her feeling like a butterfly about to break free of the cocoon. "The worst is now behind you," she hears from Spirit, yet her mind still holds doubts.

Being able to tell her story, its impact, its devastation, is so empowering. In telling it in its entirety, well ... the limited amount in court, but still more than she was previously able to, she's giving herself a voice. She believes that this is why she's had to wait so long to have her case heard. This new law had to be put in place, so she can have a voice and, more importantly, so she will be heard.

Some much-needed soul space is provided. Even though it's spring, a large amount of snow has fallen at Mt Field. She goes there to sit amid its whiteness, to be engulfed by its shhh-y-ness, to focus on joy rather than the trial, to remember to breathe and repeat.

Chapter 36

$(3 + 6 = 9)$ Completion

Its time. Ana's in Melbourne. She has no idea how she's standing; she accepts breathing as part of living; she gives thanks to her body for how she's moving.

Jacks come, thankfully, someone's hand she can dig her nails into, someone who can handle her frustrated flapping and slapping. She doesn't hurt him, not at all. She just feels all this pain, this anger, this rage inside, with each step closer to where she knows POS will be. Her body needs to allow these emotions to come out healthily, and Jack can safely hold them.

She has no idea how she even got to Melbourne. It's like she had one huge panic attack that she's not sure is over. In fact, she's pretty sure it's still happening. She's unable to recall the drive to the airport, checking in, flying, getting off the plane, breathing in the stinking foreign smell of a city, arriving at the accommodation, none of it. It's all so distant, like it's over her shoulder, behind her. She's unable to put any of it in front of her eyes, unable to allow it into her space. She feels like a zombie, numb, indifferent, ready to attack and kill for her own survival.

She and Jack spend the weekend trying to ground her, walking around the city, enjoying the good parts of being back in that space. She remembers when she rode a pedicab, how she would zoom through the city streets on her bicycle delivering parcels, or ride to work along the river, or row on the lake. She remembers school excursions to the museum and art gallery and focuses on all the things she loved about this space.

Olivia comes down and goes over their role in court along with Astrid's. Ana's feeling the support, the love, not just from those present with her in Melbourne but from all her friends and family back home. She knows this is so much more than simply her story, she needs to remember that, to keep it close, to stand strong and speak for many.

It's Monday morning, the day before the trial actually begins, the day before she's required to be physically present in the courtroom with him. Olivia and Ana are walking in the Botanical Gardens, Jack's taken some downtime before it's time for the shit to hit the fan. The gardens are a place she's always sought refuge; a place she'd bring Esi to play amongst the autumn leaves. Those images are now gracing her vision.

They sit for a coffee; Ana chooses hot chocolate. Olivia's speaking, but their voice sounds a million miles away, Ana keeps touching the cold table trying to keep herself present. The trial has started. The lawyers and judge are all in the courtroom going over everything, predetermining what will and won't be allowed in the trial. Ana doesn't understand why this wasn't done before the actual court process started. She's unable to focus with so much uncertainty floating on the wind.

#

Later, a lot later, she receives the transcript of the conversation in the court room that day. She reads the questioning of the judge:

Why is this case even in court? We're talking about something that happened 44 years ago. The complainant will be cross examined, witnesses dragged in, counsel here, money paid, court resources being used about something that happened 44 years ago, when he was possibly 14–15 years old and she was possibly 10 years. What happened to the word common sense? Can anyone in the courtroom find common sense somewhere? It would be different if we were dealing with people who had been older, say 18 or 19 years, but we're dealing with young people a long time ago.

This is what the judge thinks about her case. That her being young, that all of this happening so long ago, that she was not able to remember exact dates, all this was actually a handicap. They were trying to make sure that he was no more than 14 years old. It seems that if he was 15 years old (he was up to nearly 17 years old when it finally stopped) he would be dealing with a tougher sentencing. How is there any justice in the world?

#

But she doesn't know this right now. She just knows the waiting, the inability to focus, the inability to hear Olivia who is there waiting with her.

Her phone rings. It's the OPP. They explain that it appears it's going to be hard to convict him, to prove he was the ages she knows he was when the assaults happened. They say that her inability to remember the exact dates is letting him escape the charges. They do not say that the judge thinks this case is a waste of time and resources. This is so fucked. She feels herself melting into the ground, becoming stuck between the blades of grass, dragging their tips to the ground, covering them in mud. If she can't remember the specifics then they will throw the case out? Like, what? How? Why? Why now? Why is this only being spoken, suggested, now? The day before the actual trial starts, when she's over in Melbourne and not at home where it's safe.

Olivia's staring, wondering what's going on, hearing the changed tone in their friend's voice, but unable to offer support.

What Ana feels she's hearing, is that the last four years, all her last fifty-three years, forty-six carrying this load, can possibly be thrown out of court simply because she can't remember exact dates of something that happened to her as a 6 year old, 7, 8, 9, 10, 11 and 12 year old, where's the fucking justice in any of that?

The OPP explains the options: she can go to trial with the chance of the trial possibly being thrown out, or she can accept the plea POS has agreed to. They believe if she stays committed to the trial, then she runs the risk of it being thrown out due to lack of evidence, due to lack of exact dates. Or she can accept the pleas of two counts of indecent assault. "What exactly does that mean?" she asks. She wants him charged with sexual penetration. He did that, numerous times. She wants him held accountable for that act. Is that one of the charges? They give her forty- five minutes to decide.

This is so wrong, so FUCKED. It leaves her feeling like her head's going to explode.

She calls Kimberly who's in a session, then Melisa, who gets back within five minutes. Ana explains what's going on, Melisa then reflects it all back in a calming tone, asking how she would feel given each scenario. This is all too much. How's anyone meant to process and decide under such circumstances? Melisa reminds her of what she wanted as the outcome of all of this, what her original reasoning behind laying the charges was. She asks what she would be able to live with? These questions, all of which are great, help her head to stop spinning.

She wanted him to be held accountable. She wanted her story to be told, to be heard, validated.

"So," asks Melisa. "How will you feel if you take the plea?"

Ana thinks for a moment.

"I'll feel as though I've let myself down, as though I haven't honoured my story. And another part of me will be relieved. It will all be over, and I won't have to be present in court, in front of the jury, being questioned again and again, like in the committal. The committal nearly killed me."

Ana tries to make a decision. One she can sleep with. One hopefully her soul will be able to rest with.

Olivia's looking perplexed, hearing only one side of the conversation, asking with their eyes what the fuck is going on as they watch their friend crumble.

Ana looks around at her surroundings, grateful to be in this space, the green grass, the tall trees, the ducks splashing on the lake, while dealing with this absolute shit. Time's running out as Melisa and Ana go over different scenarios. Ana tunes into her body, listening to what it wants, what it needs. She knows what she has to do, what she needs to do for her for her sanity, her continuing life, and tells Melisa she'll take the plea, thanking them for their time, then quickly calling the OPP back.

She lets the OPP know her decision, stressing how unhappy she is about any of it, about having to make such a life-impacting decision in such a short time with no warning. They go over the plea. She wants clarity that in fact he will be charged.

"Yes," they assure her, though he won't do jail time. That was always highly unlikely, given the historical nature of the case, his age, and the laws pertaining to that time. Ana asks if her story will still be told. All of it?

"Yes." At the sentencing she'll have a chance to read out her victim impact statement. She takes a breath as the world spins around her.

Ok, she'll accept the plea of guilty on two charges of indecent assault, one of which must be sexual penetration.

They tell Ana she needs to be in court tomorrow. Like really? For fuck's sake. She just wants it all to go away, so she can go home and cuddle Big Dog and Little Dog, and breath in the cleanest air in the world. She's moving further and further from her body, leaving Earth behind, her body behind, her story behind. The rest of the day becomes a blur as Jack whisks her off to the seaside for some much-needed solitude.

#

She and Olivia sit in the OPP's room the next morning as they explain what's just happened and what will happen next.

Patrick O'Shanesy is charged with

One count of indecent assault of a girl under the age of 16 years, One count of sexual penetration of a girl under the age of 16 years.

The accused pleads **GUILTY**.

The shame Ana feels about herself stops the moment she hears that word.

GUILTY

Hearing those words, "sexual penetration" (it should be rape, that's what he did), that is what gets her. He's now been found guilty of the act he has been denying the whole time. Even if it's only one count, not the many that she knows actually happened, there it is in black and white for the world to see.

Sentencing will be in two weeks.

"Do you want to be present for that?"

Does she really want to come back and be in the same space as him? "For sure."

It's her chance to speak her story, and she wants to do that in person. She can do this, she knows she can. She's so strong now.

Guilty. Guilty. Fucking GUILTY.

Eat shit and die, motherfucker.

She can now stand with grace, even surrounded by his energy, his shit.

#

Back home, she hopes that life will regain some normality before she has to head back to Melbourne. Thankfully there's a multi-day trip on Lady Nelson, three days and two nights on the water. The sea soothes her soul, she so needs this, to be away, to be physically exhausted so that she'll sleep at night. She needs it to take her mind away from the upcoming sentencing.

The hard part, though, is the lack of space on Lady Nelson. She needs space, time alone, time to breathe. She struggles to stay present in an area that doesn't provide any space. She didn't really think this through. The close quarters, the being with strangers hadn't entered her mind. Instead, she'd only seen the open waters, the climbable masts the sea life ... now among it all she has no choice; she must make the most of it.

As often as possible she climbs to the main topgallant or to the tip of the outer jib, bouncing around on the bowsprit, removed from the deck, from others. At one point she's asked to go into the chain locker, to help with flaking the anchor chain as the anchor's raised. She looks into the space, immediately struggling. She knows she can't do that; she can't go into that closed in space. She knows she'll be a mess if she does, so she turns to the master and says, "No."

It doesn't go down well and leaves her feeling even worse than she already did. She just knows she can't get into that space. She'll feel trapped, she'll have no fresh air, no windows, no escape. Nope. Not going to happen. But she feels as though she's let the crew down, as though they think less of her now, and she wants to run away. She can't physically get away, so instead, she runs away in her head.

People don't seem to understand mental health. The limitations of someone with a physical health problem, like a broken arm for example, are much easier to accept than the unknown space of mental unease.

She's completely exhausted, tired, wrecked on the return journey, nanny napping with Patrick on deck as they head up the River Derwent after crossing Storm Bay. Now that's a patch of water. She'll be happy if she never experiences its unpredictability ever again. It's great if there's light winds, but if not, it's hell. Lady Nelson rolls one way as the swell rolls another, then add in climbing the masts. She is swiveled like a corkscrew; all she wants to do is vomit. Then it becomes calm again.

She feels much stronger after three days of constant physical activity. In some ways it's wonderful pushing her body to its limits, but the psychological part, that, she can do without.

#

Even though Ana's physically home, she feels so very far away. She's yet to come back into her body since being in Melbourne, unable to grab hold of anything tangible to bring her in. Snorkeling doesn't help, the bracing cold water that usually shocks isn't working. Nothing is. She feels numb, separate, not here. Part of her has changed forever, now preferring silence over the need to speak. She used to have to tell her story, whatever part of it was relevant (or not) to any conversation. Instead, now she remains silent, pondering, reflecting before speaking or reacting. Sometimes she chooses not to speak at all, in the emptiness of silence questions can be left hanging, uncertainties allowed to flourish.

Sometimes people feel she isn't paying attention. She is, it's just that she doesn't feel that words need to occupy the space.

In part, she feels better about taking the plea. She doesn't feel that she's betrayed herself so much after unpacking the whole pile of shit crap of Melbourne with some close friends. She's able to see it from different perspectives. Able to see it for what it is. She went through the whole legal process wanting him to take accountability, and she got that. Not perhaps in the way she foresaw, but nevertheless, he's convicted in a court of law on two charges of assault against her. That sort of takes away the sting of feeling as though she compromised herself in accepting the plea.

Melisa asks how she feels her mental health is as they sit in the second-last session. She sits in silence, reflecting, querying, checking in with herself.

"I'll be ok."

They talk about how she'd like to end their sessions, Melisa's picked up that Ana likes rituals, activities to conclude events in her life. Again, she sits a while in silence, watching the shadows of leaves play on the wall behind Melisa.

"I know. How about we go to the park and write words on leaves, then leave the leaves for the wind to carry away? How does that feel for you?"

Melisa thinks it's a great idea.

Chapter 37

A reason to live

It's back to Melbourne, Jack's with her. Astrid and Olivia are going to the sentencing too; Astrid arrives at the motel room early in the morning with some of the most divine croissants ever. They share the story behind the copious number of pastries. Astrid had told the owners about Ana and what she'd done and how today was the sentencing day. The owner was so moved by the story he gifted some divine yumminess in the form of a variety of croissants to focus on. Such a beautiful soul. Ana's eyes leak as Astrid speaks. There truly are wonderful people in this world.

They head to court and sit at the tables outside. As they wait for the court to open, her anxiety builds. Does she really need to be in the same space as him? Yes, she knows she does. She needs to do this, to stand tall, to speak her truth, to stand in her strength.

Ana's on edge. Every part of her being is awake, alert. Her spidery senses are in overdrive. She doesn't want to go anywhere near him, doesn't want to breathe the same air as him, doesn't want to walk the same path as him. When they head into court, she's a tad nervous. Around her belly, hidden in a running belt, are all her crystals – green tourmaline, green calcite, rose quartz, amethyst, black tourmaline, tektite, and of course a Shiva lingam. Somehow, she's through the other side with all the crystal energy still encasing her. She slides her hand under her top, feeling their familiarity, their energies – the smoothness of the Shiva, the rugged jagged surface of the green tourmaline full of healing properties. She's comforted by their presence, grateful for all their supportive energies. She takes a big deep breath, drawing it up into her lungs, looking to her friends, seeing their love for her reflected in their faces, but when they get into the lift, her breathing's shallow and fast. She wants to run, so far, far, far away.

The lift doors open, she knows he's there, she can sense his energy, his putridness. They turn the corner, there he is, she sees him, her body collapsing under the enormity of being so close to him. The police lead them into a private room. She can breathe, a little. She bangs her head against the wall, in that moment realising why this is something she's done all her life. She likes the pain it causes, the distraction to whatever's going on in her head. She focuses on the physical pain, the sound created by her head hitting the wall. Jack tries to stop her, but she pushes his hand away. He doesn't know, he doesn't understand, this is actually her way of coping with what's currently going on, her way of dealing with him, POS, being just there, only metres away. It's way too much for her to be able to stand in and remain normal.

It's time to go into the court room. POS has gone first; he's sitting right at the back. It's like he's in the naughty corner where he belongs. They did this so she doesn't have to have him in her field of view.

Jacks by her side, holding her hand tightly, crushing it with his big bear-like mitts. Astrid and Olivia place themselves directly behind Ana, acting as a shield between her and POS.

As she stands to read her impact statement, Jack remains seated, head bowed, tears running down his cheeks as Ana's words invade the space. Her statement, in a very little way, is representative of the many impacts the actions of POS has had over her life, especially after she became a mother, responsible for others, having to protect her children. It wasn't a stranger who had done these horrible things to her, but someone known to her family, possibly part of her family, one of her neighbours, her peers. She wasn't going to let that happen to her children. Before motherhood, her actions, her choices in how she dealt with her past affected only herself, resulting in some really dumb life-challenging activities. But her actions, her choices, affected others, once she became a mother. Her belief in herself, in her ability to parent is crap. She truly feels she's failed miserably as a parent, a mother, a mum, a human being.

Collapsing back into the chair, she lets it hold her. She's finished. She's done. Jack turns, looking at her with so much love, and right in that moment she wants to kiss him, wanting to become enveloped in his embrace. But that will have to wait. For now, she needs to try and pay attention to what the judge's saying. She can't, she's too far gone. Instead, she lets it be, hoping her friends will be able to fill the gaps.

> HER HONOUR: *Patrick O'Shaunessy, you have pleaded guilty to two charges of indecent assault. The maximum penalty for this offence is five years.*
>
> *It is well-established that sexual offending such as yours causes great psychological harm to the victim. It was abundantly clear from Ana's victim impact statement that your offending had a drastic effect on her wellbeing and her self-worth. Her victim impact statement was read to the court, and while I do not intend to repeat it again in this sentence, I will come back to it a little later.*
>
> *Your counsel tendered a psychiatric report concluding that you did not meet the criteria for paraphilia, and that there was no indication that you suffered from that condition in the past. He accepted your explanation that the offending took place when you were in emotional turmoil as a result of the continued harassment and extreme bullying from your peers. At the time you were also deeply confused about sexual matters because of issues in your family. In his opinion some 40 years later, your risk of sexual recidivism is low.*

Like how the fuck does that justify his fucking behaviour? This is so wrong; she knows the truth; she knows she wasn't the only one. This is so fucked.

> *Your plea of guilty, which was submitted, has significant utilitarian value, saving the community the cost of a trial,*

and the complainant the necessity and trauma of giving evidence at your trial.

I will take into account your genuine and deeply felt regret and remorse, which you have expressed in your interview with your counsel, in your session with your psychologist, in the police interview, and in the letter read to the court;

I will take into account your prior good character and lack of subsequent offending, the former being supported by numerous references on your behalf, tendered by your counsel.

I will take into account the delay of 41 years between your offending and charging, which meant that you have lived with the anxiety of a potential term of imprisonment and loss of employment weighing on you.

So therefore, he must be such a good person that there is justification and reasoning for his behaviour? That he has repented? Like fuck. Nothing he's done in any way shape or form has helped her, yet this obviously isn't about Ana, it's about him, it's about what he has had to live with for the last 41 years, what he's had to carry. FUCK OFF, if he was truly remorseful would you then assume that he would have taken ownership of his actions way before she found the strength to tell all. But he didn't. He also didn't admit to sexual intercourse before the trial, so how the fuck is that remorseful? Such a good guy? FUCKING BULLSHIT!

In addition, your counsel relied on two decisions of the Court of Appeal, in submitting that given your young age when you committed the offences, general deterrence and moral culpability had a far lesser role to play in sentencing. If you had been sentenced by the Children's Court at the time you committed the offences, it would have been unlikely that you would have received a conviction.

But we're not in the 1970s we're in the 2000s. It's so fucked, this legal system.

> *The prosecutor accepted that given your young age when you offended, and the long period of time that had passed since, a gaol sentence was not appropriate. In addition, the prosecution accepted that it would not have been unusual back when you offended for you to have received no conviction. It was also accepted that general deterrence was of lesser importance, albeit not extinguished completely.*
>
> *However, the prosecutor also pointed out to the great emotional suffering of Ms Suci. In doing so, she referred to Vincent J in the case of DPP v Toomey, where he said: "It is well to bear in mind the rehabilitation of the victim of sexual abuse may often be more difficult to achieve than that of the perpetrator. Frequently the damage will be profound. A long time will pass before it can be addressed at all. In the meanwhile, childhood will be destroyed and self-esteem damaged, educational and career opportunities lost, and the capacity to form and maintain relationships seriously impaired".*

Ana's so confused. They are referring to how much of an impact this has on the lives of people like her, yet she sees no reflection of that. Not in the sentencing, nor the punishment.

> *While your own difficulties at the time with respect to the bullying by your peers and your classmates do not excuse your behaviour, they offer some explanation for it.*

She's so lost, unable to comprehend what's being said. What does this mean? That he'll get a slap on the wrist? She's done, removing herself even further from being present in this fucked-up space.

In all the circumstances of this case, I consider that the most appropriate sentencing disposition is that you be released on a good behaviour bond with a condition that you pay the sum of $2,000 to the Brave Hearts Foundation.

FUCK OFF, is this real? Is she hearing this correctly?

In her victim impact statement, Ms Suci described your sexual offending as being something that had altered her whole being on every level, emotionally physically and mentally. She was filled with self-disgust and loathing. She wanted to hide, not be seen, and to wash away herself. It perpetrated and stained the core of her being.

The Brave Heart Foundation deals with children who have suffered sexual trauma and sexual assault.

But for your plea of guilty, you would have been convicted and sentenced to a community corrections order for 12 months with 180 hours of community work.

What? So, what does that mean? He's not convicted. What the fuck? This is soooooooo fucked. She feels she has nowhere to go. Her mind's exploded, her soul's shattered, her heart's broken, her faith in humanity, in the legal system, is gone.

#

Police Officer David calls her aside after the sentencing.

"I have something I wish to share with you. I feel you have every right to know this fact and we believe this witness. This particular witness stated that they saw what was being done to you, that they then went and told your parents what they'd seen. This person knows from what they observed that nothing was done about it by your parents."

Unable to comprehend what's being said, or the total feeling of betrayal running through her being, Ana simply walks away. It's all too much, she needs space right in this moment, not to try and make room for more fucked-up-ness, there will be time for that later. Before heading to the airport, she walks through the gardens. A certain tree calls her, she walks up to it and feels its energy, she hugs it, feeling its strength, listening, hearing the words, "Free to go." Her eyes start leaking, she's done.

She heads home, not wanting to be present a moment longer, needing Big Dog and Little Dog, needing her home, her space. Mother Nature has her back; there's an aurora that night. A blessing of wonder after all she's just achieved. As fucked as it was, it's something that not many people get to do, which alone is so super fucked. Her historical childhood sexual assault case made it to court. He pleaded guilty. She was heard. That alone, she needs to remind herself, is something she should feel proud of. Yet she feels that she compromised herself, and others.

#

She feels such a need to go and see Father Bullshark. She needs to see the look on his face when she tells him that POS, someone he and Mother Blobfish had in their home, someone they were told was doing shit to their daughter and yet they chose for whatever fucked up reason to do nothing about, has been found guilty of sexual assault. How fucking good do you feel now, you piece of crap? She knows it was probably wrong, but she doesn't care. It feels so good. Fuck him.

#

An admission of guilt does not result in an equal reflection within the legal system. Ana struggles to make sense of any of it, to try and rationalise, to find reason amid the chaos. She ponders, and in doing so comes across these reflections.

Her passion for the night sky, its solitude, space, and total wonderment of all that Mother Nature provides, has allowed a space to simply be present amid some of the most intense moments of life. Through that passion, she has fallen in love, both with Mother Nature and a beautiful being – Jack – a love so deep, so meaningful, so profound, it leaves her dizzy in its wake. She'd never really got friendships, never having that trust and allowance of letting others in. Happily, now though, she feels truly honoured and blessed to have the most divine souls she calls friends. She's not been alone on this journey; many have helped to carry her pain, acknowledging, embracing, and seeing her before she could even see herself.

To say that the last four years has been worth it, worth the pain, that the going to the deepest darkest recesses of her soul, the searching, the learning, the growing, has been a joy, is a big fat lie. It was fucking horrible. But she knows deep within her soul that no matter what, she did it, she spoke up, she became visible to herself and many others, she shared her pain, and in return, is honoured to share others'. She would never, ever, advise anyone to do what she did, yet in the same breath she can't help but give thanks to herself for doing so. Her faith, her belief, her love of Mother Nature, her so incredible inspiring and wonderful friends and family, her love, make up a journey that she's eternally grateful to have travelled. She's found a reason, amid all the chaos, to keep living.

Chapter 38

No more words

Talk therapies are wonderful, offering lots to lots of people, but at the moment she's over talking. She's not even sure she wants EMDR. Instead, she wants physical therapies, touch therapies, wanting to feel the healing, therapeutic safe touch of a trusted therapist. She wants lots and lots and lots of Bowen sessions with Mia. Her body is so reactive to Mia's touch. It screams out with joy as years and years of lifetime pains are released. That's what she needs right now – physical release.

#

Her time with Melisa is ending. Ana still feels that there's two separate parts of her – one part she loves, is proud of, finds peace and joy in; the other she hates, it brings pain, inner turmoil, and disgustingness, still. The last session with Melisa is rather weird and very sad. Even though they've only been present in her life for about two years, she feels as though Melisa's played such a huge role in the journey. They walk to the nearby park overlooking kunanyi/Mt Wellington, and find a big tree to sit under, bringing in the leaves already present and adding to them. They write words on the leaves about the journey, the hope, the disappointment, the anger, the happiness, the legal system, and leave them on the ground, knowing the wind will take them away, possibly resettling them on earth in another space. Then nature will proceed to do what it does best – absorb. Turning it all into nurturing goodness.

When they've finished, Ana looks at the words before her. If she'd done this exercise three years ago, she's sure the words would have been very different – negative, pain-filled. The words before her today, in this space, with the legal stuff behind, are positive. She's grateful for the journey. As hard and it was, much harder than she'd ever envisioned, as much as the roller coaster wouldn't slow, instead picking up speed, as much as the losses incurred hurt and still do, she can honestly say she's grateful she had the strength even in the weakest moments to do this, to gift herself a voice. She's done a drawing for Melisa, and hands it to her, and in doing so, knows their time together has ended. Her eyes leak tears of gratitude.

#

She sits, pondering, breathing, often shaking her head, allowing moments of anger and despair to wash over, becoming all-consuming in their rawness. There were moments, more than she'd like to recall, where a way out that didn't involve ending her life seemed distant and unobtainable. Where the darkness was never ending, the sadness and complete lack of faith in humanity and the legal system beyond comprehension, all manifesting as a black hole forming7 an abyss into the unknown. All for her to be reformed, re-created, and rebirthed into a new world full of wonderment and awe.

It took four years for her newness to come into its own, for her to be able to find a space of peace with all that she is. Four years of growth through extreme hardship, heartbreak, not knowing, frustration, tears; and immense, extreme, intense, wonderment, joy, and connections. Unfortunately, it's not a majik transformation. The path didn't suddenly become all roses. The pain of the path already trod didn't just get wiped clean. She still carries all that weight, and now it's time to try and sort through it, acknowledge what was, and allow what is. It's a process, she's aware of that, she needs to be kind to herself, to love herself …

Now *that's* the challenge.

#

When she started this whole legal process, her intention was to have POS held accountable for what he did to her, what he took from her. She has done that. So now she sits, pondering what her next lot of intentions will be.

"My intent is to write my book. To place upon the pages the emotions, lessons and growth of my journey to court. My intent is to work on my astro-photography and underwater photography to produce the results I see clearly in my mind's eye. My intent is to create works of art that speak to others. My intent is to continue to express joy and wonderment in every day, to find a sense of adventure with every step. My intent is to always have love present. My intent is to be in a healthy, balanced, expressive relationship. My intent is to live, to be happy, to create majik and wonder, to breathe and repeat, and always be grateful."

Sometimes she feels she has much to offer in helping others, talking to others, about life, about shit, about joy, about how to obtain it and maintain it. Sometimes she envisions a future where she'll be working with and talking with people, sharing her many life lessons and how through faith, trust, good friendships, and Mother Nature, she made it, tainted but still surprisingly somewhat sane.

#

It's been a busy few months on Lady Nelson. Lots and lots of sails, lots and lots of other boats gracing the River Derwent, bringing so much colour to the harbour, to her world. It's her favourite time of year. After six days straight of sailing, she wishes the floor would stop moving, that her eyes would stay level, her computer would stay still. In this time of busyness, she's managed to get all the prerequisites signed off to be a qualified deck hand on a tall ship, something she never ever thought possible in her previous life; however, in this new life she's forming, she knows anything is and will be possible.

#

A letter from VOCAT makes her question life, the fairness of it, the justice within our legal system.

SPECIAL FINANCIAL ASSISTANCE

(CATEGORY B) $2500 (as offending prior to July 2007). (Like Layla said, this doesn't even cover the first nightmare) *Legal costs $770.*

Report fee $335.50 Future
counselling $4920 Bowen
therapy $640

Camera, sky watcher, photographic accessories and second-hand campervan not allowed as not satisfied assist in recovery and not exceptional circumstances or reasonable.

Please sign and return the enclosed form by 22/2.

Look at those numbers, numerically speaking, so many twos – the number of the moon, a supremely feminine force, representing both grace and power, aiming to bring peace and balance to situations, carrying the strongest intuition. So how is any of that going to help right now? It leaves her questioning the random tangents her mind goes down.

She's asked if she'd like to talk to her psych about this before signing. Oh, how she wishes that was possible, but Kimberly's away, leaving her wholly responsible for this choice. Does she really have an option? Is there a plan B alternative compensation? She doesn't think so, in fact she knows there isn't. Perhaps she should be grateful, the special financial assistance is the most you can get.

What a load of shit. Maybe she really should get her act together, try and change things as this so suck. She signs the paperwork, returning it with mixed emotions, gratitude for what she did receive, and frustration at what seems to be the lack of acknowledgment of what childhood sexual assault actually does to a person.

#

She knows she's not back in her body … still … four months later. She wants to take risks and realises that the risk-taking behaviours of her younger years, the drinking, the promiscuity, the abusive relationships, have simply been replaced with healthier, yet sometimes still potentially life-threatening, behaviours. Like jumping off a cliff face into unknown water. But ohhhhh does it feel good. She squeals with joy as her body feels weightless, able to fly, just for that split second. It's a glimpse into not feeling connected to this earth, to this life. She's free, until the splash of cold clear water breaks her escape. Though it's unable to bring her back into her body.

All of this, the whole legal shit, the trial, the sentencing, the committal, the compensation, combined with her partnership ending, the double mastectomy, her breakdown, dealing with the kids, having to go to Melbourne to be present with POS in the same space, all of it is now truly able to surface. She no longer needs to try and hold it together, simply getting by each day, wondering what contact she'll have, wondering what or who she'll have to deal with. Now she's free, but within that freedom is uncertainty too. For so long he's ruled, dictated, directed her path. Now she's free, able to be herself. It's a matter of finding who that is.

In the process of doing so she's pushing herself, taking risks, questioning life and her place in it, while reminding herself to breathe, to have faith that one day she'll find a certain level of monotone.

Her lawyers make contact, they're looking into other ways of getting some form of compensation, they too were completely shocked by the amount awarded by the court. She hasn't asked for this, and takes it as Spirit intervening, trying to get something more symbolic in relation to what happened. Though no amount of money can ever give back her virginity, her innocence, herself, who she was. The lawyers are confident they'll find some way; she doesn't want a civil case though; she just can't be present with him again. She believes that would actually kill her, completely this time.

#

Another trip on Lady Nelson, five days sailing along the east coast of Tasmania, away from everything, the wind in her hair, the salt spray on her skin. It's just what she needs. Or is it?

It's only been three months since the last multi-day trip. It's a distant memory in her overloaded brain. She'd forgotten about the lack of space below deck, about not having any personal space. So she stays on deck, sleeping there, the morning dew on her sleeping bag just adding to the wonderment.

There's a phone call after lunch, the boat's offshore, it's the local hospital. Father Bullshark's been admitted, apparently, he's now dying, he has blood poisoning. Fuck.

"How long do they think he has?"

"Maybe two weeks," comes the reply.

"Ok, thanks. I'm on a boat in the middle of the ocean at the moment and can't dock until Monday, I'll be in then."

She's mad. People will probably think she's mean, a bitch, cold hearted, a horrible daughter, but they can all get fucked. How can she forgive him for not doing anything? For being more concerned with appearances than protecting his own child? She doesn't think she'll ever be able to forgive him and Mother Blobfish, so finding compassion for him in his last days is hard.

After the sentencing, when she was told of his complete lack of care for her, in that moment she didn't have the space nor time to process that extra bit of juicy information ... until now. Now she knows that Father Bullshark is dying, now it resurfaces, now all the feelings she's held for her parents over the years become real. She has validation of their pathetic parenting. They didn't even fulfil the basic role of a parent – to protect their child. They failed, so why the fuck should she care that Father Bullshark's dying? Fuck them both.

Standing, back to the foremast, looking across the bow, she tries to think of things that she's grateful for, the open space around, the lunge of the boat, the sounds of the albatrosses, all these helps to bring joy to the moment. She's thinking, pondering, reflecting, as the boat gently edges its way south. Thinking of things from him that she wants to keep.

She knows her love of chocolate comes from him. Though he tainted that when she was a kid. He'd buy a box of strawberry frogs and give some to the kids in the street. They'd call him "the choccy man". He'd then count the remaining frogs and place them in the fridge, giving none to his own children; she hated him for that. The other kids didn't see what he did to his own, only how wonderful he was to them, so as much as she loves chocolate, she can't thank him for that.

She's very thankful for the boxes of vegetables delivered weekly when she was homeless with the kids, and she's thankful for the relationship he shared with Esi.

She knows she carries some of his personality traits – his arrogance, his stubbornness. But also, his gift of the gab, his love for words. These are also tainted by his anger and arrogance when he corrected her spelling or a definition. His love of words ... after all, she wants to write a book. Her love of books she knows comes from him, that too has been passed onto all her kids, that she's grateful for. A memory grabs her attention, the deep body-moving tones of the double bass luring her back to a time she'd sit in the pub with Father Bullshark listening to the magical tunes of some of the most famous jazz musicians of the day. Ahhh she has him to thank for her love of jazz.

The stubbornness she'll embrace, but the arrogance she tries ever so hard to reduce. She stands, rolling with the boat, saltwater staining her cheeks as Lady Nelson makes its way back to Hobart. Rounding the point into Storm Bay, a huge pod of at least a hundred common bottle-nosed dolphins swims under the bow, they're welcoming them home, leading Lady Nelson around the point. Her eyes are leaking even more now. She's filled with conflicting, confusing emotions. She remembers to breathe, thankful for dolphin energy taking her away as she watches them swimming, jumping and tail slapping. They journey together. She's so grateful.

#

276

It seems like ages since she's dreamt, but she knows this more than likely isn't the case. Whenever she's away with a friend or on Lady Nelson, they say how they'll hear her calling out, physically lashing out, seemingly in distress, her body distorted, reflecting her dream state. She doesn't remember the dreams of those nights but it's obvious from the observations of others that the nightmares still happen. So, this particular one that she does remember must be up there with some of the worst.

She's in this space, it kind of feels or looks like it's in the country. She's in a different timeline – there are old buildings around, red brick ones, overgrown plants, and this creepy man. He tries to snap up girls; he buys bikes and uses them as bait. Somehow, she works out his plan. She's not sure if she's one of the targets or not, but she finds the bikes and figures that if she hides them then he won't be able to snap up the girls. She gets one of the bikes, hiding it in a garden shed, then the man comes back. She hasn't been able to get the other bikes and freaks out because she thinks the man is going to find her. She has a feeling there maybe someone else hiding with her. She takes the bolts off the front wheel of the bike, and leaves it in the shed, realising that she should have put it back in the same spot so it would look like it was all good to go and then have fallen apart when he was riding it. The way it's been left may show him that someone's tampered with it. There are blackberry bushes around the shed, and she's hiding in them and freaking out, not knowing if he's going to get another girl, or find her.

Feeling the shortness of breath, the terror within her being, she wakes up, grateful for Little Dog's head nudging under her hand, begging for attention, begging for Ana to come back.

Chapter 39

Life beyond

Mardi's dead. It's all so wrong. Mardi should still be here, alive, laughing, sharing, loving, but she's not.

Mardi died of cancer, cancer Ana believes was a result of the abuse Mardi suffered as a child. Apparently, Lucia and Mardi thought that they were safe, that they wouldn't get cancer. After all, it's only one in four who do, and seeing as Ana's had it three times, they thought they were immune to its horrors. Unfortunately, not.

She grieves Mardi, and it hits her hard. She was upset when Alice died, and, of course when her grandma died. But she knew that would happen, Grandma was 89 years old. But Mardi's young, a year younger than her. It's all so unfair, unjust, fucked.

#

When her grandma had died and she journeyed back to Melbourne for the funeral, POS had been there. She was struggling with the grief over losing her beloved Gran, and didn't expect to have to see POS. She had wondered why the fuck he was there, and worked to keep POS away from Esi, from herself.

A few years later it came out that POS had spoken to Troy at the funeral, telling Troy to never believe anything Ana says as she lies, she always has.

That's what POS would say all the time, whenever there was an adult within ear shot when they were all younger, "Don't listen to Ana she's just a chicken with her feathers in a flap, always lying, always making up stories."

As an adult, she realised this was POS' way of discrediting her. If everyone believed that she lied, then if she should ever tell about him, they would automatically think she was lying.

#

She visited Mardi in hospital, wanting to spend as much time together as possible. She just sat, watching Mardi breathe, ever so grateful for their presence in her life. While she was there Mardi's abuser came in. She got up to leave but Mardi grabbed her hand, pulling her back down, Mardi's eyes begging Ana to stay. She stayed, sitting on one side of the bed, Mardi's abuser on the other, Mardi's fingernails digging deeper and deeper into the palm of Ana's hand. She wanted to get up, wanted to smash his fucking head against the wall. But not before shoving it into Mardi's core, Mardi's centre of self, the place where Mardi's cancer was eating away. The space that he had invaded, where he had no right to go. The space where he tainted Mardi with his vile putridness. She so wanted to do that and yell, "You did this, you piece of fucking shit. Mardi's dying because of what you did to her. Fuck you."

But she didn't. They'd already talked about this. Mardi wanted peace while they were still alive. Didn't want more shit while they were still alive. She had to respect that.

But now that Mardi's dead, things are different. If she ever sees that piece of shit, she'll smash his fucking head into a brick wall and then continue to cause him as much pain as she possibly can. She's amazed at the strength Mardi showed in that moment. They were dying, they knew they were dying. They were weak, in enormous amounts of pain physically and mentally, leaving their life behind, their much loved and cherished children and husband, their amazing and successful career, and the many friends like Lucia and Ana. Mardi was leaving it all, yet she remained at peace, simply wanting the pain to stop, the hurt to go.

Ana can understand in a way, knowing the pain of both cancer and childhood abuse, the weight, the putridness, the shame, the guilt, the blame, the "why me?" that comes with it all. Knowing it so well, she's truly able to empathise with Mardi, with them wanting it all to simply stop. So as much as she's so overwhelmingly sad at the death of her dear friend, she believes that at least now Mardi's free, free of the pain, free of the past, free of him.

Mardi was given five years. That was ten weeks earlier. They had it all planned, Mardi and Ana, they'd open a shop, Mardi would crochet, Ana would paint and write, finding strength in Mardi's story, their presence, their being. Mardi would describe the shop: it would be little, cottage-like, looking out to or near the water, they both needed the water. Mardi's face would light up as they talked, describing how much they'll love creating all the amazing, crocheted wonders, how they'd be in the space laughing, sharing, sitting, in the hurt, the healing, the love. Ana loves that story; the one Mardi was creating in their mind's eye.

Now Ana is writing the story alone. Mardi's dead, but she can feel Mardi's presence with every word she writes. This is what she can do to help keep Mardi's dream alive, she can write this book, to give voice to so many others.

So here she is, honouring her friends, honouring strangers.

#

It's taken a few months to be able to sit at the computer, to be able to write words, to form sentences. First up, she had to go through all her journals. She's grateful she has them, the medical reports, the court transcripts, the correspondence between her and the legal team, from Melisa, from Kimberly.

As she's writing, putting her story down for others to read, she feels it all again. She smells it, hears it, feels the pain, the trauma, the despair in reliving her childhood. It's as though she's experiencing it all over, yet again. So she stops, distancing herself from it. She can maybe only do an hour or so before she feels herself reacting, her mind leaving. Then she stops. That action alone is huge, the ability to walk away from something she knows is causing unease within her. In that moment she's giving herself the space, the right, to say nope, that's enough for now, forever if she chooses.

She takes herself snorkelling, or swimming, or for a paddle, or a walk among the trees, anything that allows a space to breathe.

She hears Mardi's voice constantly in her thoughts, "You must write the book Ana, you must."

She allows her OSD to take over, trying to paint, unable to focus, binging on Netflix, even doing house cleaning. Anything that's an avoidance of sitting back down at the computer, to be present yet again in all the shit.

Then one day she says, "NO. Tomorrow I will actually sit down and physically start writing. Not researching, not trying to get court records. I will actually write my story."

And you know what? She does. The very next day she sits down at her computer and starts to write. Even though a forecast of snow is very tempting, keeping her promise to her friend is a greater commitment.

She starts with the completion of her journey, and is surprised when, after about the first ten thousand words, she realises that it isn't affecting her … well, not as severely as she thought it would. That she's present, very present and feeling very empowered.

At an appointment with Kimberly the next day, she shares what's going on, explaining she's started writing again and all the feelings she's had prior to that. Kimberly asks why she thinks it isn't affecting her as much, the actual writing, that is?

Without even thinking Ana replies, "I know this is my story, but it no longer belongs to me. Does that make sense?"

They sit for some time, pondering this realisation, allowing it to simply be.

Chapter 40

The non-ending

The #MeToo movement has been bringing truth into the world over the last few years. She's really pleased that it is, that people are talking, that some are listening, and some are being heard, believed, their stories validated.

What she doesn't get, what she can't find any logic in, is why those like herself still have to fight so hard to get their stories into a courtroom? Why the amount of compensation they receive, if they receive any, is tiny? Especially in comparison to that which those who were abused within an institution are awarded. How the fuck is there any logic in that? Yes, those abused within an institution of any kind probably did have to have interactions with their perpetrator for a number of years. But what about those who are victims of incest? They then have to live with their perpetrator, day in day out, year after fucking year, for their lifetime. They are often unable to share their story for fear of exile from the family, fear of creating drama within the family and community, fear of causing hurt to someone they love in the family. What about those abused by a friend or neighbour? They still have to have regular interaction with these people. And all of these people don't then have a safe space to go home to. They have nothing. Their world is shattered, distorted by the perverted desires and wants of another.

If they're lucky (which really isn't the right word), if their story makes it to court, then they are "awarded" a pittance of monetary compensation, if that, and most of the time their perpetrator gets to walk free with a slap on the wrist, and possibly a good behaviour bond.

The impacts of childhood sexual abuse result in the many layered complexities of PTSD and the huge varying triggers it encompasses. They don't just go away, they don't just stop, they don't just cease to be present within your being simply because time has passed, because you've done the hard yards in the psych's office, because the offender has been charged, because someone told you to just get over it. No, the impact seems to last forever. The victim never knows what's going to trigger them, and wonders when the fuck it will stop. They may feel as though things have got better, then something happens, something that puts you right back there, fifty years earlier. It's fucked and it's all so wrong.

The fact that someone is a so-called "good" member of society now, does not, nor should it in any way, take away from the reality, the truth, the trauma that they inflicted upon another, no matter how many years ago. The perpetrator now being a good person doesn't help the abused soul, doesn't help them deal with or heal from the damage that was done, in some ways it only creates more trauma, as others may find their story harder to believe.

We need to stop this segregation, this dismissal, this bullshit around abuse. Whether a perpetrator is a pillar of society, part of any form of institution, a neighbour, a friend or a family member, sexual assault is sexual assault. Whether the assault was words or actions, it was still a violation of another, and each individual will process and deal with what happened to them in their individual way. There is no "one size fits all" when it comes to how someone will live with being sexually abused, but everyone does need our compassion, our validation, and our support, through not only community and friendships, but also the legal system.

Our legal system really needs to change. It needs to validate all abuse stories, to compensate all abuse stories equally, not based on who the abuser was, but on the simple fact that a person, through no fault of their own, was abused. Simple.

We need to change; it's not just about speaking up. It can be clearly seen why so many still don't speak up when there is such an inequality within our judicial system. We need a change, let's be that change.

#

It's taken over six years and lots of self-reflection, letting go of some people and relationships, welcoming in others, finding that which brings peace and joy to her heart and soul so she can be present, but now, Ana can be happy, and most of all, she can be joy-filled. She gets sad at times, sad because humans can be really horrible. But humans can also be wondrous incredible souls who protect and save the environment, the wildlife, our fellow beings.

The past couple of years have been spent looking at her shadow side, at the Ana she's tried to hide for a lifetime. In doing so she's had to look at the behaviours and beliefs she's held onto that are no longer healthy for the new and improved version that Ana is becoming. Some beliefs were hidden so deep that she had to dig ever so far to find them. It's been tough, draining and reflective. She's spent a lot of time by herself, in quiet, in nature.

She has bid farewell to a significant, if somewhat destructive, person in her life, Father Bullshark. She has stood back as Rey has chosen their path to walk separate from her. She has listened to the tone in Esi's voice as they shared their love for their partner, her eyes watering with joy. She has watched, mainly in awe, as Zeb has matured and grown amid the crap that is being a teenager.

She's chosen to allow random strangers into her home, so she can stay in the space she knows. Sharing with others after thirty odd years is so much more than ever imagined. The joy is much to do with the beautiful souls who are placed in the space, and she's learning a lot in this process – tolerance, acceptance, differences, learning about different cultures, different personalities, different tones, different smells. Sometimes it's really hard, not having her own space, but then she reminds herself to be grateful. Grateful that she lives in a community where she feels safe, in a home where all her animal friends are welcome. A home where there's always space for others. Most importantly, a home that continues, to this day, to hold her.

She has stood back from many and in doing so discovered so much more about herself, leaving her grateful to have the life she does.

#

She thinks of angel Gianna, whose suggestion of making a plaster cast saved her soul. It was the most therapeutic and healing gift one could possibly give. Gianna provided a home for her and Big Dog and Little Dog when they needed the space. Where they would have been otherwise is unknown.

She thinks of the goddess Layla who shared their their-ness, allowing for love and laughter to enter a space usually reserved for fear. Who challenged a double dare that was so cool and so freeing. For their healing space and welcome at a time when Ana felt there was no more.

She thinks of the divine Lille who gave of their time to make sure her time didn't end, and who continues to be always present. Of Mardi, a soul sister, whose journey too was a difficult one, like so many others. Of the encouragement, the support, the thanks for Ana continually being their voice, the voice of so many. Mardi helped keep her going when it was too tough, sharing creations of wonder and joy. They brought her back to what was important, this story, Ana's story, Mardi's story, Layla's story and all the untold stories still yet to be spoken.

She thinks of Jack, whose love, passion and joy for the night sky helped her explore not only the Universe, but also Jack, and in doing so to find a soft place to fall into his huge bear hugs and non-judgement.

She thinks of her kids, who through their own fears, were still present for their mum. She hopes that they all see that no matter what, life will always, always, always provide you with positives from even the most overwhelming situations. That they'll see she's walked with dignity along her path. It's been tough at times, like real tough, but the laughs and love encountered are so much more.

She thinks of the many other friends who have shared and cared, cried, and laughed. Keeping her alive, keeping her sane, showing love, displaying non-judgement, she thanks all. A huge thanks to Mother Nature, to this Earth, to the place she calls home, a place that has allowed her to feel at peace for the first time in her life, the space that has allowed for her to heal, grow and love.

She gives thanks.

#

It's seven years since Ana's started this part of her journey. Now, not only does she feel like a new person, but her physiology is all completely new too, every cell in her body's been replaced with newer, healthier, freer cells.

With every painful step, with the breaking of every frustrating gagging of her story, of the stories of so many others, the long-lasting detrimental impacts of childhood sexual assault are being bought into the light. For the broken souls, the broken families, and the shattered lives, the wonder of Mother Nature is always holding, always uplifting, always life giving, and always, always, always has your back.

Little Dog appears by her side, sensing the emotions welling within her. Big Dog has passed. She and Little Dog have become a team. Little Dog is completely tuned into her emotions, her state of being. Little Dog's her greatest comfort as they demand attention, for her to connect to the moment, to be present with them, with the world.

The thing she can do, the thing she does, is trying to stay present. To combat the memories, she finds the majik in every day. She sees the sunlight behind a flowering Native Laurel tree, hears the waves crash on the sand at low tide, stands waist deep in button grass in the silence that is a World Heritage Area, as Venus shines brightly overhead. She feels the wind upon her face on top of a mountain covered in fresh snow, engulfed in shh-y-ness. She feels the instability of the boat upon the water as the sails billow in the breeze. She sits under the stars, remembering the planets, the constellations, and watches an aurora appear. The skirts dance and sway, beams shooting off up to the Southern Cross. She shares, hugs and cries with friends. She lives in this space, on this island, she feels safe, she breathes. For all this and more, she gives thanks.

"Because I choose joy."

Appendix

It's interesting, when Ana's stressed her dyslexia's a lot more pronounced, her vocabulary diminished. She tends to make up words as her brain can't recall the actual names. She used to have a stutter and lisp, and still does to an extent, but she noticed when she left Melbourne that within months the lisp and stutter had decreased considerably. Now it's only present when she's anxious or uncomfortable. She noticed that while going through the court process, she'd make up lots of words and her physical ability to stay on her own two feet like an able person was reduced. She fell a lot more, walking into things, things that weren't even there. Her brain was fried, resulting in the inability to coordinate either mind or body. She called herself a "gooba". One day she may write a whole dictionary of "gooba" words. Until then, here is what she came up with while traveling this road. The words are nonsensical fun, not meant to be insulting to anyone, just some light comic relief from the realities of her memories.

Gooba Dictionary

Always thoughts – things that are in your head all the time
Awewonder – to sit in total wonderment of an event of
                 nature's brilliance
Besterest – better than best
Blowey thingy – whistle
Busised – when your skin becomes colourful
Dark time – night-time
Divinlime – someone who is divinely sublime.
Epifiby – having a light bulb moment
Extremerest – a being or activity that is beyond the beyond.
Favourist – most favourite
Folts – it's yours; as in it's your fault not mine
Forthinsight – the act of seeing into the future
Friedness – being fried more than once
Gaerky – the connection between a fairy and a geek
Gelasticstar – The ability and willingness to be
completely uninhibited. To laugh by way of
snorting. To be free enough to not care. To be silly.
Gooba – Ana
Gooberisim – the act of being a gooba
Goubu – guru gone gooba
Half snap – Same thought different words
Her-ness – what makes her *Her*
Honshine – A sunny honey
Horribilist – more horrible than horrible
Hover hover – gooba equivalent to hubba hubba
Hunfgry – hungry tired
Inmapropiut – inappropriate

Labyrinthinestar – A sacred space that beckons one in, tojourney to the darkest deepest recesses of one's soul, to take all that learning, the new evolution of self, back out into the universe, to shine brightly and eternally.

Light time – daylight hours

Losterer – more lost than lost

Majikality – something that is truly magical.

Magneliciaiac – large and small Magellanic clouds which are both dwarf galaxies

Me-ness – the essential *Me*

Mosterest – more, more than more

Multichewdinous – many different things

Nonormal – not normal

Pentapus – Used to describe a person who possesses or has grown five arms ... or legs ... or a combination of both but only has one head.

Pinky purply twirly thingy – the Eta Carina

Poneeply – the act of sitting in deep contemplation, to ponder more deeply, the act of being extremely deep Profun-ditty – A deep and meaningful ditty

She-ness – the very core of self

Shhh – the wonders of super silence.

Shhh-y-ness – the act of   super shhh

Sphericaljoy – the overwhelming feeling of being completely enveloped in joy

Sponifeous – to spontaneously live life, to grasp the moment, to be present with joy. To love with openness

Tactilness – things that are tactile and their ness-e-ness

Thingy – anything

Youness – simply being you.

Directory of People

Ana Suci – victim, survivor, legend
Patrick O'Shanesy – abuser or who Ana prefers to call
    Piece of Shit, POS
Maria O'Shanesy – POS' wife
Otto Bowman – abuser/
bystander
Donny Bowman – abuser/ bystander
Donna – bystander
Troy – ex partner
Jason – ex partner
Daren – ex partner
Esi – child
Rey – child
Zeb – child
Father Bullshark – Ana's father
Mother Blobfish – Ana's
mother Mitria – Ana's step
mum Monica – first police
officer
Police Officer David – second police officer
Kimberly – psychologist
Giana – friend
Layla – friend, legend
Lucia – friend
Mardi – friend, legend (deceased)
Malia – friend from Queensland
Danika – friend
Rosemary – kinesiologist
Melisa – advocate/ support
Alice – friend (deceased)
Ariel – friend
Asia – friend from Queensland, legend
Lille – friend from Queensland

Olivia – school friend from Melbourne
Mia – Bowen therapist
Astrid – friend from Queensland
Oscar – friend
Felix – friend
Matilda – friend
Noah – friend/ aurora chasing buddy
Prof – astro buddy
Eve – star gazing friend
Peter Dombrovskis - famous photographer
Lady Nelson - pirate ship
Judy – POS' teenage girlfriend
Jack – the soul who brought joy back into Ana's world, legend

Directory of Places

Hilcock Sexual Assault Unit – the police station in Melbourne
kunanyi/Mt Wellington – the mountain in Ana's backyard
Storm Bay – the space of water Ana would be happy if she
    never crossed again.
Mt Field – Ana's favourite mountain
Mount Roland – where one can look at the stars and listen to music
Arthur River – a river with divine reflections in the Tarkine
Bluff Hill Point – where Ana found her space upon this land
Ben Lomond – Ana's other favourite mountain
Cradle Mountain – where Ana did her artist in residency,
    where the *Extreme* Exhibition was held and where Peter
    Dombrovskis' work was on display.
Scottsdale – Ana's ancestors' space
Assay Cove – where Ana and Layla sit and share
Cape Queen Elizabeth – the walk on Bruny Island where
    Danika and Ana got lost
Cygnet Folk Festival – a festival of music and hippies
Minds Do Matter – the annual art exhibition that's Ana's favourite
Bob Brown Foundation – trying to save Mother Nature
Extreme – the exhibition on at Cradle Mountain
Ten Days on the Island – the big festival for which Ana's photo
    Grandmother Tree was the banner photo.
Dark Mofo – where magic mirrors allow for fun
Puffing Billy – a joy space to visit after court
Ganlarce Work – the disability organisation meant to help Ana

Support Services

Beyond Blue 1300 22 46 36
Blue Knot Foundation 1300 657 380
Brave Hearts 1800 272 831
Breast Screen Australia 13 20 50
Cancer Council Australia 13 11 20
Domestic Violence Help Line 1800 737 732
Headspace 1800 650 890
Kids Help Line 1800 55 1800
Lifeline 131114
Men's Referral Service 1300 766 491
Mental Health Helpline 1800 332 388
QLife 1800 184 527
Relationships Australia 1300 364 277
Respect 1800 737 732
Safe Steps Crisis Line (Vic) 1800 015 188
SAMSN (Survivors and Mates Support Network) 1800 472 676
S.A.S.S after hours. 1800 697 877
Sexual Assault Crisis Line Victoria 1800 806 292
Suicide Call Back Service 1300 659 467
www.maceenergymethod.com

Authors Note-Ten Years After Guilty Verdict

It has been ten years since the court hearing, ten years of additional trauma of healing, of remembering, and of growing. As I sit in a very different space from when I first wrote this book, I feel the need to revisit it and to do so in my truth.

This story is mine, it is about incest and the insidious tentacles it infects into your very being. Your home is no longer safe; the evening dinner becomes a terrifying space as you sit across from your perpetrator, the bathroom no longer a private sanctuary. Family is not safe. The primary relationships required to teach boundaries and self-respect are non-existent. You grow up not knowing what safety feels like, what respectful, healthy relationships feel like.

I was subjected to six years of sexual and emotional abuse by my oldest brother. I named him Patrick O'Shanesy, or more commonly, POS, a "piece of shit." That is what he was and always will be to me.

Alongside many of his intrusions against my body, two brothers who lived down my street also watched and took part. I named them Otto and Donny. Living next door to them was a girl, older than everyone, Donna. She never physically touched me, but she stood by, watching and laughing as my body became a toy for others.

Sometimes I feel her inaction caused more harm than the physical abuse itself. The power of a bystander should never be dismissed. She was female, like me, yet she let them do things no child should every have to endure.

For decades I found it difficult to trust women. With men I knew their agenda, but women? The betrayal ran deep. Not only did Donna not protect me, but neither did my own mother and father, who knew what was happening and choose to remain silent, complicit. Later, as an adult, I learnt my maternal grandmother also knew. The level of betrayal and loss of faith in humanity was immense.

When my parents died, I didn't grieve, quite the opposite I became very angry, questioning their lack of parental obligations, of protection, of acknowledgement, of responsibility. My father, I must state never once denied what happened to me, though he did deny knowing about it. He supported my recovery through paying for many psychologist appointments, even attending a psychologist himself. He and my step mum moved closer to support me and be there for my eldest. He didn't choose my brother over me, he choose me Thank you, Dad. My mother on the other hand went to her grave still in denial, still choosing him over me, still showing no accountability for her role in all of it.

Over the years, I have been presented with many lessons around trust and betrayal in the relationships I have been part of. It is still difficult for me to fully trust anyone, friend or partner. I observe everything with hyper-vigilance: words, actions. I am always questioning, always alert.

For as long as I can remember I always felt there was more, knew there was more, was told there was more in dreams. I responded with "I don't want to know." What I do remember is enough. A couple of years ago in a psych session, clarity and awareness on this hidden part of my abuse surfaced. There was no denying its truth as my body responded as only those abused can. My psych stood silent as my body worked its way through its truth. Names and ages coming to me. I was I believe 8yrs, 10yrs and 15yrs old when two adult men raped men. When the clarification of those parts I had kept buried deep in my psych came to light, I found myself once again struggling with trust and relationship issues. I have since resolved to let this part of my abuse remain where it is, in distant memories, and body responses.

Recently, a friend gifted me a session in Mace Energy Method (MEM) after I asked for insight into my relationship. To say this modality changed my being is an understatement.

Within days, I noticed something profound. During a sound workshop, the self-talk that had plagued my mind for nearly sixty years was simply gone. A relief beyond words as though the space once filled with destructive chatter was now free to absorb, learn, and connect more deeply, both with people and with knowledge.

The overwhelming emotions that once consumed me no longer hold the same power. Don't get me wrong, I can still feel sadness or hurt, but that crushing urge to run, to disappear when things become too much, has left me.

My need to control has softened as inner peace embraces me.

My mind feels clearer, sharper and eager to learn.

MEM has had and continues to have a life-changing impact on me. It inspired me to become a practitioner, a title I now hold with pride. Through the training, I came to understand how essential it is to not only speak my truth but to *live* it.

I feel called to do that here with my story. The story you have now finished reading.

Perhaps one day, I will rewrite it better to reflect my truth.

For now, I leave it as is, with this added author note.